SHAME
BY PROXY

ISBN: 979-8-218-06518-8 (Paperback)
ISBN: 979-8-9870320-0-8 (eBook)
ISBN: 979-8-9870320-1-5 (Audio Book)

Cover and Interior design by Tami Boyce
www.tamiboyce.com

SHAME
BY PROXY

Book 1 in the BY PROXY trilogy

M.C. LOWE

1

The neon sign shone bright against the darkened street like a dirty Ed Hopper painting. It read, "The Dam Tavern," with a red rose featured at one end. Inside, a lone patron sat at the bar, hunched over his tall glass, looking much older than his thirty-eight years. He rubbed a tattoo on his wiry forearm, which depicted the face of the Madonna—the rock star, not the saint. His body twitched with a dark, repressed tension, like a coke addict but with the added component of giving people the unnerving impression that he was about to go for their throat.

The old barwoman, Rose, had announced last call thirty minutes ago. The few patrons remaining had downed their drinks and exited. Rose, who named The Dam Tavern for its proximity to a large beaver dam on the Wabash River, hurried into the back room. Yet, the man lingered. He didn't want to leave.

The Dam Tavern shone like a shiny silver-nickel amid the black hardscrabble landscape from which he had walked in from several hours before. Black-and-white Truman-era checkered linoleum flooring gave rise to chrome-legged, black leather-cushioned stools. Walls were lined with framed posters of a Peter Max peace sign and a Max-type rendition of a woman wearing sunglasses and bangles with the words, *she had the soul of a gypsy and the heart of a hippy.* Everything in the town—in the world—seemed to have changed over the last several years. But not this bar. It had remained very much the same, as if crystalized in coal, since he was a boy of three, peering through the screen door at his father downing beers in Rose's bar before dragging his ass home.

The man felt at ease in Rose's presence, and it wasn't only because of the five straight-up whiskeys he had guzzled in the past two hours. No, the old woman could do more than the finest whiskey ever could. She was liable to calm an angry mountain cat. Some said she had healing hands and practiced a kind of magic. He wasn't sure he believed in all that witchy stuff, but he had grown over these last few weeks to cherish the silent, early morning last calls and the intelligent conversation he spent alone with her. Those conversations were his only joy about being back in this rat-hole of a town.

He looked around the empty tavern and waited to pay up until Rose returned. In the meantime, he yawned and sighed, stretching his arms over his head, the Glock he wore pressing into the small of his back. He never left the house without the gun, no sense for him to do otherwise. Besides, he felt naked without it.

Rose entered, leaving the back door to the storeroom opened as she always did. She ran her wrinkled and age-worn hands down over the legs of her tie-dyed skirt, wiping them dry. She smiled across at him, her entire face lightening.

"Another one, Wade?" She didn't seem impatient to leave, even though the hour was late.

Wade studied the drink in front of him, not wanting the evening to end, but knowing he couldn't keep her here all night. Maybe one more for the road. "Yeah. I think so."

The howl of a pitiful whipped dog sounded in the night. Maybe it too felt the lateness of the hour. Rose set another whiskey in front of him, the lava bead bracelet round her wrist and large silver Boho rings circling each finger jangling as she did.

"You know, ol' Abe Lincoln started the fad of naming dogs Fido when he named his dog."

"Is that so? I didn't know that, Wade."

Wade smiled, taking pride in knowing something that Rose didn't. "Yeah . . . it's Latin or something... means 'faithful'. I had no idea that Lincoln had a Latino background."

"Well, Wade, Latin's not the language of Latinos. Latin is a classical language, ancient, spoken during Roman times." Rose grabbed the washcloth from her waistband and wiped down the bar.

"Is that so?" She always impressed him.

Rose nodded and walked around the bar to stack the chairs upside down on the tabletops. Even though it neared two o'clock in the morning, she still had a rise in her step.

"Well, that Lincoln guy was a genius for a man with little schooling and being raised near here and all. Sorta like me."

Rose smiled a knowing smile. "Is that right, Wade?"

"Mmm…hmm. And the interesting thing is a year after that John Wilkes Booth fellow assassinated Lincoln, Fido, that dog of Lincoln's, walks up to a drunk guy on the curb and puts his muddy paws on the man, and the mister ups and knifes him… right there… on the street. Killed Lincoln's dog, Fido, that drunk did." Wade downed his whiskey. "Bet that guy didn't do any time for that little murder." He shook his head at the injustices of life.

"Bet not." Rose responded.

"Yep. That just proves life's a mystery. Ol' Fido assassinated just like his master. One by gunshot, the other by blade. I prefer a knife killing over a gun any day. There's satisfaction in the intimacy of a stabbing."

Rose didn't even flinch at Wade's revelation. He thought she understood him, and now she seemed to ignore his comment. "You're right about the happening with Lincoln's dog," she said. "A terrible coincidence. Interesting how life can be one coincidence after another, like a repeating pattern, a cycle. If you're paying attention, you can see the links and, if necessary, make different choices."

Wade beamed at Rose's astuteness to his attention to detail.

"You're right. I'm a man for detail." He nodded, coughed, and stared at his empty shot glass, averting his eyes, embarrassed at what he understood as a compliment. "So, Rose…I got my little girl a puppy. Named him Fido. Otherwise, she'd have called it Cuddles or some baby nonsense. Found him walking around on the street. He only has one eye, but a cute dog just the same."

Rose stared at Wade suspiciously. "So, did the dog have a collar?"

"Yeah? Why?"

Rose flinched. "Well, Wade, he could've belonged to someone."

Wade waved his hand in disregard. "Nah...he was looking for a home...with that one eye of his."

"Well, Wade, Mattie's not exactly a little girl. She's almost a woman... but I bet she'll love that little dog. It'll do her good to have something loyal to love." Rose looked up from her cleaning of the bar. "And, it's the least you could do after what you've gone and done to her." Rose met Wade's gaze directly, meaningfully and without judgment, as if she caught a child doing wrong who knew no different.

Wade's eyes turned steely. "What's that supposed to mean?"

At that moment, Rose's cell rang. She turned slightly and held up a finger to Wade. She listened and then spoke into her phone. "Okay. I'll be right there. Don't you do anything to make him angrier."

Rose hung up. "Wade, can you hold down the bar for a minute? I've got to check on something. I'm closing soon, anyway. Help yourself to a beer...on the house."

Rose stepped from behind the counter, removed her apron, and hurried out of the back door. Wade needed to use the john. If he remembered right, Rose kept a stack of magazines tucked away on a shelf. He reached over the bar where he thought she had stashed them, and sure enough, there they were. He grabbed a *Reader's Digest* magazine and before he headed toward the only bathroom in The Dam Tavern, noticed the issue date, 1965. Rose needed more current magazines, he thought.

After he was done, Wade stepped out of the toilet, startled at who he saw behind the bar. A young girl, about seventeen, strode over to the sink, hips swinging confidently as she dried a glass. A snug-fitting black t-shirt with the word, *Fugazi*, printed on the front insinuated the shapeliness of her breasts.

Wade recognized her, though that wasn't a surprise in this small, god-awful town. She was one of the two girls who walked his daughter home from the bus stop that day. She was an eye-grabber alright—even by his L.A. standards. Long, curly hair framing a face that could have belonged to Phoebe from that witch show. She walked with a certain confidence and knowledge. Wade could recognize that attitude anywhere. She was no virgin. He could smell it on her, as if she were a bitch in heat, and he a feral dog.

She leaned into him, smiling brightly. She reached for his empty glass and, with a light in her eyes, nodded at him suggestively. "This one's on the house," she said, though Wade knew she wanted to say something else. Something like, *Just you wait, big man.*

"Well, all-righty, then." He drawled out the last word, spoken like the locals he had cleaved himself from all those years ago. He had returned to Taylorville from San Francisco for a short time until things cooled down, but he would soon leave and head west again.

The woman-child turned to grab the large bottle of whiskey sitting on the back bar and, within moments, faced him again, with a shot glass full of the amber liquid. He would have sworn there was a devilish twinkle in her eyes when she sat it down in front of him. She leaned forward, resting her large breast on her folded arms. He downed the drink in one swallow, desiring for her to see him as a man who could throw a drink back. He knew he would get lucky tonight. She looked young. It didn't matter that she wasn't of consenting age. This girl was asking for it.

She stood straight up, drawing her shoulders back, and glared at him intently. The seduction gone from in a flash, seriousness taking its place. "Hey! Time's up!"

He looked up at her, confused. His vision blurred before coming into focus again. He must have drunk way too much alcohol during the night because it seemed this last drink went straight to his head. He stood from his bar stool and reached into his pocket for his wallet in order to pay for his drinks. His body weaved back and forth, and the room telescoped in and out. The girl reached into her pant pocket and pulled out her cell, never once looking away from him. Before he fell to the floor, he realized he couldn't grab his wallet.

The girl tugged out his Glock. "Let me relieve you of this," she said.

He could hear the girl talking to someone as if she spoke from the end of a long tunnel. "Hey Emma, I got the scumbag. Slipped him something at the tavern." A pause. "No, give me more credit than that...I distracted Grandma Rose with a call that George had spun out-of-control. Just now texted her, telling her he settled down."

She paused.

"Hey, really… no time for the details… I need your help… now." This last word she said with forceful emphasis and a meaning of don't-you-dare-abandon-me.

Another pause.

"Okay. Meet me in front. Operation Humiliation is in play, like it or not."

2

Two weeks earlier

The softness of the handmade quilts and deep-feathered mattress had once cradled Emma, but they now confined her body. She pushed her foot out from under the frayed covers and felt liberation. If only an act of such simplicity could free her from the intangible confinement of her life.

Her mind wandered. She gave up on her morning meditating and decided she needed something greater to quiet her thoughts. She needed to go to the river. Throwing back the quilts, she half-rolled off the bed, feet first, then lifting her butt, letting her face stay buried in the pillow. The pillow muffled a groan worthy of a Broadway actress, and she reached down to grab her clothing from the floor. She dressed in her murdered-out outfit with the black, steel-toed work boots. Realizing she'd dawdled too long, she didn't take the time to lace her boots, because if she hurried, she could still meet Jolene down at the river.

She stood on the back porch. The wind slapped her face, reddened her cheeks, penetrated her thin shirt, and, before long, numbed her skin. She welcomed the numbness. This freezing blast was winter's last attempt to have its way before succumbing to spring. The sound of the river drew her attention through a spattering of trees to its rushing current. The weak, coffee-brown serpent of a river undulated around a bend, with white, creamy sprays catching the air as the water slammed into fallen logs and boulders. Her gaze traveled up to the factory smoke stacks that formed a sentry along the west bank of the river and down to a bell pit, the remains of a coal mining shaft whose unstable room had collapsed long ago.

Her seventeen-year-old mind imagined the ghosts of those coal miners from the past, covered in their dust, camouflaged against the blackened landscape, walking home slumped in a single tired line, their existence the same aboveground or under it. Those coal miners were her ancestors. They had migrated up from Appalachian country. They weren't all that different from the men of today, except that the men of today didn't work—not in mining coal, nor anything else.

Taylorville, like many other small, tucked-in pockets of fly-by-country, had been arrested in time in the seventies. Only a few miles away, the more progressive Darwin, a city of sorts, thrived. But Taylorville remained inert. The stark cultural disparity reminded her of reading about Chinatown, which existed right in the middle of Chicago. Yet, if you wandered into it, you would believe you walked in a foreign country. For Taylorville—except for the drug use and cell phones, the two things a person needed to escape—was still steeped in Appalachian ways stuck in the mid-twentieth century. To Taylorville folks, poor was a way of life, a day-to-day struggle.

Emma sprinted, like a deer toward its doe bed, to the Wabash River. She stopped at her secluded spot and braced herself. Running her fingers through her long blonde hair, she loosened the tresses from the knot. She reached down and removed her boots and her outer clothing, and then walked out to "Flattop Rock," her self-named favorite.

The river ran swiftly, about two inches over the rock. The cold numbed her feet. Confirming she stood alone, she stripped and laid down on her back, staring up at the sky through the forest of trees that leafed out.

Soon the frigid water triggered her body's autonomic nervous system, biting into her naked body. Her breath quickened. She dropped into her center and used her mind to relax her body, the way Grandma Rose had taught her. Soon, her body and mind settled. It was her way to push beyond her body's flight or fight control response. She laughed, always the conqueror, as she suppressed her body's reaction to nature. Emma stood and with her hand over her heart, a technique Grandma taught her and one that prepared her for any adversity. Then she dove into the freezing current.

Her morning swims in the Wabash were Emma's only moments of real peace. Immersed in the laminar flow of the

Wabash and surrounded by lush forest, Emma came to know the shifting of her own flow. Even with the seemingly chaotic movement of the river and its slamming into boulders, the river paled in comparison to the anxiety-provoking atmosphere of her daily life. There were the times when she flowed with the water and the wind. More often, though, she met resistance, like the boulders blocking the stream. But it was okay. She lived for the rare times when she felt loudly alive, safely insulated from the injustices surrounding her life while she immersed in her natural joy.

A million years created the Wabash and the fertile land once bordering it. The city of Darwin only took thirty years to poison it. The coal-burning factories in the city neighboring Taylorville dumped waste into the river on the east bank with abandon. In reply, when the river flooded its banks every five years or so, it covered the ground with blackened cinders. Mother Earth's revenge. Grandma said Taylorville was stubborn, because where else would grass refuse to grow? Regardless, Taylorville took the damage of the flooding river and burning factories. It carried the smell.

Though she had every right, Emma tried to avoid feeling like a victim. A victim's musing only promoted more victimization. So, instead, she wouldn't let her birthplace define her. Just like the Wabash survived the abuse of the factories, she would survive the abuse of her town, while Taylorville folk continued to suffer. Yet, she hoped the town would meander off onto a different path, one of glory rather than one of damnation. She, though, was determined to be like the river.

Over the last few weeks, Emma had watched the Wabash rising. Today, it crested high. By late summer, the river flowed about three feet beneath Flattop Rock. While most Taylorville people saw a spring flooding as a non-event—just the risk of living in a river-town — Grandpa, a man whom she considered the father figure she never really had, thought differently. He said it seemed like the Wabash just had enough. Well, she too. Emma wondered if this was the year the Wabash would even the score. If so, she'd be fine with its flooding. Flooding would be a cleansing of sorts and a reason to start over.

A splash yanked Emma out of her introspection. A slender figure—tall, dark curly hair wearing a virginal white cotton shift and painted bright red cowgirl boots running up her bare legs like raging flames from hell—lingered along the Wabash riverbank. Her friend Jolene.

Jolene, upon seeing Emma, walked toward Flattop Rock and waved, smiling. Emma smiled back. Jolene threw the remaining small rock she held into the Wabash and then she slipped out of her clothes and dove into the freezing current, making her way toward Emma in easy strokes. Emma met her and treaded water. She drew a breath, not from the cold, but at Jolene. With her dark hair slicked back, she saw Jolene's beauty for the first time, as if she hadn't looked on Jolene's face daily for the last twelve years. Her friend had changed in ways Emma didn't comprehend.

"Wow. You're becoming a strong swimmer," Jolene said. "Too bad you're not on the swim team." Jolene's words were halting, her lips turning a numbing blue.

"Being on the swim team at this point won't do me any good. You're the one with the athletic scholarship to Florida State," Emma said. "I envy you, girl."

"Don't ever say that, Emma. My life's not to be envied."

Jolene took a deep breath and looked away, closing her eyes tightly.

She opened her eyes and turned to face Emma. "I had a great time at swim practice yesterday... 1:55. I'm less than two seconds off the record."

"Florida State University Women's Swim Team is in for a helluva season next year," Emma said, happy for her friend.

"Yeah. Swimming in the frigid Wabash has conditioned my body perfectly. I think I'm going to break that collegiate record soon." Jolene looked away, slightly uncomfortable.

Emma knew Jolene treaded this subject—and Emma herself by association—tenderly. While Emma was unsure what her future held, Jolene poured her hopes into an athletic scholarship which Florida State awarded to her last month. For the first time, Emma felt inferior to Jolene. She saw Jolene's world blossoming toward exciting new adventures while she herself watched as her future seemed glued to their sad town. Emma sensed the tendrils of jealousy creep up to clutch her heart often. But, forewarned to ward them off, she pushed it down and tried to replace it with happiness for her friend.

"I'm just waiting for George to figure out a way to keep me from going. He doesn't want to lose the foster money he gets from the government," Jolene said, referencing her foster father.

"So, let him try. He can't do anything. You'll be eighteen and a high school graduate. If he tries anything crazy, I'll grab

Dad's old Remington and put an end to it myself." Emma's hate rose, causing the light in her eyes to brighten a bit.

"Come on. Enough of this. Let's get out, I'm freezing," Jolene said, laughing to lighten the mood.

Emma nodded and started a front-crawl to Flattop Rock. "I know, I know. But we have to do our Ch'Ulel Heart exercises or Grandma will be disappointed in me. Just a quick one."

They reached Flattop Rock and quickly put on their clothing. Emma stood straight in a military fashion—chin up, shoulders back—but relaxed, with her hand over her heart. She was already entuned with the vibrations of energy, seeing without using her eyes. The Blind Sight exercise strengthened her ability to read the energies.

"Warrior of Light, True of Strength, Serenity and Presence," Emma said, and took a deep breath. "Ready."

Jolene opened her eyes, "Follow me. Wait. You're peeking."

"Am not!" Emma replied. "It doesn't do me any good to peak. You can't fool Grandma. Besides, I'm tuned in now." Her voice reflected the truth of her connection to an inner state of mind by its softness and compassion. Jolene turned and softly treaded along the bank of the Wabash, making sharp turns. Emma shadowed behind her, aware of Jolene's energy, as if Jolene pressed a pillow against her chest, drawing her forward. All she needed to do was keep the soft, pillow-like pressure at her chest. Jolene circled, walking slowly, placing one foot in front of the other before jagging off in a different direction. Emma followed precisely a few feet behind her.

"Damn, you're good. I can't do that," Jolene said, the admiration shining in her eyes. "Grandma Rose will be proud. Do it again." She said this as if Emma was doing a magic trick.

Emma closed her eyes, centered, and seemed to breathe in the space around her. On Jolene's fourth crazy jag, Emma stumbled and collided into her. She pulled off the blindfold. "It seems like I can't do it either."

"I don't know...that pretty good. It's superhuman, if you ask me."

It was superhuman. Grandma Rose taught Emma to surrender her mind into her heart through practices Grandma had learned from a Mayan shaman. Grandma always emphasized that it wasn't the eyes that see; that it was the mind.

Emma tucked the bandana into her pocket.

"Won't get me into college, though. So, it's not as important as being a strong and fast swimmer." Emma wasn't really sure what use Ch'Ulel Heart did for her in life. Maybe it was just a parlor trick. But Grandma said it would hone her senses, would focus her mind, and would come in handy during a crisis. "But, I may be able to sense danger about."

"Hey, we both could use a little help in seeing danger coming our way."

Both girls laughed at the seriousness of the statement meant to be flippant. Emma understood Jolene's greatest struggle was to keep focused on her studies, but she had more to distract her than most girls her age.

The laughter dissipated. Jolene remained silent.

The silence directed Emma to reach over and hug her friend. Then she hurried down the path. "I have to go," she said, over her shoulder. "I want to help Grandpa in the store some, then head to the library." The thought of spending time in the Darwin University Library brightened her mood considerably. Quiet time in the library was what she needed alright. Not only was she away from people by finding a secluded corner somewhere, but to get lost in the writings of Carl Jung and his theories of how the mind worked fascinated her. She had her own ways of focusing her mind by delving into more scholarly things than watching the dramas that played out when people had little to occupy their minds or were needing to escape their destitute lives. She had her own creative and constructive ways to escape.

3

Jolene buried her nose into the soft brown fur of her bunny, Baby Boo, breathing in his scent. "Ah, Baby Boo, you're so much bigger than your brothers and sisters. Now, why is that when you were born the littlest?"

The other rabbits began thumping their hind legs, wanting attention too. Jolene placed Baby Boo back into his hutch, which separated the males from the females. She pulled out each of her rabbits one-by-one, loving them all in distinct and personal ways, and gave them a special treat: carrots on the verge of rot, perfectly sweet for a rabbit.

The rabbits were a godsend. She sat one rabbit, Mabel, down on the ground and watched her twitch her nose. "So, Mabel," she said. "Have you been taking care of all your children? Making sure they're safe? I bet you have. Just like the day I found you."

Jolene picked up Mabel and hugged her, lifting her to eye level and rubbing her nose against Mabel's. Jolene kept all the bunnies safe in their hutches, only letting them out when she could attend to them. Caring and protecting vulnerable things was her life purpose, as the ever-present danger lurked to torture anything looking like prey.

Jolene inhaled and froze. The old, familiar smell of rotting flesh filled her nostrils. She knew the scent, like roadkill left steaming on July pavement.

She inspected each of her bunnies, ensuring that they were okay. Nothing was amiss.

She remembered when she first smelled that foulness. A memory from twelve years ago ran shivers through her—inspiring not fear, exactly, but sorrow.

She had been walking into Frank's Grocery for the first time when she smelled it. She was six years old. New to Taylorville, and new to her foster family. She knew little about the world, and even less about Taylorville—or her new foster family, for that matter. But some instinct within her told her to be wary of that stink. There was no visual evidence of what could have caused the smell. And yet it was unmistakable.

Ironically, the first time she smelled death was also the first time she met Emma.

"How can you stand it, Grandpa?" six-year-old Emma said to the man behind the counter.

Emma's frankness fascinated Jolene. She could never speak to an adult in such a confrontational tone. She admired the girl, who stood before her wearing a worn jeans-shirt and dirty white tennis shoes, for being so brave.

Emma took shallow breaths. Jolene thought she looked as if she may vomit, and after a few more drawn breaths, Emma bent over and dry heaved into a mop bucket.

Her grandpa had placed bowls of ammonia behind cans of kidney beans on the top shelves, but his attempt at disguising the foulness failed to cut the smell. "It must've been a rat," he said. "Something's died under the crawl space. Stick your head under there and tell me if you see anything, Emma." The man pinched his nose, smiled, and exhaled through his mouth.

Emma stared at Grandpa as if he'd just asked her to part the waters of the Wabash River. "I'm not going under there. Besides, Grandpa, it's gotta be larger than a rat. Something big crawled up behind them walls and died."

The shopkeeper placed bowls of ammonia on lower shelves behind the register but, still; the ammonia did little to cover the stink. Still, she remained in the store. She liked watching the girl and the man. She sensed their closeness and admiration for each other. She liked them. She had rarely had reason to like anyone in her short life so far. But she liked these people.

To disguise the fact that the smell affected her, she took in minute, shallow breaths through her mouth, which came out like wheezes. The stink threatened to overtake her. She wheezed in slowly and puffed out quickly. Jolene hoped her breathing would allow only a little of that foulness into her body, as she believed some of those stink atoms stayed inside her, melding together with her cells. She knew she'd carry that stench with her for the rest of her life.

Emma turned her attention toward Jolene. "Hi, I'm Emma. You new here?"

Jolene nodded, surprised that anyone saw her as important enough to take notice.

"Let's go out back and get away from this awful smell," said Emma. "There's a field to pick flowers."

Emma led Jolene out the back of the aged clapboard store, where a field of flowers grew among a wall of tall weeds. The two little girls began picking a bouquet. Within minutes, the dead smell became so strong, overpowering the floral scent, that Jolene involuntarily gagged. She shifted her gaze toward the grocery's back exterior wall. And that's when she saw him.

A man lay there, slouched against the wall. At first, she thought he was sleeping. She approached slowly so as not to disturb him and noticed that he wore his hat askance. Her eyes traveled down, and she saw his hat sat on top of a bloating and blackening head.

Jolene screamed.

Later, the authorities identified the remains of the town derelict, Mr. Gasby, from his clothing, a dirty, raggedy flannel shirt and jeans with a leather belt with marijuana leaves stamped all the way around and fake turquoise jewels seated in the silver buckle. He had succumbed to his whiskey and found a nice resting place, slumped against the weathered boards of the grocery, obscured by the weeds. After he took the long sleep, scavenging animals carried away most of his flesh and bones. The police bagged his remains and took Mr. Gasby to the morgue in Darwin. No further inquiry took place. People in Taylorville rarely asked more questions than necessary.

Few people today even remembered Mr. Gasby's demise. Except Jolene. To her, it marked one of the most important days of her life. It was the day she made a lifelong friend in Emma.

After the discovery of old Mr. Gasby, Emma, Jolene and a few other Taylorville kids made a trek to the field where the old drunk had died. Emma gathered a sprig of wildflowers that she tied with a ribbon to lie at the spot. Jolene poked around the dying brown reeds and discovered among the cattails a part of Mr. Gasby's skull with a tiny patch of flesh attached and a tuft of black hair rooted in the bone.

"Oh, my God. Those police fellows didn't get all of him," Jolene said. The kids squatted down and combed the area for any more stray pieces of Mr. Gasby.

Emma said, "He needs a proper burial."

Jolene found a sturdy stick and dug a small hole. Pinching Mr. Gasby by the tips of his hair, she laid him to rest.

"I wonder what he was thinking, sitting here against Grandpa's store before Death snatched him away," Emma said.

"Probably where he was going for his next drink," said one kid.

"I wonder why he died," Jolene asked, as she cleared away the weeds around the grave.

Emma sighed. "You'ins never know why some people die. Grandma says that when Death comes, it's not leaving until it takes a living soul. She said that's why ancient people made sacrifices, so's to satisfy Death. So's Death would leave and spare them."

"Maybe so," said Jolene, her head bowed, looking at the makeshift grave. "So, you think Mr. Gasby died so another person could live?"

Emma nodded.

Reasonable Arnie stood, his finger pushing his glasses up onto the bridge of his nose. "Well, that don't make no sense. Someone still dies."

"I think Death came, and Mr. Gasby made his sacrifice in order to spare us, so we need to do him right. Everyone... gather around." Emma grabbed the hands of two children, and soon a small circle of mourners formed around the tiny grave.

Jolene squeezed her eyes so tight that she saw sparklers burst inside her eyelids.

"Now I lay me down to sleep. I pray the Lord my soul to keep." Jolene recited the prayer she knew the best, and Emma joined in.

A friendship was born that day on the heels of death. Death could be as great a bond as love, and Jolene understood that she and Emma owed Mr. Gasby a favor.

The events 12 years ago were as vivid now as they were then. Now, standing in front of her rabbit hutch, Jolene smelled the death smell yet again. Each time she smelled death, trouble soon followed. The second time, George had crept into her bedroom for the first time. The third time she smelled it, a classmate almost drowned in the school's pool during gym class. It was like her sixth sense.

Jolene looked up at the sky. The sun had risen over two hours earlier, but the moon was still visible in the sky— a children's moon, so-called because only children could distinguish it from the clouds. Jolene liked the name. She felt it was appropriate. The innocent minds of children allowed them to see many things not noticed by adults, their imaginations unrestrained by conventions of the reality of their surroundings. They could make even the most bizarre and twisted thing the most wonderful and beautiful.

Yes, Jolene remembered having an imagination like that as a child, good at keeping secrets and hoping for all sorts of better things. She had lost her ability to see a children's moon by the age of five. Living her life, she would've been blessed to have a child's imagination to untwist the dark bindings restraining her. But Jolene would do whatever she could to ensure her younger sister, Vickie, would have that child's innocence until Vickie decided Jolene's protective safety no longer served her.

4

Jolene entered her bedroom and sat on her mattress on the floor. She looked over the pamphlet for Florida State University for the hundredth time, and, for a moment, allowed herself to dream of days she would soon walk around the campus. It would be the first time in her entire life in which she wouldn't have to worry when something expected, but bad would happen. Jolene just knew she wouldn't be smelling the death smell at Florida State. She fathomed a life where her only concerns pertained to what she needed to get done for class.

She imagined living in a dorm. Nights spent chatting and doing homework, mornings spent heading to class and the campus coffee shop. She imagined swimming with only the concern that she swam her best. It felt impossible to live a life so unburdened. And yet, soon, she would be free of George, and that unburdened life would be hers.

She opened her eyes to her bare room with her bare walls except for the poster of Katie Ledecky. Jolene's gaze drifted across the hall to the new, well-made suit and hat laying out on George and Harriet's bed. It was the first of the month. The monthly cash the state sent for each foster child—both her and her sister—would have arrived. Already, as usual, it had been spent.

She closed her eyes hard enough that a tear rolled down her cheek. Jolene hated life in George and Harriet's home. But she had to suffer it all inside. If word got out, the Department of Children Services would remove and separate the two sisters into two different and unknown foster homes. Better the devil you know than the devil you don't.

The opening of the front door startled her out of her preoccupation. Jolene stashed her pamphlet, her new passport, and license into the cubbyhole behind the electrical outlet next to her bed. She took a deep breath and stealthily tiptoed into the bathroom, closing the door quietly behind her. She waited to hear a quiet footfall in the hallway outside the bathroom door. George didn't let her down. She could hear the slight creak of the floorboard, the one she had pried loose the year prior to serve as a warning signal of the approaching predator.

She stood in front of the mirror over the bathroom sink, taking in the dark circles under her eyes, and stuck her finger deep in her mouth to produce a gagging reflex and its accompanied sound. She ran the water in the sink. The second board outside her bedroom creaked and she could imagine the hesitant footfall of the man. She continued to gag, which occurred with little effort on her part. Soon, she heard the rustle of clothing brushing against clothing, and the creak at the hallway and finally the back door opening as George left to begin his day's work at the Baptist Church in Darwin. Only when she expelled her breath did she realize she was holding it during the whole time of George's exit. Another day of freedom from George and that thought brought a smile of victory to her face.

She wouldn't be able to use the gagging ruse for long. He would catch on eventually, wondering why she was always sick several times a week. For now, he had mentioned nothing, because to do so would mean that he was returning home mid-morning for no reason whatsoever and Harriet would become suspicious. Though Harriet had to know what was going on under her roof. Jolene reprimanded herself for having a momentary lapse in defending the one person who could have stopped the nightmare. Harriet did what was best for Harriet. After all, she was the adult. Not Jolene.

She opened the bathroom door when it hit her. George left the house using the back door, which made little sense, as he parked his car in the front of the house. An uneasy feeling came over her, and she hurried out the back door to her rabbit hutches. As she stepped off the porch, she caught George walking in large strides toward the house from the back. He looked at her with a stern expression, though there was also something in his face. Satisfaction? Delight? Jolene gasped. A knowing washed over her like a lead cannon ball dropping into her belly. George said not one word and stepped around the corner of their home, walking to his car parked in the front.

Jolene ran to her rabbit hutch, preparing herself for what awaited her there. The female hutch was open. Down at her feet laid Mabel, her head at an odd angle, blood oozing from her lifeless nose. Jolene threw back her head and howled as she scooped Mabel into her arms and held her at her chest, rocking back and forth. "You kept them safe, didn't you, Mabel? Only I couldn't keep you safe."

The message George gave her was clear: do not be sick the next time he came lurking. She swore that she would have her revenge, in one form or another. Getting the hell out of Taylorville was revenge enough. It would be then that she would be immune to his threats. But she wanted more. She would ensure that the minister of Taylorville Southern Baptist Church would face his day of reckoning.

She closed her eyes and her mind to the dark thoughts. She thought of sweet Mabel. Her hand searched the ground for the right tool and grabbed a stick to dig a hole, wiping tears with the back of her hand. She took a large lettuce leaf from the hutch and wrapped Mabel into it and secured it with the sturdy stem of a large weed. She placed Mabel in the hole.

"Now I lay me down to sleep," she said. "And I pray the Lord my soul to keep."

5

Wade Malone stepped off of the Greyhound bus and began his long walk west. He passed the familiar Darwin's Dollar Store and Darwin Laundromat. A dark, dirty alley separated the stores from Dolly's Diner, from which Wade contemplated grabbing a bite before heading home. He reached into his pocket and pulled out a burner phone, dialing a number.

"Yeah." A man's voice answered. "This Vega?"

Wade grunted. "I told you to stop calling me that. Wade. It's Wade, you ass-hole."

Wade took a moment, his breath hard. He tugged on his ponytail. He'd gotten the nickname Vega after John Travolta's *Pulp Fiction* character. When Wade first earned his moniker, he mistakenly thought he earned the name because Vega was a bad-ass killer. Exalted by the moniker, he even got the name tattooed on his arm with a large intracardiac needle.

Soon, though, Wade noticed the guys in his inner circle snicker and smile when using the name. He watched the film again and realized something: every time Vega was around, something helter-skelter happened. Like when Vega blew a guy's brains out by accident when he was waving around the pistol or his boss's wife's overdose when she was under his watch. The point was clear. Vega was irrelevant. Filler. A goof. He earned his alias, it seemed, because of his doltish way and manner of nervousness that introduced bedlam at times when the situation called for steadiness to get the bad deed done.

"The hit's done, and I got the money," Wade said. "You won't see hide nor hair of me neither, just until things go quiet. Don't want any Putin lovers finding my ass."

"Don't you think you should tell me where I can find you, just in case?" The man asked, drawing out his words with slight hesitated pauses.

This guy was a real wackjob. "In case of what, Senator? I'm not taking any chances and neither should you. I'm done breaking legs for a while. I'm in a place where no one talks to any law, no one ever goes to, Nowhereville, USA. Consider me a ghost. I'm ghosting." With this last statement and not waiting for a reply, Wade disconnected the call and threw his burner phone into the garbage can. Anyone who was anyone he worried about believed him to be from Chicago and not from the small hell-hole of a village on the west side of the Wabash.

Wade noticed a beefy gal in tiny shorts topped with a tight mid-drift eyeing him. He recognized her from the bus. She had yakked with her neighbor the whole time, a long-haired boy of eighteen who had sneaked sips from a Budweiser wedged between his legs. Her voice had droned on and on for the entire trip from Chicago to Darwin. Wade practically heard her whole life story, and it wasn't anything to speak about. The girl's disappointment was evident on her face when the boy remained on the bus. She turned and waved wistfully as the bus drove away. It was probably the first smart thing the boy had done in his brief life.

Wade laughed quietly to himself and waved down a taxi.

"Hey bud," Wade said to the taxi man. "Can you take me to Taylorville?"

"Absolutely not. I'm not risking damage to my cab. No siree. I'm not entering that town, no sirree, indeed."

Wade sighed. "I'll give you a twenty-dollar tip."

"No one from Darwin will drive you to Taylorville, not even for a hundred-dollar tip."

The cab sped away. Wade turned toward the sidewalk and resigned himself to walking. His first foray back in town was going just about as well as he expected.

The beefy girl from the bus had stopped at the bench and now reached into her pocket, counting her money. Wade watched her mouth moving as she tallied up the figures in her mind. Then her shoulder sagged, and she bit her bottom lip.

Wade knew exactly what would happen next, and he stepped up his pace to increase the distance between him and the girl.

"Hey Mister!"

Wade picked up his pace but stopped when he heard her stacked heels hitting the pavement in a run. His eyes rolled heavenward as he mumbled to himself. "Bloody-Jesus-Hell."

The girl caught up and stepped in front of him, blocking any attempt he would have to continue walking.

"It seems I'm short a little to make it the rest of the way home," she said. "Could you spare ten dollars or so?" She tilted her head in what she thought was a seductive manner. It came off amateurish for him. It'd taken him about fifteen minutes to run into stupid and he wasn't even in his hometown yet. He'd spent the last fifteen years in a city mingling with people who had a sophisticated air about them, even if they were begging for a buck or two. Now, he would have to deal with the stress that stupid brought.

"How old are you, girl?"

The girl pulled her shoulders back to make her breasts larger. "Eighteen going on twenty, and old enough to know what I'm doing." She glared back at him, almost as daring him to make a stink about it.

Wade pulled out a ten and folded it between two fingers. "Now, you going to say how old you really are?"

The girl's face fell and her shoulders sagged. She shifted her weight to her left stacked heel. "Fifteen. But hey, I'm no virgin. And I need the money."

Wade said nothing. He stood there for a moment, silently studying her. His eyes squinted like he formulated a plan. "That's old enough," he said, and grabbed the girl around her throat, pushing her back into the shadowed alleyway. She stumbled on her platform heels, but he held her up easily by her throat. He slammed her against the brick side of Dolly's Diner. She clawed at his hands. Her eyes registered shock. "You scream and I'll squeeze the living daylights out of you. You understand?"

She croaked out a weak, "yes." Her eyes watered, not from choking, but because she was close to crying. She continued to claw at his hands around her throat, but ineffectively, like she was swatting away a pesky fly.

It gave him a thrill to hold such power, even though he hated what he knew he must do. "Now, where's the flirting, manipulative bitch you were a few minutes ago? Don't tell me I now have a little girl in my hands who will give me all that she promised for a few bucks?"

The girl squeezed her eyes shut, and the tears flowed down her cheeks. Her face turned beet red, and she continued to struggle to breathe. Wade pressed his body against hers to quiet her struggles.

"Now, it seems to me that you need to be a little more careful traveling alone, like you've been. Like when you approached me offering something that a man, unlike me, wouldn't have passed up, no mind how old you are. You didn't even notice your surroundings and this dark alley where it would be so easy for me to take what you're offering without even a mind to pay. Not everyone you sidle up to will be as nice as me."

With that comment, Wade released his hold on the girl's neck and she bent over, coughing. Everyone needs a life lesson, he thought.

"I want you to remember this and how scared you was a moment ago."

The girl's mouth sagged open, and she continued to gasp. Spittle streamed from her open mouth, hitting the asphalt.

"Get your life in order, girl, because you're headed down a dark street going the way you're going. Just think if I was some other guy you promised to give a good time." Wade paused a moment, gathering his thoughts to drive his point home. "We crossed paths for a reason. It was fate that brought us together in this alley. Take this as a sign you must change your ways and stop struttin. Understood?"

She used her elbows to press against her knees for support and moved her head up and down. Her body shook uncontrollably as if it were winter and she was one of those tiny, hairless dogs. Her arms folded over her stomach and she slumped forward, coughing.

Wade reached into his back pocket and pulled out a money clip. He withdrew a bill and grabbed her hand, twisting her wrist around so that the palm showed. He placed the bill in her hand and clasped her fingers around it, making a fist.

"Now, here's a twenty," he said. "That may not be enough to get you where you're going, but it'll be enough to buy a meal or two." He gave her fist a squeeze and then a bump before turning to start his short walk home, happy that he could have a positive effect on one young girl.

6

Emma walked along the river bank until she reached a dirt lane. Townsfolk used the lane in equal measure as a road and boat ramp. The few rotting clapboard houses perched along the hillside of tangled and snarled vegetation were listing, but still livable by Taylorville standards. Behind them sat weathered outhouses—a stand-in against the foreseeable day that the septic tanks backed up. Emma crested the hill and saw the two old rusted signs, a smiling Clabber Girl holding up a box of baking powder and *Get Your Cold Drinks Here* there fifty years ago to patch up leaks in the weathered boards of her paternal grandpa's grocery.

The store was tiny but contained anything you could possibly need, like the bodegas of New York City, which Emma read about in social studies class. Her Grandpa's little store served the community, she knew. If New York had stores like

Grandpa's, then the Connors weren't so different from the city folk after all, and this notion gave her a sense of acceptance outside of her town.

Other than her maternal grandma's The Dam Tavern, no other commerce existed in town. A person had to travel to Darwin for any other needs. Occasionally, Emma overheard the townsfolk gossip, saying things like: *The Connor family will get your paycheck one way or another.* But what they didn't know was that, based on how Grandpa ran his business, the Connors were lucky to have any extra money at all.

Emma stepped up onto the porch of the grocery and stomped off the small amount of mud that had gathered on the bottom of her boots. Grandpa's grocery might not look like anything from the outside with its weathered, mismatched boards, but as soon as she stepped inside, the smell of the oiled oak floor and long oak counter warmed her. The pressed tin ceiling with a carved disk in the center painted with small flowers and cupids drew her eyes upward. The accumulation of blackened coal dirt, cinders, and melt trafficked in on the bottoms of boots and bare feet layered the wood and silenced footsteps. The wear looked an eyesore but reminded her of the store's popularity. If you were sad in San Francisco, you could go to the beach. But if you were sad in Taylorville, you could go to Frank's Grocery. And people did.

"Good morning, Sweet Pea." Grandpa croaked in his bullfrog voice from behind the meat counter where he always sat reading his books. His white apron shown, about the only thing Emma could make out in the dim light of early evening. He reached up and easily placed several cans of beans on to the top shelf.

"River's cresting," Emma said.

Grandpa pulled a cigar out of his shirt pocket from under his butcher apron. He held the ends of the cigar between the fingers and thumbs of his hands, studied it, and then, looking as if he didn't know what to do with the thing, placed it back in his pocket. The familiar gesture, which Emma understood comforted him, brought warmth to her heart for reasons she couldn't fathom.

"The city's forgot us. Hell, the country has, too. They don't want to be touched where this town touches you." Grandpa placed his forearms on top of the meat counter and clasped his large hands with their delicate, long fingers. He nodded east toward Darwin. "Folks over there don't want to remember what poor is like here. No way. You mark my word, poor with no hope breeds a special kind of anger."

Grandpa was a man of a few words. He had seen all the world he wanted to see during the Vietnam war. He carried a somber aloofness brought about by witnessing the worst of what men can do to other men. He had purchased the old store after the war and had kept it opened day after day all those years. Some of those days, he and his good friend Bill sat behind the meat counter, puffing on their cigars, drinking, then hiding their Four Roses whiskey from the women and children who came to shop. They would reminisce over their time spent in the jungle, including the day Grandpa saved the men in his platoon from an ambush, earning him a Purple Heart and Medal of Honor. But most of the time he spent behind the meat counter was to read his series of books—chronicles of war and tales of the heroic deeds of simple average people. He stayed inside the store during the days and walked across the street to his tiny one room home at night and never went nowhere.

The bell tinkled, and a small boy and girl entered. The Harvell kids. The coal dirt dusted their clothing and smudged their skin, the genetic inheritance of the town. Snot ran down the little girl's face and she had a red chafe around her mouth.

"Mom says to get a loaf of bread and bologna. And to put it on the tab," the boy said. His eyes shifted to his left to the candy counter beside the register, attempting to not appear obvious. Emma's heart went out to the kids. They came into the store often, always buying groceries for their mom, and always hopefully glancing at the candy counters even though they never had the money to slide them open.

Grandpa reached into the meat case and palmed the bologna, pulling it out. Emma grabbed the store's iPad and logged in the amount owed. These folks always bought on credit. And their tally was running up. Glancing through the large storefront window, Emma saw the children's mother, arms folded across her chest and her hand to her mouth, chewing her fingernails. She paced back and forth in the street. She wore her T-shirt inside out. No coat.

"How would you two like a Clark Bar?" Emma asked the stringy-haired Harvell children. Both heads bobbed up and down and their eyes lit up. The little girl licked her chapped lips and left her tongue out, the tip pointing heavenward, a perpetual hanky. Emma reached into the glass case and pulled out two Clark Bars. The little girl's eyes followed the movement of the candy bar from the case and into the hands of her brother like a hungry puppy. She reached to grasp the candy Emma held out for her. "Are you on your way home from school?" Emma asked.

The children's heads continued to bob, although she didn't think her question registered. Their small heads bobbed in the affirmative no matter what she asked. The girl's ponytail swung over her head like a whip.

Emma tested her theory of how overly agreeable children answered yes to anything. She looked at the girl and her chafed mouth, "Are you really Pennywise the Clown and you're mysteriously manipulating the townsfolk to do your evil bidding?"

The entranced little girl continued to nod and stuck her tongue further to touch her snotty nose tip. She eyed her brother and his candy bar, as if she received so much pleasure watching him consume his treat.

Emma noticed the girl's tongue was dark, like she had eaten coffee grounds. "What's that on your tongue?"

The little girl looked confused and teared up as if she had done something wrong. The boy stepped in to answer. "It's dirt," he said. "Lillie was crying this morning because her stomach hurt from being hungry and Momma told her to eat dirt to help the hunger."

Emma, shocked, looked over at Grandpa, who shook his head. She walked to the meat case and Grandpa handed her two slices of bologna and cheese that he folded into a meat roll-up.

"Here you go guys. A little breakfast to start off your morning with a happy tummy." The children had the bologna-wrapped cheese in their mouths and chewing within five seconds.

Emma repeated the cost of the items in her mind, added the total with tax without grabbing a calculator. "Okay, that'll be $7.12 for the bread and packaged bologna. I'll put it on the tab." She handed the bag to the boy.

"Thank you, Emma," said the boy, turning to leave.

"Tank you," said Lillie, spinning around to hurry after her brother, her eyes glued to his Clark Bar and grasping her own high above her head. The boy stopped before reaching the door and peeled the last of the wrapper off, breaking off a piece of his candy to give to her. Once outside, the boy gave the brown sack to his mother, and she grabbed it from his hands, opening it wide to see its contents.

Parents often sent in their children to shoulder their shame, because they had no money for the essentials, like food. Grandpa called it "shame by proxy" to explain the behaviors of the adults in town. It made no difference to Grandpa if parents sometimes unwisely spent some of their cash on drugs or alcohol. He saw those things as a necessity to dull the pain of living. He continued to avoid collecting their overdue accounts.

"But don't you think you're contributing to the problem by not holding their parents responsible for their debt? Most aren't even appreciative."

"I'm only responsible for my ways. Besides, I'm not looking at getting anything in return for helping. That don't make sense to me—giving to receive," said Grandpa.

Emma sighed. "Maybe you can give it to me, then. I need to get as far away from here as possible and I'm thinking college is the sensible way to do that. This is just a town full of... full of vampires."

Grandpa laughed. "Vampires! I think you've been reading Anne Rice and not Hemingway. Anyways, I think it's going to take more than leaving Taylorville or going to college to run away from the injustices in the world."

Emma opened up the ledger and ran the numbers of the children's purchase in her mind and wrote the amount in the ledger under the counter, even though she had an electronic copy in the iPad.

"You amaze me with that calculator you have in your brain," Grandpa said, shaking his head. "Just like your dad, you are. Adding things up, figuring out the tax and all, and coming up with the total. I used to check your numbers with a calculator and found out you were right on the penny every-time."

"Of course, but why did you ever doubt me, Grandpa?" She opened the iPad and wrote the total in the Harvell's account. "Was it because I was only ten?" She laughed, wanting to make a point.

Emma got a disgruntled "humph" back in reply. After a few more moments in silence, Grandpa elaborated on the children shopping while their mom waited outside. "Yep... those kids...shame-by-proxy, that's really all it is."

Grandpa reached behind the cans of beans and pulled out his Four Roses and took a swig, then placed it behind the cans of creamed corn.

"Grandpa, don't you think it's a little early for that?"

"Define early. And no, I don't think it's a little early...need the swig to help with the day, that's all." Grandpa retired to his seat behind the meat counter and returned to his reading the day's newspaper. Even though Emma tried to get him to read it from the iPad she convinced him to purchase for the store (and her own personal use), he refused. He said he liked the feel of the paper in his hands and the ability to look at the full page at once. Emma soon joined Grandpa and opened her book he had given her. Emma was reading *The Old Man and the Sea*. She gazed over at Grandpa's book on his stand by his chair. *Nineteen Eighty-Four*.

His book told the story of a man working for The Ministry of Truth and where the man alters his past to fit the future and the erosion of free will through fear. Emma had read the novel and thought the theory presented an interesting concept. She likened it to what a person does when they heal emotionally from past traumas. She and Jolene had toyed with the concept of time happening simultaneously, so it made sense that when you tend to your past trauma and release the pain surrounding it, that you can re-write your history, and therefore, create a new present self—a self that hadn't lived the trauma and could make different choices. Jolene had said she wanted to believe this life theory was true, because Jolene had a great deal of trauma to rewrite. But Emma thought *Nineteen Eighty-Four* had an oppressive premise.

Grandpa would want her to read it again after he finished and would quiz her to see if she understood something more in the book—a political message, she guessed. Grandpa was more of a man of the times and didn't want to understand that maybe time is fluid. Emma had difficulty detecting the political undertones in the book. She had no interest in politics, and the mere ominous political themes of the book were enough to challenge the most sophisticated of readers; nonetheless, she would stick with it. She never put a book down before finishing it, no matter how disinterested or badly written it was. Maybe she would discover a new idea to perceive her life, even from a political basis. Heaven knows, she understood the drive for total control and pure power. For her current book, *The Old Man and the Sea*, a slender book, Grandpa would grill her soon enough about her thoughts and understanding of the simple but profound story.

"So...analysis of your read?" Grandpa must have read her thoughts.

Emma sighed.

Grandpa snorted. "Hey, you're polishing your brain by reading and talking about what you read," he said.

"Well, then...oh...I don't know. It's about an old guy and his fishing habits. Not exactly an interesting or profound topic for discussion, Grandpa. Not much polishing going on here." She sat her book down on her lap and pointed at her head. "Next time pick something more exciting...like...Simone de Beauvoir."

"See? Unable to find the profundity in simplicity, eh?" Grandpa said, chuckling. "Like, for example, a man making a living doing what he loves and facing his largest adversary at his old age."

"Doesn't seem that adversarial to me. I witness children facing adversity...you know, living with drugged-out parents, poverty, hunger, and abuse. I don't need to read about an old man encountering a large fish. His problem doesn't seem so serious to me."

Emma's cell vibrated, and she picked up.

"Emma, George done and killed Mabel," Jolene said from the other end of the line, her voice heavy with grief.

"No, oh no," Emma said, her eyes tearing. She slumped over the counter. Grandpa put his book down at the sound of alarm in her voice.

"I hate him, I hate him! Who does this sort of thing?" Jolene's voice was near screaming at the other end of the call.

"I can't believe he'd threaten you like this. Oh, poor Mabel, innocent little thing." Emma's voice cracked. Grandpa had a look of concern in his eyes, and he waited to hear the bad news he knew would come.

"Do you think Grandma Rose would mind if I move their hutch to your backyard?" Jolene asked, haltingly, between sobs.

"Absolutely, not mind at all. I'll ask her, but I know she'll be fine with it. Let's move the poor babies after we walk Mattie home, okay? They won't spend another night near that man." Emma's eyes met Grandpa's, and she shook her head.

Jolene sighed her relief over the phone. "I feel better knowing that the other bunnies will be safe. I swear to God, Emma, I will find a way to make George pay for what he's done. One way or another."

"I know, you will. One way or another." Emma paused. "Are you okay?"

"Yes," Jolene said, settling her voice. "I'm better now, knowing we can move the hutch. Later, okay?"

"You bet."

Emma stood and looked down at Grandpa and relayed the news to him. "See Grandpa, Jolene faces a great deal of adversity in her life; she doesn't have to fish for it."

Grandpa frowned and studied the floor, refusing to look Emma in her eyes. He nodded, then spoke. "That girl has a world of trouble on her shoulders. The law does nothing, and we have our hands tied."

Grandpa was right about the law. One time, Jolene mentioned to her first-grade teacher that she wasn't sleeping at night because George would wake her up. The teacher, concerned and observant, called Department of Children Services who interviewed Jolene and visited the home to speak with George and Harriet. But before the interview by DCS, George threatened Jolene. So, she said nothing. She kept the truth about the nightly visits under her tongue. The case manager closed the case, probably in relief, glad to avoid added work to her caseload.

Emma felt a deep sadness overcoming her. "Grandpa, is it alright to take the Ford to the library for a few hours after I walk Mattie home?"

Jolene's predicament drove an urge to go to the Darwin University Library to the psychology section for two hours for solace right now. To focus her mind in a Jungian psychology book allowed the stress of the day to drop away. When she read Jung's work, she could almost grasp a larger picture of all the suffering of people around her and then she wouldn't be so victimized by things she had little influence over, like Mabel dying at the hands of a mean old man.

Grandpa grunted and nodded in reply and Emma grabbed the keys off of the hook behind the meat counter and headed out the door, leaving Grandpa to find his own solace engrossed in his book in the quiet store.

7

Wade walked by the cemetery at Taylorville's town limits. The town cemetery sat on a rise of acreage and loomed over the town...the truly dead, in Wade's opinion. Their loved ones placed markers wanting to absolve fears of their own mortality. Headstones rose from overgrown weeds. Some of the older headstones had turned gray-green, some had split at sharp angles, and some had toppled over, breaking into shards that scattered. More stones had fallen than stood upright. One freshly dug grave with red roses nicely arranged caught his eye.

"Welcome home," he mumbled. Passing alongside the few graves near the road, one grave with flowers and a child's stuff dog reminded him that maybe it would be nice to get his sister some flowers and the girl a gift, to soften the blow of his unexpected visit. Wade entered the graveyard and weaved through the graves before walking to the head-stone of the nicely cared for grave that he had spied. He read, "Suzie Hempshaw, born July 8th, 2000 and died June 10th, 2009." Wade thought a moment and spoke out loud. "Suzie Hempshaw? I remember you. You were Gary Hempshaw's brat. I gave you a Tootsie Pop when I passed by your stoop on my way out of town all those years ago."

Wade stood looking down upon the neatly decorated grave. "Hmmm...wonder what happened to you." He thought for a moment. "Hell, I know what happened. You're lying in a tiny coffin for all eternity. My kinda hell." He caught his breath when the beginnings of panic rose from his belly, and he felt closed in upon, as if the sides of Suzi's grave were pressing in. Images of himself, 14 years old, when his father had shoved him inside the trunk of a 1971 Chevy Chevelle SS as a lesson taught because he'd gotten his ass kicked by the town bully earlier that day. When his father and brother finally opened the trunk a couple of hours later, they broke out in laughter, seeing Wade trembling in fear, sobbing and piss-soaked. He could not live that one down with his father and brother, something they had never let him forget.

He squatted down and rolled a joint, his attention finely focused, thinking of nothing but the task at hand, not too tight and not too loose. It was, after all, a really potent strain. Only after he had taken a long drag that he looked at the tombstone once more and shook his head before he reached and rifled through the flowers. He stood and smiled, his task completed, and he set off for the walk home. Soon, he crossed the Wabash and turned down a short lane, then his stomach spasmed at the familiar sight that never changed. Wrecks lined up in the yard leading up to his family's front door, sparking a walk down memory lane as he passed by the older of the heaps first.

Some people kept photo albums that triggered nostalgia. Wade's family had a lot of old wrecked cars. Good memories and bad memories both lingered here amidst the wreckage. An old school bus sat on flat tires. The body had rusted in places and insects flew in and out of broken windows. His father had dreams for that old bus of turning it into an RV, and the old man would speak to his boys about trekking across the country in it. To a boy of ten, the dream of an adventure occupied most of his mind. Inactivity, though, had beaten his dream down when, year after year, his father made no movement toward transforming the bus.

Then Wade passed a 1940s Ford truck parked next to the bus that had rusted to the point that the original blue paint had completely disappeared behind a coat of filthy brown and red. The truck's round headlights and grill had morphed into an exaggerated cartoon character's face that seemed to express shock as to why any visitor would walk up this lane. The tall weeds growing up between wrecked and abandoned cars rising out of the black cinder hardscrabble would serve as a fit destination for any horror movie taking place in Chernobyl. He remembered running that Ford up to Sugar Creek and pinning Becky, his old flame, down in the bed of that truck, having his way with her. A mind-blowing experience, that. She'd been his first. She had fun, too. They were thirteen. Even then, the old truck ran good. Now, it too joined the auto graveyard.

Then he stopped short, as once again today, he was reminded of the one shameful memory he hated most. The 1971 Chevelle SS sat on four cinder blocks, the tires and wheels gone and rust eroded most of the original shiny red paint. Wade's sharp intake of breath drew in the acrid smell that he swore was the piss-soaked floorboards of the trunk. He hurried along.

The models of the cars became newer and less corroded when he neared the house until he reached the last vehicle— an old bulldozer with a large shovel resting on the ground, tall weeds growing around it. Looking at the bulldozer, two things concerned him. One, by the looks of the old vehicle, his brother hadn't done a lick of construction work in years. Two, the line of wrecks stopped with the 1970 El Camino that Wade himself had driven before he left for L.A. That could only mean one thing: his brother and sister were driving wrecks instead of retiring them to the auto graveyard.

At the top of the lane stood the Malone family house, a house standing for generations of Malones and a testament to their shotty workmanship. The Malone family house had been built room by room from scraps of wood and other material. Smoke rose from the stovepipe on a roof badly in need of repair. They built chicken coops better than his home. Although the house was little more than a shack, it had kept a roof over the Malones' heads for decades. Now, holes the size of baseballs rotted right through the asphalt shingles and plywood. Wade's lungs clenched when he thought of walking into the house and taking a deep, moldy breath.

He placed the bunch of flowers he grasped up to his nose to overcome his image of mold. He shoved the tiny stuffed dog he had picked up in the cemetery deep into his pocket to present at the right time and took another deep breath as he walked toward the front door. One of his sister Dottie's dogs barked from under the porch. The mutt ventured out, its head low, eyes intent, hackles rippling over its back. Wade's approach slowed. A gun's report sounded in the distance and echoed in the hollows. Another shot rang out. The shots did not sound as if fired from a rifle used for hunting, but from a handgun. At least, the timing of the shots indicated the gun wasn't aimed at a person. Maybe a shooter doing target practice on a set of cans placed on a log. Maybe something else.

The dog hunched over and growled. A first warning. Wade's stride shortened and his walk slowed. Then, as he approached, he gave the dog a swift kick before it had time to lunge. A woman in her forties came out of the house and stood on the front porch, whistling once. The dog tucked his tail and retreated under the porch to curl up next to its companion. The woman's bleached blonde, shoulder-length hair blew in front of her eyes. She tucked the strands behind her ears and mashed the hair down at the part, which emphasized more the two inches of new growth. She folded her arms under her ample bosom to keep her flannel shirt from blowing open with the occasional gust of wind.

"What do you want?" the woman said, squinting at Wade, to shield her eyes from the glare of sunshine. "I don't think I know you."

"It's Wade, Dottie. You know, *your brother*," he said, the bunch of flowers dropping at his side.

The woman's eyes narrowed slightly. "Wade?" Her tone sounded incredulous. She stepped off of the porch and grabbed him by his shoulders, drawing him in for a hug and then pushing him away, all in one continuous motion. "What are you doing here?"

"Came for a visit. I'm allowed, don't you think?" Before she could respond, he added, "Good thing for me—you know, with the little girl—that the FBI Witness Protection Program wasn't for you."

"Yeah, well, things didn't work out there." Dottie smiled smugly. "Besides, I got tired of someone telling me what to do and where I could go. I don't need to hide. I mean, you have to be crazy as a bat in a peppermint patch to piss off a Malone."

"Damn straight." Wade laughed. "There's no safer place than home."

Dottie fired a Camel from her pocket and leaned back against the porch railing. "Damn straight," she repeated. She held the cigarette between three fingertips and her thumb, almost the same way a man would hold one, and then took a deep drag from it.

Dottie, at sixteen, found herself in a relationship with a married man forty years her senior. They had planned to marry, but first they had to get through one obstacle: his wife, who had all the money. So, the dumbass killed her, and roped Dottie into dismembering the woman and burning her body down by the river. Dottie, the smarter of the two, turned State's witness against the man. She swore she'd forever love him. But, in the end, a get-out-of-jail-free card won out.

Wade thrust the bunch of flowers toward Dottie. She looked at them suspiciously.

"They're for you. I picked them up on the way here from Darwin."

"Picked them up...from where? The Darwin Memorial Cemetery?"

Wade didn't answer her. "Hey it's the thought that counts, isn't it?"

He reached into his pocket for the stuffed dog, pulling it out and rolling it over in his hands.

"Really Wade? You took the stuffed animal from the headstone of a child's grave?" Dottie's eyes narrowed again before she met Wade's stare and took another drag, blowing her smoke straight at his face. She had startling blue eyes, fearless and cunning, made even more so by the heavy black eyeliner unsuccessful at corralling all that blue. Like the dominant dog earlier that showed its teeth, Dottie used her eyes to back anyone into submission. There were two types of women in these parts. One type gave in and was submissive. Those types of women never gave you a lick of trouble, but you wondered if those women were maybe born too soft for their world. Then, the other type who was harder than granite and stood their ground no matter what, a meanness bred in or added later by circumstance. A person needn't guess which type Dottie was.

"So, what brings you back?" she asked, her eyes narrowing even more. "I don't want no trouble, Wade."

"There won't be no trouble," he said, dragging out his words. He had only been in town a couple hours and already his hillbilly diction had returned. He felt a twinge of shame, noticing it. Though, in truth, that accent never completely left. In San Francisco, in his mind, he spoke with the eloquence of a sophisticated, metro man. But that's not how other people always saw him. "Hell, from the looks of things, if it wasn't for me sending money, you'd all be up shit creek," he said to Dottie.

Dottie nodded in agreement. "And without a paddle." She laughed. "I guess you're right there, but I would say I earned it." She looked at him pointedly. "I cleaned up your mess and I'm still cleaning up your mess. And by the way, speaking of that mess, she's not so little anymore." Dottie looked at him as if her eyes would bore straight into his brain and then to the stuffed dog he clasped. "She's a beauty, Wade, and she looks just like you."

Wade didn't want to continue down that rabbit hole.

"Well, ain't you going to invite me in? Where's everybody, anyway?" Throwing out the questions over his shoulder while his arms flew open, and he stomped onto the porch and pulled open the front door.

8

Wade walked into the dank front room. Once his eyes adjusted from the brightness of the day to the darkness of the Malone home, he surveyed his surroundings. Nothing had changed. The same pleather couch jammed against one wall with a scratched and ringed stained coffee table in front of it. An overstuffed La-Z-Boy took up one corner of the room. The table held several beanbag ashtrays that overflowed with half-smoked cigarettes. Several empty beer bottles and a few half empties lay scattered on the table and the floor. Ashes and cigarette butts had been pushed down into the opened necks to lay at the bottom of the bottles. A soft yellow glow came from a floor lamp next to the recliner. An old flatscreen television hung suspended on one wall of the room, blaring an old episode of some reality show. The smell of stale beer, cigarette smoke, and sweaty socks filled the house.

Nothing was different, except everything was. Of course, he'd changed, trading his hillbilly slump for a west-coast swagger. But what about Dottie? She looked the same, though there was a difference about her he couldn't put a finger on.

Her eyes glinted, and she brought her cigarette to her mouth, took a long drag, walked to the coffee table and put the cigarette out in an open beer bottle. "Your daughter Mattie is a beauty, Wade," Dottie said. "A little slow, but sweet all the same." Dottie delivered this piece of information with a natural cadence and calm. "Even though I raised her from a baby, she knows who her real daddy is. She'll be here soon from school. And she'll love to meet you."

Mattie spawned Wade's regret. He skipped town before her birth. In fact, he hadn't known he had a kid until her mother died when Mattie turned three, forcing Dottie to track him down. Dottie took Mattie in on his behalf and raised her best she could on the money that Wade sent from California. He enjoyed receiving updates every few years from Dottie about the girl. But mostly, he had wanted to keep his distance. He couldn't shoulder the burden. A child complicated his life. He liked coming and going without feeling worried over another.

The sound of the back door closing and footsteps echoing from the doorway off the kitchen drew Wade's attention. His eyes eventually landed on a man with long black hair tied into a ponytail, the hair graying at the temples. The man entered the room and threw down a 9mm revolver into the center of the kitchen table. Heavy shadows framed his eyes. He had deep-seated dimples like parentheses, not on his cheeks, but around a dimpled chin. His white T-shirt hung over green sweatpants he tucked into western-style boots. He dropped at the table and stared at the gun without blinking, almost as if he would nod off to a wide-eyed sleep right there.

The man's slender body belied a rage and danger that could unleash at any provocation; much like the soft appearance of a slow loris with hidden sharp teeth concealing a potential ferocious attack, if one reached out for a cuddle. The sight of the gun did not startle Wade, but the jailhouse-inked tattoo on his bicep did. In the towns of Taylorville and Toad Hop, where surface always serves as substance, this man's body spoke danger in spades.

But his creed was not seeded from these parts; he wouldn't easily buy into the common ways of presentation, nor the laws of the town. His body tattoos were not armor like most men wore to scare. No, siree, Wade sensed that. This man's restrained cruelty shown in his tats told the reliable story of his past dark deeds. No need to display the tattoo for boasting rights. He wore his ink because he had earned the right to brag. The hair on the back of Wade's neck stood at attention like the hackles of a dog facing off with an adversary.

The man's tattoo depicted a dagger piercing a faceless clock, the hard edges curvy and running, much like a Dalí painting. Three droplets of blood dripped from the tip of the dagger. A prison tattoo if ever Wade saw one, although done with an artist's flare. He either had served a long bid for killing someone, or he had killed someone while serving time in prison. The number of blood droplets depicted the number of people he had killed, or the number of bad deeds done. Whether the killing had occurred in or out of prison, in Wade's mind, no difference existed. Killing was killing, and this man had done it. He needed to keep an eye on this guy.

As Dottie talked about Mattie, the man sucked slow and deep from his cigarette, blowing a plume of smoke toward the ceiling. The plume traveled languorously upward, as if affected by the man's aloof personality. He did not glance Wade's way nor take any interest in what Dottie said. But Wade sensed that the man had heard every word since he entered the house.

The man reached over and lifted a baggie of white powder that lay on the table. With a long pinky fingernail painted black, he scooped out some white powder, pinched his right nostril, and snorted with his left. He repeated the process into the right nostril. He closed the bag and pinched the tip of his nose, wiped and snorted again. The man then stood, stretched his arms upward, and Wade noted his gaunt physique and sunken stomach—the sign of a heavy drug diet.

Then, the man grabbed his revolver from the table and palmed it, passing it from one hand to the other. He came from outside the Taylorville world, Wade knew it. He had an air of violent sophistication to him, one that didn't abide by Taylorville's hilly code or any set of rules. Wade's eyes continued to stay focused on Dottie. His head nodded now and then with her conversation. She droned on about how Mattie contributed to housework or how Mattie achieved an "A" in Special Education class, but his mind attended to the stranger in the next room.

"Who's that?" Wade finally asked, tipping his head toward the kitchen.

"Oh, that's Sy, my man." Dottie's voice dropped to a whisper that continued to carry through the house. "Word has it he stabbed his pregnant prostitute girlfriend in the belly. He got time. Sy even scares me. He's one son-of-a-bitch." Dottie sighed. "He's the love of my life."

This, from a woman not queasy regarding the dismemberment of her ex's ex. Wade realized, even from the darkness he arose from, that this man appeared unlike any other. This unknown element made his situation more dangerous for himself. Not that he was afraid of Sy. No, Wade could hold his own. Besides, he saw an opportunity to not be bored with this man. Maybe they could liven Taylorville up a little. Yet, this guy could create a different sort of problem for Wade. He was here in Taylorville to lay low. Now, he wondered if he'd chosen the wrong town.

9

Behind Grandpa's house, Emma rolled the rusted shed doors open and jumped into the seat of the red and white Ford truck. She pressed the clutch with one foot and started the ignition, easing the truck out and onto the road. The 1986 Ford had belonged to her dead father. Other than his work boots, he valued his truck most. It was all she had left of the days when they would hunt for squirrels, rabbits, deer and mushrooms that hid in secret places in the forest. During those hunts, the truck transformed into an all-terrain Jeep, and they into African safari trackers, scouring the plains for a rare white elephant. She did not look back on Dad and his death with sadness. Her father died trying to stop a bar fight at The Dam Tavern. When Emma grieved him, she also felt buoyant with pride. Her father died as he lived his life, standing up for others.

Her mother, though, lived another story. Anger simmered at the bottom of Emma's gut when she thought of *that* woman, and she threw the truck into a grinding third gear. For some reason, when she became nostalgic for her first few years with her father, the image of her mother filled her head. After giving birth to Emma, her mother decided that having a screaming daughter in her arms pushed her to the limits of responsibility. Soon after leaving the hospital, her mom left the state. She'd only return home when Emma turned four—and then, only for one year, because her mom soon felt the call of adventure again and left town with a stranger. Beyond that, aside from one other brief visit, no one had heard from her since.

Emma surmised her mom lived hell-bent on a drug-fueled quest for a better life without responsibilities. She had last seen her mom at the age of five. Then, after her father's death, Grandma and Grandpa raised Emma much like an old married couple would, even though they were not in fact married, and they lived on the opposite sides of their small village. They parented with zeal and love, lathering Emma with what their own children could not provide—Grandpa rectifying for the untimely death of his son and Grandma atoning for her wayward and irresponsible daughter.

The drive to the edge of Darwin took only five minutes and to the university library another fifteen. The city built Darwin University Library in the late 1800s to be the home of the owner of an ironworks foundry. The mansion kept its original fabric wall coverings with elaborate murals depicting life in that era, the same Tiffany gas light fixtures, mosaic fireplaces and hand-carved wood floors, trim, and doors. It was a beautiful place to get lost in thought.

The students crowded the library at this time of evening. Seeing kids near her age going about their day with a purpose and drive triggered in Emma an emotion that maybe she, too, could develop a part of her that was of something good and purposeful. The wooden floor creaked as she crept to the psychology section on the third floor. No students sat at her favorite tucked-away spot at a table, so she sat and opened *The Collected Works of Carl Jung*. Before delving into the thoughts of this brilliant theorist of the mind, the experience of having her own small corner in the huge mansion-library washed over her. She felt the gooseflesh run down her back from the pure pleasure of belonging. This place felt like home, but better. Here she had hope that maybe one day she could escape her town.

Emma's satisfaction was short-lived, though. Soon after she sat down to read, someone intruded into her space, dropping into the seat beside her. This person had the whole empty section of the library to use, but he chose to sit at her table. Her lips pressed together when the intruder grunted a most obnoxious sound, and the cover of his book dropped against the table as he opened it and flipped the pages, somewhat aggressively.

Emma stole a furtive, angry glance. She saw black wavy hair like stormy dark swells rolling toward shore. She saw skin smooth enough to inspire envy in many women. He looked at his book as if she didn't exist. Long lashes contrasted with his skin. She didn't need for him to lift his eyes from the book he read to know that his gaze would certainly disturb her. And yet, she lingered on his face too long.

Their eyes met. His lips expanded into a wide, sudden smile upon contact. Her eyes lowered to her book, knowing he had caught her studying him and then, after rereading a sentence for the third time, she realized she feared to look up from her book. She didn't want him to know he interest her. This interest in a guy was a feeling she was unfamiliar so, she dared herself to do what she compulsively resisted, which was an urge to ignore him. She could never say no to a dare, even if a self-directed one. She would dare herself to push against her uncomfortableness with this college boy and look at him. When she looked up, she gasped. Irresistible blue eyes stared back at her and held her enthralled. He was that magnetic.

She could hear Jolene say, "Why, his eyes are like Liam Hemsworth's from *The Hunger Games*. And those dimples!" She and Jolene always compared people to actors in the movies. It was a game they play between them. And for the moment, Emma barely took in anything else. Then she glanced at his book cover that elicited such a sigh from him, *The Pragmatic Programmer*, a book at least two decades old, the T-shirt with the faded picture of Che Guevara on the front stretched across a muscular chest and a Tommy Hilfiger down-filled jacket slung over the back of his chair, both symbols of capitalism, one ironically so. She diverted her glance once more, but not before she caught his large open smile once again. He'd noticed her studying him. Was he laughing at her?

Suddenly, the awareness of her shabby black shirt tucked into her black jeans, which she had stuffed into dead father's black steel toed work boots and her long blonde hair pulled back into a messy ponytail made her feel unsophisticated. She hurried to gather her belongings, pulling them to her chest and pushing away from the table. Anger replaced her self-consciousness. This college boy ruined the precious few minutes she stole from her day, making this time pointless. Yet, she had to be honest with herself and know that her anger arose from the realization that she felt didn't fit here at the university or at the side of a college boy. She wasn't a college student and probably would never be one. She didn't fit anywhere, really. Not in Darwin, nor really in Taylorville. Not west of the river, and definitely not on the east bank, where opportunities for girls were more prevalent.

She closed her book and stood up. She had to walk by him and she wouldn't be able to avoid not looking at him unless she risked accidentally bumping into his chair. The college guy's eyes met hers, her face reddened, and she hurried past him. She placed Jung back on the shelf and walked out the door of the library, her head down, while wondering if his eyes followed her. Once in the truck, she laid her head on the steering wheel in shame. Unbelievable! Living her life west of the river, she acted all brave and everything, but put her on the east side and suddenly she trembled bunny-like. The shame that a boy's attraction to her would have this effect surprised her. She wouldn't be able to live this one down, so she wouldn't tell a soul, not even Jolene.

10

Emma waited on the grocery porch, licking at her favorite raspberry-chocolate ice cream waffle cone, dressed in her black jeans, studded belt, black hoodie, and her father's black steel-toed boots. An outfit that always gave her distance from others. She enjoyed controlling people's rejection of her by her aversive clothing, so then she would know that they didn't reject her for her soul. After her library experience with the college boy, she desired to drown herself in a tub of ice cream. She settled with the cone from the grocery. The raspberry sauce started to melt and drip over her hand, creating a grotesque look. Somehow, the messiness of the dripping cone parroted her emotions from the morning at the library.

She stood when the small bus arrived, licking her cone quickly to completion. This bus transported the special needs kids from the Darwin school to Taylorville, and this day,

Saturday, it contained only one passenger: Mattie, a fifteen-year-old. Mattie had a special field trip to the museum. Two years ago, Emma and Jolene befriended the single bus passenger after they witnessed several young boys pummeling Mattie with their fists and feet like army commandos when she exited the bus. From then on, Emma and Jolene designated themselves as Mattie's protectors. They had walked her back and forth from the bus stop every day over the last two years.

A commotion down the road drew Emma's attention as a group of teen boys walked toward her, laughing. She licked her ice cream, slower now, with long easy strokes, her eyes focused on the boys. She couldn't hear their conversation, but she understood it as another attempt to demean a girl or someone different. Heat rose in her neck and cheeks. Just let them say something to her. She wasn't in the mood. She witnessed the intention of their conversations by a certain strut the boy she knew as Jeff had, and the thrusting of his friend's hips offensively as a response to what Jeff said that tipped her off. The boys now stopped in their approach while they watched Jeff's mimicking. Jeff, his long hair flopping over his face, hobbled pigeon-toed with his hand limp at his chest and making a slack face like he slobbered. The boys followed close behind him, laughing.

"Emma," Jeff said, and he dug his thumbs into the front pockets of his jeans, his fingers pointing in the direction of his penis, and he shoved out his hips in a back-and-forth motion. The other boys, laughing, stepped back, leaving Jeff standing in front of the group. "How about you and I have a little fun? You know, so you can do the walk of shame tomorrow?" He looked at his crotch, "and if you're lucky, you won't be able to walk at all."

Emma observed Jeff for a long, silent moment and the sniggering group of guys in another moment, not saying a word, the raspberry sauce running down her arm. The boys sobered upon her demeanor and straightened their spines, which expanded their body mass like pufferfish trying to give the illusion of a stronger presence, but failing in the process to do so.

Emma stared calmly and continued to lick her ice cream cone without missing a stroke. The guys shifted uncomfortably, a little embarrassed, red shading their ears and faces. They slowly backed away. Jeff shuffled his feet a little. Then, mustering courage, he stood his ground, with his arms folded across his chest in what she saw as an effort to ward off her dark mojo she sent his way.

"Whatcha lookin' at? Can't you take a joke?" He looked back at the guys, "Yo, bros! Just peep this shit out."

Emma observed them for a long while, holding her cone as the raspberry sauce dripped along her arm. She stood askance, staring. She felt better already after her library experience, where the college boy rendered her helpless and shy. Emma remained staring.

The town boys moved on, somehow knowing that if they stayed longer, there'd be a reckoning. Heads down, defeated in their effort to get a rise from her.

Emma smiled, satisfied.

Jolene walked around the corner and joined her on the porch with eyes that were puffy and swollen, and she watched the boys retreat down the street. Emma reached over and gave her a hug.

"Okay?"

Jolene nodded and looked away as if to say there was no need to bring up the image of her dead bunny, Mabel. She couldn't go there yet.

The small yellow school bus drove up to the front of the grocery. Two scuffed tennis shoes stepped from the bus's folding door. When her eyes registered her friends, Mattie's face lit up. Her honey blond hair hung straight around her shoulders, having come out of her ponytail in the day. She wore under her jacket, a T-shirt with sequined hearts on the front and jeans emphasizing the curviness of her body. She showed signs of becoming a beautiful woman, but when the boys caught sight of her vacant stare, they gave her a wide berth. Her simple mind saved her from the same treatment many women got growing up in Taylorville, Emma and Jolene included.

Mattie shoved her hand into the pocket of her pants and pulled it out, opening her fist to reveal coins. Her mouth moved as she counted her money. Her face turned upward toward the sky, as if the computations she performed slowly in her mind would write themselves in a celestial body floating by to give her the answer.

"Hey, girlfriends," she said. "Can I go in the store and grab a Coke before we walk? Dottie gave me my allowance that Dad sent."

Mattie spoke in a nasal, loud, and stilted voice, its impact softened by a smile luminating her face and the interest she held in her eyes that she found in everything. Whenever Mattie spoke of her father, she brightened in a different, dreamier way than her normal state. Having a father *out there* allowed Mattie to sustain the belief that a guardian angel overlooked her every day, Emma believed. If only it were true.

"You saving for our visit to the tattoo artist?" asked Jolene. Mattie nodded, and Jolene smiled in return.

"Why don't you go and have a raspberry ice cream cone... on Grandpa? We'll be back in a moment. Jolene and I are going to ask Grandma about moving the rabbits to Grandma's yard." Emma smiled, taking pleasure in removing George's threat to Jolene. No way would George take action against Grandma and harm any rabbit living on her land,

Mattie's eyes lit up as if someone had given her a birthday gift, the gift of having her friends walk her home, and a free ice cream cone to boot.

With her attention redirected to a purposeful activity, Mattie turned and skipped into the store, an enormous smile lighting her freckled face. Emma could understand why people thought Mattie strange. She had a carefree way of moving from one moment to the next, always smiling like a girl without a care or worry in the world. It was as if Mattie wore an invisibility cloak that shielded her from the harshness of Taylorville. Emma marveled at that ability. She wished she could discover Mattie's secret for herself. Maybe she'd be able to return to the library and not feel the need to run out because she met a boy.

11

The two friends walked Mattie past the wrecks. A little pug-terrier mutt, Rascal, ran up ahead, a neighbor's dog that met the girls on their walk. Rascal greeted the girls at the top of the lane every day after school with his characteristic sideways running style, a product of his mixed genes. Emma made sure Mattie had a piece of ham from Grandpa's store to give him. It was possible that the slice of meat was Rascal's only meal of the day. Or maybe he was conning the entire neighborhood. Either way, the mutt grew devoted to Mattie. And Mattie grew enamored with the faithful dog who walked her home every day.

"We'll see you in the morning to walk you to the bus stop, okay?" Jolene said.

"Yes, and can I call you tonight if I need to?" asked Mattie. Her eyes searched Jolene's face, even though she asked the same question every day and received the same answer.

"Of course. You call me anytime you need me, you hear?"

Mattie nodded, the largest smile on her face, her eyes downcast.

"And don't forget, tomorrow we have our meeting at the studio. Bring your money."

As the girls approached the Malone house, a group of four men wearing wife beater t-shirts and baggy jeans with carpenter belts hammered new shingles on the roof.

"Well, isn't that something?" Emma asked, wondering if Dottie had come into a little money. It could have only come from Wade. Emma knew Dottie only ever made adjustments to her life if a little dough came in from California. Emma recalled the time Dottie bought the old truck she drove. She was all smiles for months, stating that her brother finally came through with a little support cash.

The worker's hammering drew Mattie's attention upwards. The moment she saw the men on the roof, Mattie transformed from a thoughtful, gentle girl into a seductress. She walked ahead of Emma and Jolene in a few quick strides. She swung her hips as she went, shoulders pushed back, strawberry blonde hair twirled around her finger. The jeans she wore that day with her blue T-shirt tucked in accentuated her hips. The men on the roof, sweat dropping off their brows despite the coolness of the day, stopped hammering and gawked at the vision below.

"Hello, guys. What'cha all doing up there?" she said.

The men didn't respond, but they scooted to the roof's edge for a closer look.

The door opened. Dottie and a man Emma didn't recognize walked out. He had curly dark hair, sinewy arms and taut legs. He resembled a rattlesnake, coiled and ready to strike.

"Mattie, guess who's here?" Dottie asked. "It's your daddy. He's back from San Francisco for a visit."

Emma tried her best to hide her shock, knowing all too well that the Malones viewed shock as a sign of weakness. You wouldn't want a Malone to think you were weak.

The women in these parts were accustomed to never having enough, making one sacrifice after another. They were used to being degraded by men, and especially the men of their own families. The life of a pawn. When the weaker sex endured those acts, it sometimes bred a woman made of stone, rebellious and resilient to any adversity. Jolene embodied the image of those women.

Emma witnessed Jolene's stone-faced expression as Mattie went from seductress to little girl instantly. Mattie didn't have Jolene's resourcefulness. Unfortunately, she would walk the path of the victim, appearing helpless at times and manipulative the next.

Mattie pulled down at her hoodie, twisting the ends into tight coils. In a shaky voice, she said, "Daddy?"

The man stepped off the porch and approached, shaking his head, but smiling. "Maybe, but you can call me Wade."

Mattie gave a nervous smile, one that Emma had grown to understand as her way of sending a message to everyone that everything was fine with her. No harm done. No need for anyone to rock the boat.

Dottie smiled. Her arms folded over her chest as she leaned against the porch pole, her legs crossed at the ankles.

Emma felt her body go into high alert at Mattie's anxious smile and noticed that Jolene stiffened at her side. Emma stepped forward, standing somewhat in front of Mattie and holding out her hand to Wade. "Hi, I'm Emma Connor and this is Jolene. We're very close friends of Mattie's."

Wade stopped in his approach to Mattie and looked at Emma. He didn't accept the shake. "You're—what—the granddaughter of Frank Connor and Rose Ford?"

"Yep. That I am," Emma said, dropping her outstretched hand.

Wade stood looking Emma up and down and nodding. He assessed her value and abruptly turned his attention back to Mattie. "So, honey, how about we get a little acquainted?" He dismissed Emma with the turn of his back.

Emma stiffened when he referred to Mattie as 'honey'. Sy slid through the door and leaned against the house, like an afternoon shadow, void of any light, falling against the outer wall, flat but ominous.

"Uncle Sy!" Mattie cried out and a seductive quality washed over her, turning her from awkward teen to an alluring woman as she sashayed over to the front porch and looked up at her "uncle", smiling, with her hand on a hip that she jutted out to the side. "Will you help me with my homework tonight?" She asked, batting her eyelashes at him.

Dottie stiffened, and her smiling face turned sour. Emma could sense the tense vibrations coming off of her in waves.

Sy didn't respond, giving Mattie a blank stare before nodding to the crowd on the porch and slithering back into the house. He, at least, appeared to not want any part of the drama unfolding.

Emma watched as Wade's body tensed and his jaw muscle flexed. Light flickered in his eyes as if he was striking matches from an internal matchbook and his fingers pulled into tight fists and then flexed, extending, reminding Emma of a gunslinger readying himself for a gunfight at the O.K. Corral. It was at that moment she realized Wade was wary of Sy. Dottie hurriedly followed Sy into the house, like a canary befriending a cat. It was the first time Emma had known Dottie to cater to any man.

12

Emma observed the unspoken exchanges and a story of this household not mentioned out loud came together in her mind, a hierarchical shift in power. Dottie, always in charge, now relegated to third on the totem pole. The sign of Dottie's insecurity of her man's lack of attention toward her when another woman was present revealed that even childish Mattie could threaten a dangerous woman.

Not that Sy behaved all handsy and grab-assed. He spent some time at The Dam Tavern and hardly left a mark. Wade had done more to make Mattie, Jolene, and Emma uncomfortable in the hours of his arrival than Sy. Actually, since he arrived, Sy stayed pretty much to himself, as far as Emma had seen. She wondered how many more edgy men could live under one roof without one taking the others out?

The air crackled between Wade and the girls.

Blood was blood, after all, and Sy wasn't blood. No one knew what role Sy played in this household except as a boyfriend of Dottie. Still, Emma and Jolene would always err on the side of protecting Mattie, whether against the boyfriend or father.

"Come on, girl. Let's go," Wade said, speaking to Mattie as he turned toward the door.

"Okay, guys. See you tomorrow, okay?" Mattie, oblivious to the telegraphed messages, turned and looked back at Emma and Jolene. Only when she received the nod from Jolene and a hand wave from Emma did she step over to Wade. Jolene and Emma watched while Wade and Mattie ambled back toward the house, Mattie's head bowed.

Yet, as she approached the porch and the sweaty men working on the roof, her mood changed. She cocked her head seductively and said, in a sultry voice, "Hey guys, it sure looks hot up there."

Wade stopped short before the opened screen door. He breathed under his bitten top lip for a brief moment and then slammed the screen door, stepping back onto the edge of the porch, his jaw working. He grabbed a hammer off of the porch railing for want of busying his hands.

"Damn it, Mattie, git your ass in the house," he said. He swung the hammer in a wide arc and landing it in the porch post, the claw end anchoring deep into the wood.

Mattie stood, her mouth slacked and shoulders slumped. She made no movement toward the house, as if she froze in her spot.

Emma didn't know what to do. The unexpected violence from Wade triggered an unusual response in her: helplessness.

The fear she may do something that would spin things out of control immobilized her. Only her eyes moved to glance over at Jolene, who also stood muted—but not as tensed—as Emma. Jolene, experienced to unexpected rage from a man, knew when to step down and scrutinize the situation first before acting.

"You girls go on home now." Wade's voice had a quiet tone to it that belied his mood moments ago.

Silence hung in the air. Emma studied Wade with morose recalcitrance. The workers said nothing but also remained looking at the scene unfolding below them, standing at the roof's edge. Jolene's eyes met Emma's; a silent code transmitted: *best to leave things be.* Slowly, Emma nodded, unsure but resigned. Jolene dropped her eyes and pivoted, as if to escape some horror. Emma called out to Mattie in a voice as normal as she could muster. "We'll see you tomorrow, Mattie." Mattie didn't respond. She remained rooted in her place, head bowed.

Emma followed behind Jolene, increasing her pace with a hop and skip to catch up. When they reached the end of the lane and were no longer in eye and earshot, they turned to each other.

"What do you think?" Emma asked.

Jolene looked into Emma's eyes, her own indecisiveness reflecting Emma's state, and tears welled up. She looked back up the lane and spoke out what Emma thought. "I'm not getting a good vibe from this man, Emma." She studied the ground for a moment. "Let's go back and tell Wade that we need to speak to Mattie about her homework assignment for tomorrow...that we forgot to go over it with her."

Emma nodded. "We can make sure she's okay." The girls jogged, which then sped into a sprint back to the Malone house.

13

Within earshot of the home, they heard Wade, and slowed their pace to a cautious walk.

"Do it, do it now, girl."

The ominous tone in his voice inspired Emma and Jolene to quicken their pace into a jog. When the house came into view, they saw Mattie standing in the same spot in which they had left her, head bowed and arms crossed lengthwise. Wade stood in front of her with a garden hose in his hand. Dottie stood on the porch, leaning against the post. A slight smile drew her expression, much like Pennywise about to drag a child by the ankles into the sewer. Sy came out, closing the screen door silently behind him so as not to disturb and draw attention to himself, although his presence alone pulsated out a vibe of a mixture of doom and excitement.

The four men on the rooftop now stood at the edge of the roof with shoulders slumping, a dramatic shift from the preening, sexually charged stances of the previous moment. Emma took in the scene within seconds. She and Jolene slowed their pace as they neared Mattie, not wanting to push an already intense situation over the edge. Both girls stopped a few yards from Mattie's side. Wade didn't seem to notice. He drew his attention solely to Mattie.

"Go on, now, take them off." He ordered.

Emma couldn't follow what he referred to. *Take what off?*

Mattie began whimpering like a wounded puppy.

"I said now. If you want to strut your stuff, we might as well give the guys a show."

"Pleaassse... Wade...don't make me do it. I'll be good, I promise." She wiped away her tears and ran the back of her hand under her nose to wipe away the snot. "I was just born backwards, is all."

"Well, I shouldn't expect you to know how a proper girl acts. But you still need a lesson. Take them clothes off now."

Emma couldn't believe the horror unfolding in front of her. Surely, he wasn't serious. She'd lost her voice for the first time in her life. Mattie pulled her t-shirt over her head, revealing her bra, and pulled her pants down over her panties. Her body shook from the sheer helplessness and humiliation she experienced. Her knees almost buckled.

"Take off those undergarments, too." Wade ordered.

Mattie reached behind her to unleash her bra when Emma screamed, directed toward the one person she thought could hold some control over Wade. "Dottie! My God, Dottie, stop him."

Dottie eyed Emma, but said nothing.

"What's the matter with you?" Emma screamed.

Dottie remained leaning against the post, not appearing to want to reach out and interfere. "Her daddy's giving her a lesson to not be so flirty," she said, giving a half nod and a tight grin.

Emma turned toward Wade. "Wade, please don't do this. Let me help Mattie find the right way."

Wade looked at Emma, her presence registering in his eyes for the first time. Emma saw in her side vision that Mattie had stripped herself naked and stood with her arms crossing her body to hide as much as possible her intimate parts, tears streaming down her face.

Emma ran over to cover Mattie with her body in a large hug. Mattie melted into her arms, her knees sagging, Emma holding her up and pressing her face onto the top of Mattie's head. She smelled the honeysuckle Suave shampoo that she knew Dottie bought at the Dollar Store. Emma's back faced Wade. She thought she just needed to walk Mattie to the lane. *Why wasn't Jolene helping her?*

"Get away from her, now." Wade said in a slow, deliberate rhythm, his tone turning a deeper shade.

Emma didn't move, but tried to lift Mattie onto her feet to steer her away from the nightmare and down the lane.

"Emma, stop," said Jolene. The quiet forcefulness with which Jolene spoke broke through Emma's psyche. She couldn't believe her friend would succumb so easily and let Mattie continue to suffer. But then she glanced over her shoulder and understood why.

Wade had his 9mm Glock pointed straight at her. The blood drained from her face and settled in her gut. All she could see in her mind was a bullet going through her head. She let go of Mattie and turned to face Wade. Mattie remained in a semi-collapsed stance. Emma continued to shield Mattie, blocking her from the view of the men.

"I said to get away from her once. Next time, I'll say it with my Glock."

Emma stepped away.

Wade pointed the hose in Mattie's direction and sprayed. Mattie stayed in her crouch stance, head bowed, soaked in hose water and tears. "Now, turn around girl, so's I can get your backside."

Mattie turned, one foot stumbling over the other, her knees knocking.

Tears ran down Emma's face. She had seen a lot of raw living in Taylorville. She had seen grown men weeping over their beers or pissing themselves without knowing, couples carrying drag-out fights in their front yards, women yelling and throwing out clothing and possessions from windows, young women shooting heroin on the side of the road, and much more. But this display of degradation superseded anything else she'd seen in her seventeen years. What Wade did enraged her completely, consuming her like the fire in Grandpa's potbelly stove consumed paper. She wanted nothing more than to make Wade regret ever coming back to Taylorville.

"All right, guys," Wade yelled up to the men working on the roof. "Show's over. Get back to work."

Jolene and Emma simultaneously ran to Mattie's side, using their bodies to form a blanket protecting, and warming their shivering friend. Emma glowered at Wade over her shoulder as he watched. "If it's alright with you Wade, we want Mattie to spend the night with us." Her voice shook slightly, either from rage or just the foulness of the experience.

Wade scowled. "I don't care where the hell she sleeps." He turned to follow Dottie and Sy into the house.

Emma took off her hoodie and placed it around Mattie's shoulders, zipping it up. Jolene did the same with hers and tied the arms around Mattie's waist to form a makeshift skirt. They then both wrapped their arms around Mattie, embracing her tightly between them like a thunder shirt for a dog. The three friends eventually made their way silently and stumbling, taking little baby steps down the lane.

14

The trio stopped in front of Jolene's house before proceeding to Emma's, where Mattie and Jolene would spend the night. A night of respite from men wanting a repugnant need met from their children would be welcomed in this moment. Jolene believed Mattie would mend in the safety of Grandma Rose.

Jolene's family house had a spattering of clumps of brown grass among the black cinders that covered the ground, similar to all the yards of the neighbors. When the Wabash flooded in prior years, the river dumped cinder debris that nearby factories disposed of during the night and away from prying regulatory eyes. This cinder debris left a blackened hardscrabble landscape where nothing would grow but weeds. A white porch swing hung from the gable roof, suggesting a certain family wholesomeness and presenting a stark contrast against the darkened backdrop. Behind the home, though, a different story—weeds grew in oversized variations and in one corner of the yard, a mountain of scrap metal comprised of open and used cans and metal appliances took on heights greater than any man. George promised every year to cart the junk away for cash, and every year, the mounds grew higher.

Jolene gave Emma a nod. Emma responded with a tug to her ear. They settled Mattie on the porch in the swing before walking back toward the street for privacy.

"She'll be all right, won't she?" asked Emma, looking back at Mattie shivering on the porch. "I couldn't do a thing to help her. I froze in fear."

"Em, Wade had a Glock. What did you expect?" Jolene breathed deeply, composing her own nerves.

"I don't know. I should have done something. What good is all this stuff Grandma teaches us if we can't use it when it matters. She'll be alright, don't you think?"

"She'll be fine," Jolene said. "Trust me. I understand her situation the most, don't you agree? What happened today will be another nightmare. She'll add the horror to her file and lock it away in a deep recess of her brain. You learn to do that living here. Maybe she'll be different, act smarter toward men. Some learn that."

Jolene understood Emma's doubt of Grandma Rose's teaching of holding a center and shifting the brain out of the victim in order to engage a crisis more effectively. Both she and Emma could only stand and watch their friend stripped and humiliated, with no real intervention to prevent the crisis.

Even Emma's last question of Mattie's well-being brought about a feeling of impatience in Jolene. Mattie would never be alright, but she would survive. No one understood why she didn't tell on the abuse, or why she continued to live in such an abusive house. Yet, she understood why others looked the other way. She would take the path of least resistance, which was to suffer to keep things as they were for now. She was at the homestretch and no need to upset things for Vickie.

Emma nodded, her gesture at odds with the confused look on her face, as if she understood what Jolene meant by 'acting smarter'. Jolene knew she had her swimming ability to get a scholarship to a university. Emma had her intelligence and a supporting family to find her way out of a challenging situation. But what did Mattie have? Their friendship offered some support. But maybe Jolene and Emma were Mattie's only means of keeping safe.

"You don't sound convinced she'll pull through this," Emma said, her eyes still watching Mattie.

"Damn, I don't think I'll recover from seeing it."

"She needs to leave that house."

Jolene considered Emma with disbelief in her eyes. "Do you really believe she can just do that? Where's she going to go, Emma? Do you think she can just do *whatever*?"

Emma's head snapped back by Jolene's angry confrontation. Confusion swept across her face.

"No, I don't think Mattie can just leave and just do *whatever*."

"That's right, Emma. Mattie and I can't always just do *whatever*."

They stood there in silence for a moment, Jolene fuming and Emma brooding.

"We have to do something so that Wade Malone thinks twice before hurting another girl," Emma said. "If he thinks at all."

"We have to come up with a plan that will square this with Wade without having the Malones retaliate."

Jolene nodded again. Emma's suggestion was a good idea. There was no need to take on the whole family.

"And that Sy person, he scares me. He never speaks a word and you never know where he stands," Emma said, biting her lower lip in thought. "The plan needs to be revenge-proof. The kind of plan that shames the family so much that they don't even think to retaliate or they would risk further humiliation."

"That's it. A plan with an insurance pity policy," Jolene said.

Both girls laughed, and then nodded, deep in thought and agreement.

15

The next morning, Emma and Jolene walked Mattie to her bus stop. The three friends remained silent, taking Mattie's lead as to what she needed to get through her day. Jolene and Emma walked on either side of Mattie, hooking their arms through hers, holding her up.

Mattie remained weak but stoic. She was no longer the girl who could endure abuse one moment and yet laugh with blissful ignorance the very next.

"How do you think she did last night?"

"How do you think she did?" Jolene asked, surprised at the little bite in her response.

Emma recoiled, but then her face softened. Jolene found it difficult to comfort Mattie. The situation brought up all the rawness inside of Jolene. She'd face George's abuse from a place of reticence, whereas Mattie suffered a more helpless victimization. Mattie's need to please exposed her. Jolene didn't care at all. Jolene had the bite it took to live in a place like Taylorville and not feel victimized. Mattie just rolled over and exposed her belly. Jolene was tougher than even she herself wanted to be.

Jolene continued in a softer voice. "First, she suffers years of emotional abuse at the hands of Dottie, her only real mother figure. Then, she's scarred by Wade, the father she has long revered in absentia. That girl's never known real love. Wade stole any hope she might've had to get some."

"I couldn't sleep thinking it would not get any better for Mattie," Emma said, pensively pacing, until an idea came to her. "How about we take her to the quarry after school?"

"That's a great idea! I don't think she's ever been. It'll be an adventure."

"It'll be an initiation into a new Mattie."

Jolene smiled. To have Mattie jump off of Bird's Eyrie would be the right amount of risk to bring the life back into her deadened eyes. Jolene and Emma were excited about the solution they came up with to lift Mattie's spirit and maybe recover the girl they knew from before the hosing down.

16

Emma had her chance of sneaking away to the library the following evening. She couldn't stay away from her place of refuge and her readings of Jung for long, so she took a few deep breaths to quiet her nerves. The lateness of the evening would indicate that perhaps the college boy with Liam Hemsworth's eyes wouldn't be around, as he would have other activities to do this night. She was sure of that. She walked to her spot in the Psychology section and found her favorite corner. No college boy around to disturb her. She sat down to a quiet time with Jung.

After reading for a few hours, she thought she'd better get home, as Grandma would worry. She stepped a few feet away from the table when a low voice reverberated down her spine. "Excuse me?"

She turned to find the boy extending his hand, within which he held her pen. A glimpse of a smile tugged at his lips.

She had not noticed him anywhere around her vicinity earlier and she had been watching.

"You left this," he said. Their fingers touched, and the electricity shot up her arm and tingled her in areas that had never tingled before. "I'm Nate," he said.

"Emma." She took the pen and turned to leave, not wanting to prolong the meeting or to create a greater chance to embarrass herself.

"Wait!" His smile widened to reveal bright teeth, but his confidence beguiled her more. "I think I noticed you coming here several mornings ago. Actually, I hoped I'd run into you here again."

He paused for a moment, waiting for her to say something. Maybe he considered she believed him to be a stalker, which skirted through her mind. So, when she offered nothing else, he exhaled, took a deep breath and asked, "How about getting a pizza with me later this week?"

The question, once asked, froze them in awkward silence. She didn't expect the question, but nodded anyway—not because she wanted the date, but because any other response evaded her. She could only muster up the bare minimum answer, as she wanted this whole incident to go away. If only she could escape his devouring eyes. Emma didn't trust him. What could he possibly see in her?

Then, as if reading her mind, he said, "Any woman who reads Jung in the evening is someone I want to get to know."

An unfamiliar flush of heat spread up her neck and into her face. His good looks not merely dumbfounded her, but the manner in which he called her a "woman" threw her completely off centered. No one referred to her as a woman, and no boy had ever asked her out—in a proper way. Dating wasn't something normally done in Taylorville. You just hung out with someone. His good looks aside, Nate quickened her heart and made her self-conscious. He was the first boy who took an interest, and the first she ever saw actually reading a book—other than her father and Grandpa, of course. So, in response, she just nodded, all she could muster up in the moment.

After he entered her number into his cell, Emma quickly escaped from the building before she could make a bigger fool of herself. Once back inside the truck, her head rested on the steering wheel. What had she done? The thought of an outsider coming into Taylorville and her home rattled her nerves. He won't make it to the front door before the glaring stares of the townspeople send him back to Darwin, and him wondering why he had a lapse of common sense to ask out a poor, unsophisticated girl from the west side of the river. What would he think of her and her home?

It was the first time she felt some shame of living in Taylorville and that she cared what another person thought. Well, the incident was done. She had committed to going on her first date. Her nerves balled up in her belly and she started the truck for the drive home.

She pulled out her cell and texted Jolene.

You won't believe what just happened...

Then she attached a .gif of a cute gorilla in a zoo sitting quietly eating a banana before unexpectedly flinging itself at the glass partition and towards the children who watched.

17

Jolene rushed to catch up with Emma as they walked to her house to move the bunnies the next evening. "So, did you make a date with the college boy? Or should I say 'man'?" Jolene's smile lingered in stark contrast to her puffy eyes.

"Yes. He's going to pick me up on Friday at The Dam Tavern and we're going to do something. Maybe go for pizza."

"He's going to pick you up? Here? In Taylorville? Isn't he from Darwin?" The alarm in Jolene's voice brought Emma to a fleeting thought that she didn't want to linger on because she would lose the courage to go out on this date.

"I think so." Emma bit her lower lip in thought, afraid to give voice to her insecurities, even to Jolene. "Well, I suppose he'll find out sooner or later where I live, so why not on the first date?" Emma was well-aware that Jolene expressed her first inclination to have Nate pick her up in Taylorville.

Jolene's forehead wrinkled in thought. "Makes sense. At least he'll pick you up at the tavern and won't know right away that you live next door. I don't want to yak all over your yum, but be prepared that he might just turn the car around and speed away."

"Yeah, I thought about that...but like I said, better to find out now if he can brave Taylorville to date a girl from the west side of the Wabash."

"Makes sense to me. Better for him to reject you because of where you live, versus rejecting you after getting to know you."

Of course, she had thought of Nate rejecting her because of her roots. She hoped he was a bigger man than that.

As they walked to Jolene's house, Emma looked at the neighborhood with fresh eyes. One house had layers of dirty brown blankets over the opening where a front door should be. Chickens ran in the yard freely. The neighboring house had weathered clapboards, but on this house, a piece of plywood served as a front door. Someone stacked layers of clothing and discarded appliances against windows, triggering the imagination that this house belonged to a family of hoarders. In their backyard, a small camper trailer was shoved up cozy-like against a wooden fence and rested on flat tires, maybe serving as a reserved place to sleep when there was no more space in the home. There were two eight-foot heaps of discarded items such as metal chairs, tires, hubcaps, a rusted refrigerator, several broken washers, all from trash the owners collected from the neighboring homes. Beer cans were scattered around the man-made mounds like stray flowers filling the backyard space. If only the owners had arranged all the trash carefully, it could be considered art, maybe making a statement of consumerism, because the junk pile reminded Emma of considerable human waste.

Emma felt torn between fearing Nate's judgment of her when she herself judged others of their struggles in life and ways they used to get through the day. Maybe Grandma was right regarding a person's need for a place to unwind with drink, something simple, no responsibility demanded of them other than to sit and be served. Sometimes reaching for the sauce to find solace required less effort than dropping to your knees in prayer.

18

Jolene and Emma dragged a hutch over to the side of Grandma Rose's shed behind the house. They hoisted it to sit on top of a makeshift wooden table they found while rummaging through the discarded items in the shed. Jolene decided on a spot under a big, beautiful oak tree. With the table placed next to the shed, the tree provided a wind block and canopy against the elements, a cozy and sheltered existence. Jolene handed Emma the smallest rabbit, Baby Boo, nuzzling him and stroking his soft bunny fur.

"You know, you were always rescuing the helpless," Emma said. "Remember when we were little and playing in the woods? That day you saved Mabel."

Jolene nodded. She remembered all too well. That day, she and Emma had been running in the field next to Emma's grandpa's house when she spied the two coyotes crouched down and creeping up toward a bunny, twitching her nose in the tall grass, just like Mabel had done that day. She thought it strange that the bunny allowed the coyotes to approach; even as a little girl of ten, she knew what predator behavior looked like. As the coyotes gathered tension in their hind-quarters, ready to pounce and run at the helpless creature at top speed, Jolene let out a war cry and sprinted past the head coyote. As the second coyote closed in to grab the bunny in its mouth, Jolene snatched the bunny into her arms. Emma ran up behind, screaming at the second coyote like a banshee and waving her arms. Both animals ran off toward the river.

Emma studied Jolene, and Jolene smiled. "You did a good thing, Jolene. You gave Mabel another eight years with her kiddies."

"You're right. That kinda thing is instinctual for me. Doing what I can so another can live harm free...at least for a while longer. Sacrificing for another." Jolene buried her nose in Baby Boo's fur. Tears filled her eyes again. She endured George's abuse so that her sister wouldn't need to. When DHS removed her and her sister from their natural mother's trailer to come and live with George and Harriet, she had cried hard. George, though, became angry and yelled at her to stop crying because they were giving her and her sister a suitable home and they should feel apprecia-tive. Over time, she had learned that tears made things worse. People either couldn't handle another's suffering or they pun-ished you for it. Either way, things didn't get better.

Emma pulled Jolene into her arms, along with Baby Boo. It felt nice to Jolene to experience the touch of another person without them wanting something forbidden in return.

19

Grandma Rose entertained her patrons with her witty stories. The jovial mood was rare amongst folk, considering the suffering most lived, but that was Grandma Rose's way to lighten the mood. Besides, Grandma Rose's life was far from mundane and she had many tales to tell. Her personality flowed with an in-tune with-the-cosmos thing. Jolene contributed Rose's light in her eyes to her way of thinking. She entered her life during the laid-back hippie era and never saw reason to exit from it.

This evening, Tim McGraw belted out "Live Like You Were Dying." The song played from Grandma Rose's iPad, which she had reluctantly wired into the vintage jukebox. She no longer used the vinyl 45's from the 60s. Those records sat abandoned under the glass dome of the jukebox, with one record frozen in place, ready to slot into play.

Emma threw the back screen door wide so it would slam shut, like she always did, to test Old Miss Henry. A fixture in the tavern, Miss Henry wore one of her floral cotton dresses, a light sweater, and heavy, black orthopedic shoes, with thick nylon stockings rolled down just past her knees. Every day and into the evening, Miss Henry sat perched in front of the nickel slot machines, her back straight, her knees pressed tightly together, and her feet planted on the rungs of a stool. Her purse laid on her lap primly, as if she was a devotee sitting in the front pew of a church. She sat as she once did when she was a proper lady, but now she lived out the rest of her days as a companion to the slot machine in the corner of a tavern.

Today, Old Miss Henry failed the test again. She sat perched on her shiny, chrome-legged stool in front of the poker machine, completely still, entirely unfazed by the loud sound of the door slamming open and shut. She didn't even look Emma's way. The old woman's eyes remained fastened on the spinning of the reels, her hands clasped together, her fingers gracing the bottom of her chin in prayer-like fashion as each reel clicked into place, the bells clamoring and the coins dropping into the pan below. Nothing tore Miss Henry's attention away from her one-armed bandit. Miss Henry didn't give Emma and Jolene any mind at all, because she had no mind to give.

Miss Henry pulled the lever of the machine and swooped into the tray to gather her coins, almost in a continuous motion with a rhythm to her playing. Jolene and Emma looked at each other and smirked. Secretly, they suspected Miss Henry of faking dementia so that her family wouldn't interfere with her gambling. One day, they knew they'd catch the old woman playing her devious game.

"Miss Henry, you winning at the slots today?" Jolene said, smiling and throwing her arms around the old lady in a hug. Miss Henry stopped her gaming for a minute to rest her hands over Jolene's arms, relaxing back into Jolene's embrace, a quiet smile of her own on her face.

Grandma Rose believed that Miss Henry had a lot more going on in her head than she let on, too. "She'll probably win Jeopardy somehow," Grandma Rose would say. "Just look at them eyes...they shine with intelligence."

Grandma Rose leaned over the heavy mahogany bar that braced one side of the tavern. The same cabinetmaker who had designed Grandpa Frank's counter in the grocery built this relic in the tavern. The artisan woodworker carved elaborate and intricate scrolling designs into the wood and tried to accommodate Grandma Rose's stature; at only four-foot-eight, Grandma Rose barely stood higher than the bar.

Emma approached, and Grandma Rose waved a white rag in her left hand as a greeting. She wore one of her floral button-down tops with jeans and a white half-apron tied around her middle. Her eyes lit up, grinning her typically blissful and Zen smile, being in-tune with nature and the cosmos and all.

Grandma Rose's most startling feature was her eyes. Their sparkle sometimes shone part blue and sometimes part grey. The changing shades captivated Jolene. It was as if those cosmic forces Grandma Rose balanced through meditation breathed a light force within her that her eyes let out, like windows. Those eyes could bore into a person's core; no thought remained hidden from Grandma Rose. The serenity emanating from Grandma Rose's eyes bore the truth of a long, wise life, and Jolene understood she could get through another tough challenge just by connecting with Grandma's gaze and allowing a profound peace to penetrate what ailed her.

"So, were you able to move the rabbit hutches to the side of the shed?"

Emma and Jolene lowered their eyes in a sullen nod.

"I'm sorry about Mabel. I know how special she was to you, Jolene."

Jolene nodded and sighed. She used the back of her hand to wipe away a tear falling from her eye. She wanted to dissociate from the experience of that morning, feeling in some bizarre way that Mabel's death was her responsibility.

"You know, the Mayans believe an unexpected death is a sacrificial death for a person or the village. Maybe Mabel, when she protected her young the best she could from the coyotes, became the symbol of the mother who sacrifices to protect her child."

Grandma Rose had Jolene's attention now.

"Jolene, you have always been the protective mother to your sister Vickie, willing to put your life on the line to rescue her from any hurt."

Jolene nodded. She held back her tears, fearing they might run down her face, starting a crying jag. Jolene, listening intently to Grandma Rose speaking in her quiet voice, calmed her running thoughts. Sometimes Grandma's perspective shifted the hurt of a situation to one of a deep acceptance and peace.

"Mabel represents the protective mother in you that needs to die. She has sacrificed herself to free up the mother's energy in you so that it doesn't have to manifest. You need to free yourself so that you can live the life you're meant to live. Go. Follow your dreams."

Jolene looked at Emma with a feeling of excitement bubbling up deep inside of her at her realization. "Emma, you spoke about this sacrifice when we buried the pieces of Mr. Gasby. I remembered it after all these years. And I remembered Mr. Gasby's story when Mabel died," Jolene said, eager to have Mabel's death mean something more than George's attempt to manipulate her for sex.

"Do you really think so, Grandma? Do you think Mabel died so that Jolene can free herself from George?"

Grandma Rose looked at Emma, puzzled. "No, Mabel died so Jolene can free herself from the burden of having to be everyone's protector."

Now the tears ran down Jolene's cheeks unchecked. To have a living thing die so that she could live freely never happened in her life. Grandma Rose identified a pain so directly within her that the acknowledgement released something inside her.

Grandma Rose studied Jolene with concern. "Jolene, I want you to know that when you leave for school, Vickie can come and live with us. We'll work something out."

Relief rushed through Jolene, knowing her sister would be safe.

"You mean we can threaten George that his church will learn of his vile ways if he doesn't back away and let us have Vickie?" Emma asked.

Grandma Rose regarded Emma for a moment. "I don't see exposure to the truth as a threat. It's the intention in your heart that matters. But, having said that, taking charge of karmic justice seems to be the way of the women in this town. Clearly, the law doesn't take the time."

The girls nodded in agreement. Sometimes karmic justice was the only kind one could wish for.

Jolene looked at Grandma Rose. Pain marked her eyes so deep it was a darkened color that turned her blue eyes black before gratitude turned them blue again. "Thank you, Grandma Rose. That's mighty kind of you taking Vickie in. Knowing my sister's safe will take a load off my mind. But I've got to warn you: George needs the government money he gets for us. He won't let go as easy as you make it sound."

"Like I said, we'll work something out. He can keep the money and no one needs to know that she's living with me." Grandma Rose stood up and clapped her hands, ready to move on from a difficult subject. "Okay, girls, clear the floor. It's time to practice Ch'Ulel Heart."

20

Emma and Jolene and the few remaining patrons of The Dam Tavern pulled the tables and chairs back, forming a perimeter around the center of the main barroom. The three men at the bar stood from their stools and moved to the edge of the makeshift stage, each readying themselves for the performance about to take place.

Grandma pogoed into her Sumo warrior stance with her hands clasped at her heart center. Jolene and Emma joined in similar stances, facing her like two fierce warriors.

"Ch'Ulel! Center Yourself!" Grandma yelled.

"Ch'Ulel! Center Ourself!" Emma and Jolene shouted back.

"Align the chakras," instructed Grandma.

The female viragos twirled in a clockwise manner seven times, with their speed picking up upon each completion of a spin. Emma thought she would throw up her lunch, but then she heard the clap of Grandma's hands, signaling to drop to their knees. Emma dropped, and the momentum of her body's inertia continued to move her upper torso in a circular motion. It was at this point that she surrendered her body to the movement, releasing all control to resist. Her body moved in a polyrhythmic fashion, like an African Xhosa dance.

"Jolene, surrender your body," Grandma said, directing the girls.

They moved as if compelled by an invisible puppeteer.

Grandma clapped her hands again, signaling for Emma and Jolene to lie prone on the floor for a few moments of silence.

But Emma was far from silent. She felt a thousand points of light spread across the insides of her eyelids. Those pinpricks started at her hands and feet and advanced their way to her torso. She felt her head grow to the size of a balloon at a Macy's Parade, and she drifted along the wave of her consciousness. The clap of Grandma's hands alerted her to the tavern.

"All righty then, enough tripping, ladies. This isn't a psychedelic high. Bring your brain into coherence with heart. Remember, your heart is five hundred times more powerful than the brain. Now, push your energy field beyond and into this room." Grandma clapped again. "Belly up to the bar, now."

Both girls sat up and walked to the bar. Jolene reached for a bandana and tied it around Emma's eyes. Grandma reached under the bar and pulled out a set of colored pencils. Grandma held up a yellow pencil in front of Emma's blindfolded eyes. She shook her head at Jolene, warning her to not prompt Emma with any words or a light gesture.

"Yellow," Emma said.

"Right." Grandma pulled out a red pencil.

"Red," Emma responded.

Next, Grandma selected a purple pencil.

"Blue."

"No," Grandma Rose said. "Pull the blindfold down and look at the pencil. Take in energy of it, then close your eyes and expand your senses without the sight to discern the subtleties of the object."

Emma lifted the edge of the handkerchief enough to peek and let her eyes absorbed the purple hue, in the old, practiced way of seeing. Then she opened to the sensation the purple pencil evoked within her and closed her eyes to pick up the nuances of the energy. The energy was delicate, yet billowing, like silk threads fluttering around until they settled.

"Okay, I'm ready," Emma said.

This time, Grandma ran through all the color pencils with Emma missing only one more. She had honed this skill that Grandma had taught her for over two years now. The Ch'Ulel heart technique lent Emma the ability to read the energy frequencies of many objects, and even people. Grandma, the ultimate practitioner, exemplified that skill more than anyone. Rose had a knack for seeing people beneath their facades and down through their layers to their true intentions.

Emma admired Grandma and wanted to study the world with as much clarity. However, sometimes she wondered how or why this skill could serve her towards her primary goal: university. The Ch'Ulel heart helped her navigate life in Taylorville, but it wouldn't help her get out of Taylorville.

After the practice session, the men sitting at the perimeter of the bar murmured about the magical scene unfolding before their eyes, even though they had watched Emma and Jolene practice many times. These were men who witnessed or practiced a skill of shooting a shotgun, but never had observed someone, animal or man, who could see without their eyes.

"Rose, you have magical qualities that are superhuman, if you ask me," Charlie said, as he walked to take a seat at the bar.

"Well, Charlie, no one asked you," Grandma said, the light dancing in her eyes after her session of settling into the heart.

Charlie grunted, a slight smile on his face, clearly pleased that she teased him.

Emma understood the men observing them daily in their training with the heightened energies she, Jolene, and Grandma brought about were passively healing their own ailments, whether emotional or physical. Charlie himself was told he had to have a stent placed in his heart. After a month of daily observation of the Ch'Ulel, though, his surgeon reviewed his X-Rays to discover there were no clogged arteries.

Charlie didn't have a clue what had transpired to heal his clogged artery. He contributed it to only drinking a six-pack of beer daily and not the twelve he normally paced himself during the day and giving up French fried potatoes. Grandma Rose's eyes twinkled when Emma asked if the heightened energy of Ch'Ulel heart helped Charlie's heart, but Grandma didn't verbally acknowledge that power of the energy. Emma didn't understand how the healing took place. She believed Grandma taught her and Jolene to increase the vibrational frequency of their body and therefore assisted others to increase theirs. Mostly, she trusted Grandma, who told her that Emma would need her skills to meet her life challenges, not to heal physically, but to change the course of her life's events. All of this, though, added to the mystery of what she and Jolene experienced during their daily trainings in the Dam Tavern.

21

After school, the friends met up for their tattoo, to seal their friendship in forever ink. Emma drove Mattie and Jolene in the Ford to Darwin and their meeting with a tattoo artist. The three girls squeezed into the seat but didn't mind. They were too excited. And a little nervous. Jolene felt the nerves up in her mouth. Luckily, the tattoo artist's name was Angel, which calmed Jolene's jitters a bit. So did talking with her friends.

"Okay, fam," she said, as they rolled along in the Ford. "This tattoo will be our initiation into womanhood. It's also an ironclad commitment. We are blood sisters. Now, we will be blood and ink sisters. We will have each other's backs, no matter what."

Emma parked the truck a few blocks from the address of the studio. The friends walked at a quicken pace. "You'uns as fraid as I am right now?"

Emma always lapsed into her hillbilly speak with anxious or self-conscious.

"Nah. Let's go get our tramp stamp before we miss our appointment time," said Jolene, throwing her arm around her friend's shoulder.

"Don't call it *a tramp stamp.* It cheapens the reason we're doing this," Emma said, turning to move out of Jolene's arm.

"Maybe you're right. Besides, we're placing it on our back shoulder, so it really isn't trampy," said Jolene, her eyes searched ahead for the building. "George and Harriet would be angry about the tattoo. It wouldn't look right to the high-and-mighty church elites. But no one will know it's there, especially George, as he only has me on my back."

Rarely did Jolene allude to the events that went on inside her home. She didn't want to trouble her friends. They were wise enough not to pry or too uncomfortable to ask Jolene about it. Jolene knew Emma would be there for her if she ever needed someone to share the darkness of her adoptive parents.

"Jolene, are things getting *worse* at home? As if that could be possible."

"Not worse. I've found ways to hold George off. I've only a few months left and then I'm out of there.

Even Jolene wasn't comfortable after dark in the part of town where the tattoo parlor resided. The part of town where the factories and warehouses were was close to the east bank of the Wabash. The three girls walked by an auto repair warehouse, where someone parked rusted wrecked cars bumper to bumper, a marble and granite store housed in a small warehouse with pealing painted mortar, and a business called Scrap It, a metal recycling dump site crushing metals into small squares in a wire-fenced area. The noise from the sound of cars being crushed made Jolene's nerves jump. She wondered if getting a tattoo had been a good idea. Or, if getting one *here* had been a good idea.

A large, two-story warehouse with large multi-paned windows loomed ahead. Vandals had broken some panes of glass on the second floor. The first floor was in the process of renovations, as the windows were new and the red brick restored. A large sign came into view that read "Tattoo," with an arrow pointing next to a red painted steel door.

"Okay, this looks to be it," Jolene said, reaching for the door handle and pulling the door wide open to hold for Emma. Emma gave her the evil eye, letting Jolene know she was on to her trick.

"How about y'all go ahead first? Or are y'all going to just stand in the doorway?" Emma asked, smiling.

"I'm fixin to." Jolene responded and took an exaggerated enormous step inside, laughing.

22

Upon entering, a narrow staircase led downwards into a basement, toward another "Tattoo," sign. Walking toward the basement, the temperature dropped about fifteen degrees. At the end of a long hallway was a two-panel wooden door with the stainless-steel sign and the words, "Good Faith Tattoo," and "Angel" stenciled under the business name. The three girls stood in front of the door, looking at each other. No one attempted to open the door.

"Should we knock?" Emma asked, as she turned the door handle, which was locked. Before Emma could raise her hand, she heard the scrape of a chair and steps approaching, then the sound of a lock sliding back. The door swung open, revealing a small man with dark curly hair tucked under a St. Louis Cardinals baseball cap. He had a large smile with white straight teeth that reflected with his white wife beater t-shirt.

The thing that drew Emma's attention was the beautiful angel tattoo on his left shoulder. The angel was female, her hair cascading over one shoulder, her arms crossed in front of her chest, crouched down with a knee drawn up. Her hands were in a relaxed position, while her wings extended upwards, as if to take flight, though she could not rise because of the shackle and chain at her ankle. Angel had drawn the rendition beautifully in a subdued black ink, with realistic detail.

Emma liked him immediately because of his tattoo. His tat expressed her sentiments of what she felt living in her home-town and having her unknown future looming ahead. Emma, like the angel, felt like she wanted to take flight, surrendered into acceptance of her circumstance, but yet remained shack-led to the ground that had given rise to her.

Angel pivoted sideways, letting the girls into the small room.

"Hi, I'm Emma. Love the tat," Emma said, stepping into the room and glancing around.

The loft-style room was freshly painted white. Off to the side was a small, tufted red leather loveseat and an oriental rug. A beautiful chandelier hung from the ceiling, its crystals catching the light of eight light bulbs, casting out beams of light in different directions. In the room's center, Angel had placed a dentist chair with a retractable arm holding a lamp on the end. At the side of the chair was a stainless-steel tray with small plastic containers the size of a thimble contain-ing colored ink and an instrument with a needle. The site of the chair reminded Emma of pictures she saw in her history books of the chairs the Nazis used to torture the Jews in the concentration camps during World War II. Angel turned his attention to her and smiled his warmest smile.

"Your angel tat confirms for me that we have found the right man for the job," Emma said, speaking with confidence.

Angel glanced down at his tat and rubbed his hand over it, then looked at Emma when he spoke. "Yes. It's my finest creation. I didn't lay down the ink, of course, but the stencil's all me."

"You have a delightful place here, not at all what it would appear to be from the outside." Emma remarked, looking around his studio with appreciation.

He smiled. "Can't always judge a book from its cover now, can you? It's a quiet place. Nobody hears much of anything down here."

"Beautiful chandelier," Emma said, walking nearer to the light fixture, her eyes fixated on the light, and avoiding Angel's last comment.

Angel nodded toward the chandelier. "Found that in one of the abandoned spaces, hidden in a dark corner under a mound of construction wood. Apparently, it survived the scavengers looking for hidden treasures. They missed this one." He admired his own good fortune for a moment, a twinkle in his eye, before shifting back to business matters. "So, did you bring your finished drawing so I can prepare the stencil with the changes?"

Emma nodded and reached into her back pocket, pulling out a folded sheet of paper and smoothing it flat on a wooden desk. The changes to the image Emma had sketched were an angel dropping her head back in surrender, her arms thrown wide, and her heart emanating light, as three doves lifted her by cords held in their beaks. It represented surrendering to your soul's will and discovering the unconditional love, silence, and peace of doing so. Each dove represented one friend and how the friendship promised to support and lift one another through life.

Angel pulled out his stencil and began inking the design. Jolene watched, a fascinated look on her face, admiring Angel's delicate but confident pen strokes. He took the sketch that Emma had labored hours over to draw and, within minutes, completed a new design. Emma and Jolene compared the drawings. Mattie looked over their shoulders.

"Wow, it looks good, Angel," said Emma, stepping back for Mattie to inspect.

"Yes...it's so beautiful." Mattie hovered her hand over the drawing, reverently, as if she could absorb all the goodness from the angel.

"That's so sick," said Jolene, before turning and looking at Emma. "Are we good, everyone?" Each girl nodded vigorously, both excited and trepidatious. Even though Emma remained steadfast, she still felt the anxiety rise within her. She fought the subtle urge to run out of the studio screaming. But, thinking of Grandma Rose, her awareness dropped into her heart center and she took a few deep breaths in to her belly. Slowly, her anxiety subsided.

"So, who's the bravest?" Angel asked. He sat on his stool with rollers and rolled it up to his tray. He slid his hands into black latex gloves, stretching his fingers into the latex and snapping the glove against his wrists to ensure a tight fit.

"Emma drew the short straw," said Jolene. "She will be our sacrificial lamb. By the time you reach me, the tattoo will be perfection."

"She's right. I'm to be the original and they'll be copies," Emma said, laughing. Jolene's laughter drained Emma's anxiety even more.

"Whoaaaa...That's a slam," Mattie said, smiling and taking Emma by the shoulders and guiding her to the table. It didn't seem Mattie felt one iota of stress regarding the tattoo.

Angel turned his back and ready his instruments, pulling out the ink he would use.

"Okay, remove your top and lay face down on the table," Angel said, preparing his tray with the needles and black ink he would be using. "When I apply the ink, it'll hurt initially, like a thousand bee stings, but the endorphins will eventually kick in and deaden the pain. Before long, you won't feel a thing."

Emma climbed onto the table and placed her face into the head cradle. Jolene pushed a chair to the head of the table and grabbed Emma's hand for support.

"No, I can't have you too close to where I'm working," Angel said, taking the stencil and positioning the stencil ink down onto Emma's right shoulder.

"Can we hold her feet?" asked Jolene.

"Yes, as long as Emma's not bothered."

"That'll be fine. It'll comfort me." Emma's voice became muffled as her face buried into the headrest of the table, breathing through the paper towel protector that Angel had placed for her to rest her head.

"Great. If it becomes uncomfortable, raise your left hand," Angel said.

In the next moment, Emma felt the tension in her feet let go and she could not raise any hand.

23

*E*mma buried her nose in the grass, breathing in the fresh-dirt scent and enjoying the moment. She loved being outside, near the woods.

Dad strode out of the forest of trees, indiscernible in his camouflaged outerwear, his shotgun strapped over his shoulder, a string of furry squirrels dangling at his side, "Okay, Em. Come on, I need help."

"No, Dad! Do I have to go? Don't make me."

"Come on, it's your job to help me skin these squirrels." Dad took his string of four squirrels and dropped them to the ground inside the wooden shed. He released one rodent by pulling the line out from its back paw. "Here," he said, handing her the squirrel. Its tiny paws felt cool in her five-year-old hand. She wanted to warm the squirrel's feet a bit. She imagined that paw running along tree bark and limbs just moments before. Her fingers rubbed his paw. She wondered how this squirrel would be as a pet. She'd name him Rocky, and Rocky would eat peanuts from her fingers and sit on her shoulder.

"Good eatin' here. Hold the legs tight, Em. You got a hold on it?"

Emma nodded.

Her father expertly handled the knife, talking each step of the way. "See, cut here along the waistline," he said, making the first cut along the squirrel's belly. "You take hold of the fur at the cut and tug. It's like pulling off his pants. Now, flip him over so I can remove the other half of the fur."

She grabbed the squirrel's front legs. The blood smelled like pennies in her piggy bank. "Now you tug from the waist up and over his head and pull off his shirt." As Dad pulled the skin and fur back over the legs and head, she held onto the squirrel by the underside of his skin. It felt sticky, like half-eaten chewing gum set out to be retrieved later. The blood on her hands increased the difficulty of holding tight.

"Hold it, Em, so I can gut him."

"Yes, Daddy," she said, tightening her grip on the slippery underside of the skin. Dad cut down the middle and, using two fingers, scooped out the innards. He plopped the naked, bloody squirrel on a sheet of newspaper at her feet. The skinned body lay bow-legged, the arms raised high in the air. "Look Daddy. He looks like a headless cowboy and we're holding him up for money."

"Hmm...yeah," said Dad, not looking up while he unhooked the next squirrel. He handed Emma the back legs, and she grasped the new squirrel's tiny paws between her fingers, the toenails pushing into her skin. "Emma! Grab hold, Em."

"Okay, Daddy," said Emma, *annoyance and reluctance in her tone.*

"Emma!" Yelled Dad.

"Emma!"

She heard her name called from a distance and felt confusion about where she was and how Dad could be here. He was dead. A breath tickled against her ear, and Angel called her name again. The recent past flooded into her mind. She remembered she was getting a tattoo. Her eyes opened, and she turned her head to the side and stared into the eyes of Angel, whose face was inches from her face. Relief flooded into his expression.

"You okay?"

She nodded. "I'm fine. Why?"

"Because you passed out," Angel said.

"You must have fallen asleep and dreamed about your father," said Jolene, who had remained at her feet and rubbed her legs. "You were talking to him about cowboys and needing money. Sounded like you were having a nightmare."

"It wasn't like you passed out. There were no signs of it, no sweating or twitching or moving about. It was like you were here and then you weren't, and your whole body relaxed. Like you entered another dimension," said Angel, shaking his head in confusion. "That's never happened to me before with a client. But, no worries." He bent closer to her face to read her expression in her eyes. "I'm almost done. Are you good at continuing?"

"Yes. I'm good. I'm fine." She wasn't afraid that she had entered some nightmare world, or that she worried the dream would return, because it wasn't a dream, just a memory. The tattoo triggered her memory of another time she was initiated into a new mode: when her father introduced her to the violent, raw reality of the world.

Angel swabbed the area over her shoulder. She couldn't feel any sensation near the wound. "I'm done," he said, patting the tat with his cloth.

Mattie and Jolene released her feet.

Angel assisted Emma from the table. Her shoulder felt tight and hot. He reached over and grabbed a hand-held mirror, handing it to her, and helping her off the table to a mirror attached to the wall. She held the mirror with her left hand and raised it above her head to get a good angle on her right shoulder and tattoo. The angel hung in a complete surrender by cords, her beautiful face lifted and back stretching, displaying her slender and elegant neck. The angel's frail wings fell limply behind her shoulders, useless to lift her. But the three doves carried her upwards by the cords.

"An angel inked by Angel," Emma said, twisting her body to get a better look.

Mattie and then Jolene received their tattoos with no problems. Mattie whimpered a little, though Emma believed she did so out of pleasure, luxuriating in a specialty Jolene foot massage; it was probably the first time anyone had touched Mattie in a loving and supportive way. Jolene, meanwhile, kept tensing her muscles and Angel had to keep asking her to relax so he could lay the ink easier. Emma could only believe that Jolene had difficulty allowing anyone to restrain her, even if it were friends gently and lovingly holding her feet.

24

The sky was dark, with a streak of red light slightly above the horizon when the girls left the tattoo parlor. Mattie, Jolene, and Emma chatted about their tattoo experiences. They each looked at the others' tattoos to ensure the healing was occurring fine. They applied the cream Angel gave them to each other's tattoo so the wounds wouldn't scab and pull ink off the tat. Their bond grew deeper as they all tended to one another, each reveling in the excitement of their new tattoos.

Emma though struggle to remain focused on their conversation. Her mind wandered to Nate. Nate and his dark good looks and dimpled smile and books. He consumed her mind.

"Hey, Emma, Mattie asked you a question about three times," said Jolene, giggling. "I'm guessing you're thinking of someone. I'm thinking this guy's wow factor has to be off the charts."

"I've never been on an actual date before. Maybe I should text him and tell him I've work to do." Emma didn't find the guys who lived anywhere near Taylorville interesting and thought most of them uncouth. She just assumed she would never date, or even marry, either. Most of Taylorville's married young girls presented to her a woman living a life in a double-wide, raising several kids, and dark roots sprouting up out of her head, which contained ruminations of bettering her life. Maybe there was another type of woman who grew up without the opportunities given to others living elsewhere. Someone she could model her life after. Then, she remembered her grandma.

Grandma had lived alone since her late twenties. She owned The Dam Tavern herself, free and clear. She held her own against drunk, out-of-control men with a baseball bat stowed under the bar—and, for the more violent fights, a shotgun. Maybe Grandma, being her blood, gave her ideas that went beyond the norm for females in her town. In fact, last year in Psychology class, Emma heard a deep, masculine voice inside her head that spoke a directive so forceful that she had to attend to it: *Emma, you need to figure out what you need to do, because you'll be supporting yourself for your whole life.* When she told Grandma about it, she said it was an important message delivered from her guardian angel and that Emma needed to follow its advice.

Emma turned to her friends. "I need to focus on more important things in my life right now, like getting into the university. I should text him to cancel the date."

"Is that fear I hear in your voice, Emma Rose, The Noncommittal One?" Jolene said. "I've never heard you backing down from anything you've agreed to do. Your word is your word. Go on, girl. Go out and do you, and you'll be fine."

"That's right," Mattie said. "Go. Have fun, Emma. There's always time to work and this may be the only chance to date a college guy."

Emma glanced over at Mattie and smiled. The way Mattie said this simple statement to just focus on having fun contained wisdom that, otherwise, Emma thought might be out of Mattie's reach. It brought a warmth into Emma's chest, and she wondered again how this soft-hearted girl rose out of the darkness of the Malone family and how quickly she was bouncing back from the humiliation and abuse she had suffered only days ago. Mattie inspired her. But she still held some doubt.

"I don't know," Emma said. "When I think of Nate reaching over to kiss me, I want to throw up. Dating makes my nerves shot. I've never kissed a guy in college. And then there's the chance that maybe he won't want to kiss me at all. Do you kiss someone on the first date?"

"You're looking at me to give you advice? I have dated no one," Jolene said, laughing. "You'll be fine. Don't be so lame. Plus, you can always shake his hand after the date."

Jolene gave Emma a shove down the road in front of her.

Emma offered a smile, but she noticed the shove came from a sensitive place. Jolene must have felt insecure about Emma's date. Probably because it opened the door to intimacy of the emotional, and the physical kind.

"You could take him on a boat ride on the Wabash," Mattie said. "You enjoy being on the river."

"Actually, that's a thought. Have Nate see you in your natural environment." Jolene laughed.

Joy abounded in Mattie's face at being included in a substantial conversation with her friends talking about guys.

Emma ruminated. "The river may be a good idea. Thanks, Mattie." A sensible solution from a simple mind, and Emma felt pride and a protective urge toward her friend.

Mattie's shoulders lifted at the acknowledgement of her contribution to the conversation, and she skipped ahead. Mattie's mood was slowly becoming more Mattie-like. Emma contributed it to hanging out with her friends.

"Well, Grandma says she has a feeling about this one," Emma said.

"What one? He's been the only one." Jolene laughed again and Emma and Mattie soon joined in, although the laughter could not ease the tensions of the past few days.

25

The Darwin limestone quarry provided the stone to construct the Empire State Building and the Pentagon. The extraction process had left deep pools of luminescent green waters surrounded by sixty-foot-tall limestone walls. A high ledge loomed above the quarry the locals called "Bird's Eyrie," which hung over a four-hundred-foot-deep pool. Bird's Eyrie was the highest peak of the stone quarry. The locals named the peak after the state's hero, Larry Bird, and also, because of the peak's brute presence emerging above the stone face like the eagle nests of the birds of prey. Everyone called the jump off of Bird's Eyrie and into the deep pool below as the *leap off of Bird's head.*

Emma met Jolene and Mattie at Grandpa's store in the old Ford truck before driving off for a day at Bird's Eyrie. She noticed Mattie showed signs of joy by the light in her eyes with their newest adventure. Emma drove the truck as far up the road to the Darwin limestone quarry as possible before meeting an enormous pile of broken up limestone rocks, which forced them to hike to the top. The girls walked in single file along a narrow rocky foot path while Jolene told stories about past summers swimming in the cool waters of the quarry, a favorite place for teens to hang out.

The sound of masculine laughter erupted from the direction of the quarry's edge and interrupted Jolene's chatter.

"Jump! Jump! Jump!"

When Emma reached the clearing at the top of Bird's Eyrie, she saw three boys looking over the edge, clapping, cheering, pumping the air with their fists.

Jolene ran over to the edge and looked down. "Did someone jump?"

A lanky boy looked over at her. "He sure did. He better have. Can't have a man-gina in Sigma Alpha."

The guys, psyched of the mention of their fraternity, chanted, "Sigma Alpha! Sigma Alpha! Sigma Alpha!"

Jolene scoffed. "Some sort of bro-code-mantra guys?"

The air was heavy with weed. A short, muscular boy held a flask. He looked Jolene up and down. His need to challenge her confidence overcame him and he blurted out, "Bet you twenty dollars that you won't be able to make that jump."

A nice-looking and smiling boy who had kept quiet until now looked over at Jolene. "I wouldn't take that bet. You stand on that edge and you'll say goodbye to your money."

Another kid nodded and looked at the short boy. "It'll be an easy twenty for you." Then he turned and looked at Jolene. "Look over the edge before you take the dare."

"Don't need to," Jolene said. "You're on. Better be ready to part from your money."

An impressed look washed over the short boy's face. "So, where you girls from?" he asked. "I haven't seen you on campus before."

Jolene looked at her friends, amazed that they could pass as college girls.

"You wouldn't have. We're from Taylorville and not in college yet," said Jolene.

"River Rats?" The short guy asked, not waiting for an answer, his lip curling into a derisive expression. He turned to look at his friends. "So, guess we wouldn't have seen these girls on campus... since they're River Rats, a few zip codes over from campus. Maybe we would've seen them in one of the downtown dive bars."

Emma blushed while Jolene flushed with anger. Meanwhile, Mattie appeared not to follow the conversation, maintaining her deadpan stare. Emma was grateful for that, at least.

Jolene couldn't contain herself. "One thing's for sure, a River Rat doesn't walk back from a bet because they're too afraid. Or too weak with no backbone." She glared at him. "You're on."

"Maybe I'm a fool to take that bet now. I'd lose for sure against a River Rat. They're half cray-cray." He looked at Jolene, "And *you* were offended by the man-gina comment?"

He scoffed. "I'm sure people have called you a lot worse." He flushed with rising anger, swiped his towel against his leg, turning away from Jolene.

Jolene quickly turned to scrutinize Emma, a look of disbelief on Jolene's face as she mouthed the words, "What's wrong with you?" Apparently, Emma's non-action against these boys was off-putting. But what Jolene didn't know was that Emma felt useless in the moment. Any semblance of grit or guile Emma may have had vanished at the sight of one person she didn't want to encounter emerging from the path to the clearing, a six-pack of beer in his hand, as he dried his chest with a towel.

26

Nate's laughter sounded virile and deep in his accomplishment. The lanky boy ran to clap him on his back and handed him the flask for a drink. "That was awesome, Bro. Wow!"

Emma's mind tried to make sense of things. Could it be that Nate was part of this group of guys? She struggled to square the kind boy in the library with one who would have these guys as his friends. Emma trembled as she forced herself to gather the strength to stand up to the guys who crossed a boundary, even though Nate now featured astride that boundary as well.

Nate dried his hair before running the towel over his muscular body. He must exercise daily, she thought.

It was then that Nate noticed the girls standing by the edge. His eyes widened when he recognized Emma. Warmth emanated from them, calming Emma, and his smile broadened, which eased her mind even more. Maybe he wasn't like these boys.

"Emma! I didn't expect you to be here."

"It was a spontaneous decision. My friends and I had...we wanted to make the jump." She rambled, trying to pull it together. She felt pulled in two directions—one moment looked upon with disgust, the next with pleasure.

"Well, your spontaneity is a welcomed surprise. Are you going to jump?"

Emma nodded. "We all are, together."

"Really? So, you're about to sacrifice yourselves to the icy pool below Bird's Head?"

"Yep, except it's more of a surrendering and letting go rather than a sacrifice. We're ready to make this leap."

"Point taken. Kinda different from us. We're here to complete a hazing requirement for our fraternity. We'll be shamed if we fail."

The boys, upon hearing mention of the fraternity, cheered and pumped their fists into the air again.

"Congratulations," Emma said. "on making it through the hazing." She wasn't feeling the congratulatory moment for Nate after witnessing the behaviors of his friends.

"So, you must be Nate?" Jolene said, sauntering over, clearly having figured out the identity of the mystery jumper.

Nate nodded.

"I'm Jolene, Emma's best friend."

The tall, nice-looking boy walked over to join Emma and Nate. Even though Nate was tall, this boy towered three inches above all the others. "So, you two know each other?"

Nate responded, "This is the girl I spoke of earlier."

The tall boy turned to the group, smiling a gentle smile and deciding to take a more gentlemanly approach. "So... ladies. Are you ready to take the leap? Would you like a support team to watch? So, you can immortalize it forever in the minds of men?"

Mattie smiled shyly, but nodded her head.

Emma looked at her friends. "You'uns, ready?" As soon as she uttered the words, blood burned her cheeks. She always checked her language before speaking when outside of Taylorville. She never wanted to sound like a hick.

The short, muscular kid sneered. "You'uns? What the hell? Is that redneck secret code? Hillbilly speak?" He scoffed again.

Emma flushed red-hot with embarrassment. Jolene straightened her shoulders at seeing her friend's wounding humiliation.

Jolene turned toward him. "And you're an asshole. That is universal code, though I'm sure you don't need your college degree to know the meaning." She turned toward Emma and Mattie, softening her expression but reflecting her determination. "Y'all ready, ladies?"

Jolene swung around to the guys and extended out a fake olive branch by giving her best fake sweet smile. "Let's go, ladies!" She yelled over her shoulder, declaring her decision to leap, as she pulled her hoodie off and removed her t-shirt over her head, revealing the top of her swim team swimsuit. "I'm going to win me twenty dollars."

Mattie removed her own clothes, down to her bikini. Soon, they both stood in their bathing suits. Emma walked over to them and, with her back to the guys, hurriedly removed her clothes, feeling the boys' eyes on her undressing movements.

"Shake off the dark side of men who only want to remain boys, ladies. This is for us!" Jolene smiled at her friends, and Emma and Mattie smiled and giggled back in response.

Each girl grabbed at the other's hands, placing Mattie in-between. The bonded-soul friends stood on the edge of Bird's Head, looking down at the long distance to the surface of the gleaming pool below. The guys swept up in the moment, chanted, but in a more somber voice than before, echoing like a deep drum beat. *Jump, jump, jump.* The girls stood shoulder-to-shoulder, calm, breathing deep on the inhale, and long on the exhale. Emma closed her eyes and Mattie's fingers tightened their grasp on hers. A brief laugh of excitement escaped to vibrate around her. A little scream of terror came from Mattie. Emma squeezed Mattie's hand in reassurance.

Nate started the countdown. "Four, three…"

Her father's voice rushed into her head, wanting to impart some wisdom, strong and independent. *Always walk to the edge and jump.*

So much for the wisdom of her father in spirit.

"Jump!"

27

Their bodies lurched forward and upward, arms flung high, still grasping hands. They remained suspended in the air for a moment, shrieking, before dropping and letting go, becoming their separate selves and hurling down to the deep constructed pond. Emma's stomach followed behind, trying to catch up with the rest of her body. Then, all three girls squealed before breaking through the surface of the freezing water.

The coldness pierced Emma's skin and the air bubbles tickled as the trapped air rushed past her body to the surface. The deeper she dropped, the quieter her world became. She let herself sink down, closing her eyes to the murky blackness and the water's density to drown out the voices from above. Her friends made no movement, caught in their own experiences. The silence was inviting. So peaceful, a quiet world.

Emma sensed thrashing from Mattie as she pulled her way to the top. She understood Jolene would remain under the surface for as long as she could, as she loved the freezing shock of cold water and would see it as a test of her resolve. Jolene proved her sense of power when confronted with adversity, while Emma pushed through distress, longing for the silence and peaceful realm of harmony. She relished in that silence and harmony now.

"Emma," Mattie called, her voice muddled by the denseness of the water. Emma dropped another few feet before she scissored her legs and reached up with her arms to propel herself upward. She broke the surface and gasped for air to the cheers of the guys above for their accomplishment of the region's long-standing, initiatory practice of "the leap off of Bird's head". She turned and caught the exquisite smile of Mattie, which made the risk they took worth the effort. Mattie reveled hearing the guys standing on Bird's Eyrie cheering her.

Jolene raised her arm in a fisted acknowledgement. There was a renewed round of applause and cheering from above. The three friends, bonded even more in their shared risk-taking, swam together to join in a tight hug, teeth chattering, before swimming to the quarry's edge.

Nate's powerful hands pulled each girl out. Jolene first, as she was the faster swimmer. Second came Mattie, who giggled excitedly. Then Emma. As Nate's arms pulled her up and close to his body, he held her for a moment longer. She looked into his eyes and his prideful warmth filled her. Emma's legs trembled and she couldn't stop her teeth from chattering, but she didn't think it was all from the cold. Nate's hand remained steady on her back as he handed her a towel, roughly rubbing another towel along her back to get the blood flowing and warming the skin. The thoughtfulness of his act of meeting the girls at the edge and bringing their towels stood out in her mind. Other than her father and Grandpa, never had a man in her recent memory made such a thoughtful gesture to her.

"Wow, all you girls needed was a count of three and you jumped without hesitating," Nate said, shaking his head. "The bravest women I've ever seen."

The small group ran in overdrive speed to the top to warm their bodies and retrieve their clothes. The excitement of everyone completing their separate and unique initiation rites energized the air. Emma noticed her toe and fingernails were blue and she quickly grabbed her discarded clothing, putting her top on and removing her bathing top undercover. Soon she donned her thick socks and work boots, luxuriating in the warmth of thick clothes and wonderful friendship.

Jolene stretched out her hand, palm upwards toward the betting boy who, in the midst of laugher from his friends, reached into his pocket to withdraw a twenty-dollar bill and handed it to her. She then, in turn, tucked it into her pocket and held out her hand for a shake, all forgiven in the success and exhilaration of the jump.

As evening drew to a close, the girls retreated down the trail, impatient to get to the truck for additional warmth and before darkness made the trek dangerous. Talking and laughter pushed through purple numb lips and chattering teeth.

Jolene and Mattie climb into the truck's front seat and Emma walked over to the driver's side. Nate followed her to open the door.

"Are we still on for tomorrow?" He asked, a hopeful look on his face as his eyes searched hers.

"Of course. I'm looking forward to it." Emma smiled, shaking a bit, either due to the cold or her nerves. Or, more likely, both. She turned the key, and the truck responded by jolting forward because Emma had let off of the clutch too quickly. The girls squealed. As Emma steered the truck down the quarry road, Mattie chatted excitedly about her jump off of Bird's Head. Jolene smiled at Emma knowingly. Their idea accomplished its magic on their friend.

The truck sped onto the Wabash Bridge, where a billboard loomed above. A larger-than-life business executive carried a woman dressed in a short, tight black skirt over his shoulder. The message read, "Don't hold back, carry your work home!" The billboard effectively turned the thought of her accomplishment into something profane.

While the day ended on a high note at the quarry, something dark and dangerous broke into Emma's peace. The disregard and repulsion from the frat boys stirred a repressed rage in her that smoldered beneath her surfaces. Those boys didn't change their demeanors until Nate arrived, doting on her. Only then had they backed off. Pathetic. Their attitude was infuriating, and she felt her rebellious side kick in.

Emma pushed her foot on the accelerator, speeding the truck across the bridge and onto the rutted road, entering

Taylorville. Her friends screamed at their thrill of the ride, a ride that nearly matched the excitement of the jump.

But Emma wasn't enjoying the drive. Her thoughts turned to Wade. Mattie was a symbol of all things innocent. Emma understood she and Jolene needed to meet and decide how to handle Wade. How to handle all the Taylorville men who used vulnerable girls for their own power trips. It was time Taylorville had a reckoning.

28

Late the next evening, after Jolene and Emma dropped Mattie at her home from the bus stop, the two girls silently walked to The Dam Tavern.

"We've got to make this right. I'm so freaking tired of people who're supposed to care for you in this town and don't. It's abusive...foisting their problems onto children. Children carrying that kind of load soon lose hope." Emma huffed her frustration. "Grandpa calls it shame-by-proxy."

"Children, women from Taylorville, dogs or bunnies... it don't matter none. Someone carries the load for others. Someone carries another's shame," Jolene added, her own indignation rising and coloring her face.

"Yeah. People just need to figure matters out for themselves, deal with their own baggage, and stop making others pay for their ineptitude." The anger raged within Emma until her head pounded. Her rage consumed her like a fire burning through the forest on a dry August day.

"So, why now, Emma? Why so angry now?" Jolene looked at Emma accusingly. "Wade's hosing of Mattie wasn't enough?"

Emma felt as if Jolene applied a bellows to her rage. She didn't understand how Jolene now focused her anger on her. She stopped before quickly responding and thought for a moment. The guys at the quarry triggered something else within her. She wasn't sure why she was so angry now. She desired action, otherwise her rage would eat all the good left inside, and she would be another victim of the acts of men or boys. She felt driven to action, as she had a purpose now. "Those boys at the quarry were disrespectful. They judged us for something we've no control over, for just being girls who lived west of the Wabash. We need to do something."

Jolene drew her head back in surprise. "Wow, Emma, I didn't think you completely bought into the whole revenge thing against Wade."

Emma remained quiet for a moment before responding. "Maybe, not initially, but yesterday, those Darwin boy's behaviors at the quarry brought a degradation that I felt personally, and I thought Nate would be swayed by his friend's attitudes and not want to follow through with our date. I'm tired of boys dumping their own insecurities onto me."

"You mean the boys, in an effort to feel superior, degraded us and pushed us to feel less than them?" Jolene asked.

"Yeah. That's how I see it." Emma said, a little defiance creeping into her attitude.

Jolene looked confused. "Or is it truer that unless the abuse affects you, then it's not enough to do anything about it?'

Emma looked down in shame. Jolene was always the straight shooter in her appraisal of situations. "Maybe you're partially right. I distance myself when bad things happen to others, because I'm not living with the consequences. Maybe, it's because I feel helpless in not knowing what to do or unable to do anything at all. But, to have someone outside our town direct the contempt at you...then at me? It just piled up on top of everything we went through with Mattie's hosing down. Well, I'm ashamed to say, but it held a whole new meaning of shame-by-proxy."

Jolene considered Emma for a moment and then looked away and nodded. "I get what you're saying." She reached over and grabbed Emma's hand, holding it for a moment.

Emma glanced at Jolene and then looked away to stare at The Dam Tavern neon sign. "I'm on board. Let's make a plan for Wade."

A slight smile turned up Jolene's lips. "Okay. Let's do it."

"But first," Emma said, returning her smile. "First, we shake on it."

They stopped, and with their clasped hands, did their secret handshake. They hadn't done the handshake in years. They made it up when they first brought Mabel home and hid her in Jolene's bedroom. Whenever they saw an injustice done, they made it right, or at least made the victim feel not alone. Flashes of when a friend's father had passed out from one whiskey too many in the middle of the living room floor during her friend's birthday slumber party, and Jolene had the idea to paint his nails red. Her friend's father had red nails the whole of the next day before realizing it and blowing a gasket.

Or the time a neighborhood jerk sped down the road in his shiny newly waxed car and almost hit Jolene and Emma. Emma's idea was to place bird seed over his car, which he had left parked under a tree late that night. The next morning, the birds had left a nice, white, gooey mess for him when he walked out to his car for work. Both girls simultaneously laughed at all the antics of their childhood and how they felt that their partnership righted the wrongs in the world.

29

Wade walked across the Wabash River Bridge and back into Taylorville. He had walked to the Dollar Store as he wanted supplies for a few weeks. Dottie sure kept nothing extra around the house. A simple woman with simple needs, he figured.

He passed an alley and walked over to an old wreck parked alongside the alleyway. He fired up a Lucky, taking a long drag, and sat on the hood, thinking. He could get used to this lifestyle—easy going, no demands. It just spoke to him in an agreeable fashion. His *joie de vivre*. Damn, if he wasn't a sophisticated man. He looked around the cinder-blackened alleyway. Too bad he only reached this state of easy living while here in Taylorville. He'd like it more if he had this perspective and lived this way in L.A.

A scraggly dog running in the backyard of a fenced area snuck under the wires and trotted over, wagging his tail, his head close to the ground, like dogs do around him when acknowledging his superiority. Wade noticed the dog's missing eye.

"Well, lookie here. You like me, buddy?"

The dog lifted and tilted his head as if listening to what Wade said, a smart dog. Wade thought of Mattie. It might do him good to gift her a dog. He was in a generous nature of late. Mattie was doing better after her lesson, more reserved. She had earned a reward. And this dog listened, too.

Listening was a good quality in a dog, cause you could be having a conversation with the animal and if the pup paid no attention, you'd be wasting your time. A dog that listened made all the difference. A passerby seeing you talk to a dog would assume you were a person of tenderness and mercy, whereas if you were speaking to yourself, they'd give you a wide berth in passing. Yes, a good dog made all the difference in a lone man's life.

"You seem to be looking for a new home, buddy. You want to come home with me and be a pet for my little girl? She'd be sweet to you."

The dog wagged its tail. That was confirmation enough for Wade. He scooped up the pup, who barely weighed fifteen pounds, and walked home.

30

Emma and Jolene entered from the rear of the tavern in order to avoid any distractions from their mission. "Hey Grandma, we'll hang out in the back room," Emma said, turning before Grandma could put her rare eyes on them.

Grandma nodded while she swiped the top of the bar with her white dish cloth. "Hello to you, too," she shouted out.

"Hello." Both girls flung back over their shoulders as they walked around the corner to the storage room.

Once there, the grand conspirators shut the door, looking for a more private place to hide. Jolene walked to the place among the scented smells of herbs, plants and weeds. They moved two large cardboard boxes closer together, tucking themselves among cases of Johnnie, Jose, and, of course, Jack—the only men who played a constant role in Rose's life, as the joke went.

Jolene leaned in, elbows on her knees, eyes glistening with interest as Emma laid out her plan to the last detail. Jolene sat up with her shoulders hunched and hand covering a smile of delight. "OMG, this is perfect, absolutely perfect. It's the Circle of Life. The perfect 'Time's Up' scenario. The Malones would no way seek retribution." She laughed, her eyes shining. "You're a freaking genius, Emma."

"Thank you. But there are some holes. Like, for example: how're we to separate Wade from his Glock?"

"Maybe we can point that rifle Grandma Rose hides in plain sight behind the bar," said Jolene, half serious. "Right in the middle of his forehead. It wouldn't be the first time that gun's been pointed at someone's head."

Emma's mind flashed to an old rumor about Grandma toting her rifle along with a few armed men before re-focusing on the problem at hand. "Well, let's not do that." She thought for a moment. "But preparation is key. We need to be ready to act spontaneously, not rashly."

At that moment, the friends heard the storage room door open.

Grandma Rose, of course. How much had she heard?

"You two aren't planning some evil-doings now, are you? I thought we discussed this." Grandma weaved around stacked cartons of liquor and her stash of mushrooms, hanging herbs, dandelions, and other flowers left out to dry on tables under shelves holding jars of labeled liquids. Grandma concocted all kinds of mixtures for ailments derived from plants she gathered throughout the year. Other than the medicine practice and the Ch'Ulel Heart she learned while studying under a Mayan Shaman as a young woman, she also practiced her meditation and a Filipino martial art called Kali, which was rooted in survival.

Emma's face twisted in a grimace when she looked up at Grandma. Why did she have to interfere?

Silence hung heavy in the air, which answered Grandma's question. Emma watched as the old woman's eyes narrowed and chin dropped. Emma wondered if she could spin off the evil part of her question to tell the truth, but not the whole truth.

"No Grandma, we're not planning anything evil. Who do you think we are?"

"Girl, I didn't fall off of the turnip truck yesterday. I'm on to that trick," said Grandma, looking sternly at Emma. "Divert the meaning of my question and throw in an accusatory question back at me. Now, tell me. What's going on?"

31

The smells of lavender and sage Grandma had left drying near the window of the back room overwhelmed Emma, and she felt a little lightheaded and sick under the scrutiny of Grandma's all-seeing-eyes. She sat staring at Grandma and blinking her eyes, not knowing how to respond. She'd told Grandma almost everything except the actual step-by-step plan. Grandma, though, didn't leave Emma long in her uncomfortable, silent moment.

"Let me tell you... you can't mean to settle this for Mattie by answering Wade's violence with a retribution violence. Fighting hate with hate only produces more hate. Wade's an unpredictable and dangerous man. I don't think I'm telling you something you don't know yourself. It will not be as simple as whatever plan you've got going in your head. This'll not bode well for you... or you. You'll only escalate the danger." Grandma looked at Jolene. "You need not follow some eye-for-an-eye town code. The town won't abide two young teenagers involving themselves with matters not concerning them. There are other ways to handle Mattie's situation. Going after Wade isn't one of them."

Silence filled the room. Each person waited for someone to confess to a plan or give in and leave others to go about their business.

"You're not clear with your intention. There's judgment, anger, and fear all over this." Grandma regarded Emma and Jolene. "Your choices will cause a boomerang karmic effect if you continue down the path your vengeful minds take you."

"But how is that fair? Should abuse happen in front of me and I cry inside, but not do a lick about it?" Emma asked. She was stuck between a rock and a hard place of having no way of understanding Grandma's position or the inability to convince Grandma differently. Grandma knew the score.

"So, Grandma, what solution have you for Mattie's situation? What solution doesn't bring about karma? She's living with a daddy who would do abusive things to her, you know? We've witnessed that." Emma's tone implied that even Grandma wouldn't have a solution that would right this injustice.

Grandma studied her. Then Grandma's shoulders dropped, the anger and tension draining from her body. "I don't know the answer. You interfere, and it's worse for Mattie, that much I know. Revenge is not the answer."

"Well, an eye for an eye is in the Bible," said Jolene. "Matthew 5, Verse 38. 'Ye have heard that it have been said, An eye for an eye, and a tooth for a tooth, that ye resist not evil.'" Jolene knew her Bible verses better than anyone. She had years of weekly Bible study and home study of the good book, the only good George ever brought her.

"Yes. You're right, it's in the Bible," said Grandma Rose. "But, remember the rest of that verse, which goes something like this: 'but whosoever shall smite thee on thy right cheek, turn to him the other as well.'"

"Grandma, you believe that, really? To turn the other cheek? What does that mean, anyway, in our situation? And how does that solve anything?"

Grandma looked at Emma and then at Jolene. "That verse means to understand your intent behind what you do. If you strike out of anger or fear, then you won't find empathy for the other's suffering. Yet, if you identify the vulnerability driving the bad actor, then you can find compassion. Compassion changes situations. That's the only thing that will make the change at the deepest levels. With Mattie and Wade's situation, you'll understand that Wade is as much a victim as Mattie. So, find what he's a victim to. In that case, the fight leaves you, and then it leaves him, as well. Action taken from clarity is the only right action to take. Solutions come to you at the moment."

Emma scoffed. "I'm struggling to see Wade's being a victim when he stripped Mattie naked in front of those men and hosed her down. How does his action compare to anything that's been done to him? Why do I have to be the one to sympathize with Wade to right this wrong?"

A strong resistance built up inside of Emma to near exploding. Here it was again. She hated always having to be the responsible one. She hated the presumption that she would be good. Other people lived their life freely, made choices, powered over the weak, and avoided consequences. Turn the other cheek in order to be slapped again. Why didn't the guy doing the slapping feel obliged to find peace with the situation? She was just plain tired of being the responsible one.

Emma shot Grandma a glowering look and clenched her jaw, speaking volumes in silence. She wasn't about to let Grandma off the hook, spouting off spiritual wisdom as if Grandma was an innocent.

The three women sat on cases of liquor, their bodies tensed with anger, confusion, and helplessness.

"What about Dwight Green, who terrorized the town in his alcohol-cocaine-knife-wielding binges?" Emma couldn't help herself, and the question fell out of her mouth before her brain had time to mull it over and reframe it without the angry tone.

The Dwight Green rumor was a legend in Taylorville. The undisputed fact was someone—or several someones—shot Dwight dead after one of his many drinking bouts. Rumor had it he filled the nights with bootleg booze and tormenting women and children; when he reached a respectful level of drunk, he even harassed a man now and then. The Darwin courts did little to set matters right. Dwight always found a way out. He never spent a day in jail, even when his victims showed up at the police station with evidence of their bruises, cuts, or stab wounds. Several of the town's people saw fit to take matters into their own hands, to put Green out of his misery, and to free the town from his terrorizing ways. Supposedly, Grandma was among them.

Emma didn't want to know the truth about the Green rumor. Grandma would have been nineteen when that incident occurred. The Darwin police investigated, but no one in town outed the shooter. Truth be known, the entire town was in cahoots with the crime. It was in the genetics of our hillbilly selves; no one hunkered down before authority. From the Darwin's law side, like any illegal situation in Taylorville, it was not worth the time and money and the law considered the case a cold one.

Grandma studied Emma before answering. "Don't think I'll be getting into any of those rumors. I admit I took part in things during my youth of which I'm not proud and about which I will carry a burden for the rest of my life. But I've grown from my mistakes. Hopefully, you won't have to. Hopefully, you won't carry such regrets later in your life." Grandma stood for a moment, staring at Emma and then Jolene, before taking her white rag and swiping at a carton of booze.

"Grandma, what's going on? It seems you're asking me to walk away and allow Mattie to suffer."

"Maybe because I'm not the one fighting. It's you two," Grandma said, nodding first at Emma, then Jolene, "and it frightens me. Heaven knows I've struggled to know what to do for Jolene and now Mattie." Tears filled Grandma's eyes. "Whatever you do, you may end up causing more trouble for that girl, making it worse for her. We don't know how long Wade's going to be living there, or that Sy fellow, either. Knowing Wade, it won't be long before he moves on. Mattie won't survive if she's taken from her home. Jolene, you know this if anyone does."

For the first time, Emma remained silent, and her silence gave weight to the possibility that Grandma was right.

Even though silence hung heavy in the room, it belied the heaviness of the tension between the women. Grandma switched her attention to Emma. "Your Grandpa and I've protected you too much, and Wade has a danger to him I've not seen in this town before. Maybe because he's lived elsewhere and has done dark deeds in some powerful places with some powerful men. I'm ordering you to stay away from Wade."

"Even when Wade comes into the bar and we need to serve him? A man who abuses others?" Emma said this with a meaningful stare. "He can *still* buy beer at The Dam Tavern."

"Girl, don't tempt me here. You won't like what comes of it. I'll serve anyone I damn well like in my own damn tavern. If I only served angels, there would be no business, now would there?" Grandma paused to compose herself. Quietness filled the backroom and everyone stared at the floor, deep in their own thoughts.

Grandma spoke, continuing in a different vein to make her point. "There is an old story I heard while in Mexico from my shaman. It's about a man named Don Juan, who lived in Spain with his young daughter and a bull, whom he called Civilon. Don Juan bred Civilon for bullfighting. One day Don Juan spied Civilon gently eating flowers from his daughter's hand, who was only eight. From that day on, the children came and fed and petted the bull who became beloved by the country." Grandma paused in her telling, and Emma jumped in.

"Yeah... what about it?" Emma was hard put in understanding the relevance and sudden leap to another insignificant topic. "How's this relate, Grandma?"

Jolene looked confused. "You've lost me, Grandma Rose. I don't understand your point. We're not children living in Spain and petting a bull."

"Well, give me time to tell the story and maybe you'll see what I mean." Grandma sighed and continued her story. "When the Fascist forces threatened to attack Barcelona, the city held a bullfight in Barcelona's historic bull ring in an effort to raise national pride. The promoters took Civilon from his pasture and carted him to the arena. At the beginning of the bullfight, picadors stabbed Civilon between his shoulders and Civilon, even with his gentle nature, acted as any reasonable animal would, by charging back at the picadors, driving them behind the barriers. But then, a whistle sounds out over the arena and the wounded Civilon trotted over to his old owner, the rancher, and leaned in for a caress—the violence and pain he suffered didn't wipe away his memory of kindness and his trust in his own reason."

"Civilon's action of gentle kindness and submission moved the onlookers, and the crowd cheered. They chanted his name, indicating a desire of a pardon. The president voted in favor of his people and waved his handkerchief, granting the bull his pardon. The people sent Civilon home to recover in his peaceful pasture."

"Still not seeing your point here, Grandma." Emma said, feeling exasperated, maybe because the story moved her far more than she like to admit, while it offered her a challenge in her reactions to Wade.

"The point is, that when you meet an ultimate adversary, in your case, Wade, you find the kindness and courage in your dealings with him. First, don't give up the fight to find that compassion within you, even when all is lost. Then, use your training and find the deeper part within you that feels weak. Hold that part in your heart. Then see that deeper part within Wade which feels vulnerable and you hold that part of him in your heart as well. Trust the compassion, then the fight leaves, and then you can take action from that space of inner resolve."

"Grandma, really, do you think my having compassion for Wade's weakness would change anything? He's not a man that understands kindness. He's all about powering over someone. He'll just want to power over me or Jolene." Emma's tone was laden with indignation.

Grandma shrugged. "But a person who holds genuine power doesn't need to power over another. The real question is which part of you greets the fight? Is it part within you who gives in to her fear, the one who fights by grabbing power to power over, or the one who finds compassion for the weaknesses in both? That's the real question. Is there a part within you that doesn't want to take advantage of Wade's impotence, shown in his fight? Because, in my eyes, Wade has that last part of powering over something covered. He'll fight. Remember, he's walking around and not sitting in a jail cell somewhere, so he can't be as much a halfwit as you think. Wade, on the surface, refuses to see his weaknesses because he's not strong enough to go within and take notice. So, he misses out on knowing any true strength without fear. He misses out on knowing himself."

"So, what crime did Jolene—or Mattie—do, for that matter? They seem to carry the sins of others? Are they living some type of karma?"

"Yeah, I'm not sure the type of crime I committed to live a life with George," Jolene said, anger tingeing her voice. "I'm not sure what my karma was at age six.

"I don't think I'm wise enough to understand what purpose you serve in carrying the shame of your perpetrators," Grandma said, sadness in her tone. "I just know it happens."

"Maybe it's Jolene's path to experience vengeance? Maybe she was a victim of something early in her life, you know, like at age four her mother abandoning her so that she has to play out a role with power," Emma said, trying to grasp the philosophy herself and also realizing she spoke of her own past pain of her mother's abandonment as well.

"You may be right. But understand that when you operate at the frequency or the resistance of the problem, you only express one side of the situation—or as that guy you're always reading, Jung, would say, 'expressing the darkness'—then the result of integrating the opposites, such as, coming into a oneness with your darkness doesn't occur. Without the view of both opposites, you won't see the other creative possibilities that bring new solutions to the situation. Like Civilon, moving past his pain and his aggression toward the picadors, he felt his kindness toward the rancher and a new solution of gaining the crowd's support appeared. He didn't make that happen. He didn't have power over the crowd.

He only trusted his kindness toward the rancher and acted upon that."

"So, tell me, Grandma, what do you know of Jung? You've not read any of his work." There was a tinge of anger in Emma's voice and her rebellion nature pushed-back at Grandma's all-knowingness attitude.

Grandma Rose smiled. "I don't need to read him to understand a universal principle which underlies his philosophical theory. During my time in Mexico, I learned it. I was a little older than you are now."

Emma knew how far she could push Grandma and she hung her head and watched herself pick at her fingernails while resignation sat in. Grandma's advice had merit and when she brought in Jung...well, Emma could only flail. But the unresolved feeling remained within herself, so she tried another angle, a play on words.

"Alright, I promise," Emma said. "I won't do anything *violent* to Wade or the Malones."

"There's a theory behind the martial art practice of Kali, where you have an opposing force coming at you...say, a fist. Your first reaction would be to counter the force...say, with your hand to push back. If you take that action, you're battling to have the greater force and prevent the fist from connecting with your face. In Kali, they train you to embrace the fist and surrender to its force and become one with it—and then influence its redirection away from your face. The surrendering is the key."

"Okay, Grandma." Emma felt irritated. What good were these fortune cooking-sounding proverbs? She was done with the anecdotes and the conversation. "I don't understand how to apply the logic of Kali or Civilon to the situation with Wade. But I promise, I'll try."

"You've heard me say that everything is divine. Even if the actions you take are from a vengeful heart and are among the darkest deeds. Those actions also serve in ways we can't even grasp. But, I ask again, which mind do you engage in the situation?"

"The only mind I have," said Emma, exasperated at how everything Grandma said had to have a wise advice attached to it. She resisted any lesson Grandma was about to spout off. Emma just wasn't in the mood, but she took note that Grandma had been on the uptick with her advice giving and having her and Jolene do their lessons every day now. She wondered why the shift? It made her uneasy.

Grandma sighed.

"Why don't you just tell me what to do instead of throwing out allegorical messages?"

Emma noticed by Jolene's vacant, yet wide-eyed stare that their philosophical banter baffled Jolene. She could barely hold the understanding herself.

"I don't know...this is for you and Jolene. That's why it's better for you to figure out the solution of liberating yourself from escalating this violence. I know your rebellious side; you'll create a larger crisis." Grandma looked at Emma, and then Jolene, her eyes rimmed with tears. "But I'm telling you, your generation is unlike any generation that's come before. You're wise at such an early age. I've never seen that before. You know, in my generation, we might find that knowledge at thirty, if we're lucky. But more likely at fifty. With your grandpa, he found wisdom from all that reading, being inside the heads of thousands through his books. I found mine in my study with a teacher in the Mayan world. Your generation seems to have received some kind of understanding of things whilst you were baking in the belly of your mamas. Then you popped into this world with it, a knowledge stored in your DNA, from all the generations before and the current times you're living. I'm amazed by you and what you can do."

Emma fell silent to hear Grandma talk about her in such a reverential tone. She always respected Grandma's views, even though at times she defied them and their authority over her own thoughts. But, to hear Grandma say that she was amazed by her abilities, well, there was no greater praise than that.

Grandma appeared wistful, almost as if she would have liked to have been born fifty years later. Emma decided, for the sake of Grandma's wishes, that she would tweak her plan and remove any violence toward Wade. She and Jolene would right the situation with Mattie and send out a message to the town without violence.

"I love hearing your stories and it may give us an idea of how to deal with our situation in a better way because all the theories you talk about just confuses me," Jolene said. "Have you ever met a threat of violence in which you didn't fight back or give up?"

Grandma's eyes had a faraway reminiscent look. "I don't know about myself. But Emma here did, and she encountered that violence without pushing back. Can you tell it, dear? About the time you faced adversity in your grandpa's store."

32

Grandma swung her body around on her box of Jack Daniels to face Emma and Jolene more directly. An enormous smile lightened her face, shifting the mood in the room away from tension to curiosity. Jolene's interest initially focused on Grandma, turned to Emma with a surprise look on her face. Emma's mind raced as to what exactly Grandma knew. Maybe it wasn't the story Emma thought Grandma referred to, at least she hoped not. But Grandma's next statement dashed Emma's hopes to not have to share the most adverse and dangerous situation she'd ever encountered.

"Well, Emma had just turned fourteen and her grandpa allowed her to work the grocery by herself one day." Grandma started the telling.

Emma interrupted. "Grandma, how did you find out about this?"

"Girl, did you not think your grandpa wouldn't call me to give me a heads-up about the situation?"

Jolene regarded Emma, her look of surprised replaced with a questioning and shocked expression. "What? How could you not tell me? I thought we told each other everything."

Emma looked at Jolene with amazement. "Really, Jolene? I figure you of all people know that even the closest friends don't tell everything. Sometimes, it's best to have our secrets." There was a long pause before Emma added in a softer voice. "Although it's not really a secret. I didn't want Grandma to worry or, more likely, interfere like she does." Emma returned Grandma's pointed look, before turning toward Jolene and softly continuing. "And I didn't want to add to your problems with my own." In actuality, Emma thought Jolene would have involved herself and she didn't want to put Jolene in danger. She watched Jolene's expression to ensure Jolene wasn't upset with her silence on the matter. "Besides, I had it figured out. It wasn't a problem."

Jolene's chin lifted defiantly, and a few moments of deadened silence fell between the three. She glanced at Emma, before looking at the floor and composing herself. She met Emma's gaze. "You're right. It's rarely someone thinks of me first. But, since Grandma Rose opened up this can of worms, can you tell your story, please? I would really like to hear it now, as it somehow relates to Wade."

Emma nodded and pulled up the memory—the ornate counter of the grocery's main room, the three gang boys standing on the other side, somewhat intimidating and borderline menacing, the scene as vivid as if she were there yesterday. On this day, her grandpa was in the back room, carving up a ham.

"So, one day, these three gang members wondered in from Darwin and came into the store. They wore grey clothes and bandanas with their gang symbols. The tallest guy threw down all kinds of merchandise—a garden hose, a hammer and a hunting knife. 'Bitch, I want a refund,' he said, an anger he thought would translate into an agreement from me to just hand over the money.

"The three teens were slightly older than me, around eighteen, and they just glared from the other side of the counter. I wondered if the guy was going to fling himself onto the countertop and grab me by the throat. He had such a deep, repressed anger. Yet I held my cool, because I was going to have to tell him the truth."

"You go, girl. Of course, I could see you doing that." Jolene said, totally captivated by the story.

"'I'm sorry, we don't carry those items for you to return for a refund.' I said, trying to hold his glare, you know, look him directly in the eyes.

"I remembered the guy just gritted his teeth and pressed his lips together." Emma's face was contorting into the expression of the gang member. "I could see his fist flexing, open and close. 'I want a refund,' he said, more forcefully this time.

"'Okay, but we don't sell those items in the store. Maybe you purchased them somewhere else?' I got a little anxious, you know. My hand was shaking, so I braced it against the counter.

"Then, the boy pointed his finger and jabbed it in my face. He spat out, in a forceful, loud voice, and his spit splashed across the counter, 'I don't care, bitch, give me the money.'

"I shook my head no.

"'Bitch, watch your back. You've got one more chance to give me that money. If not, then we are going to have a bitch of a problem. You don't want to be screwing with me, and you can believe that shit.' The hate leapt from this guy's eyes. Then he made a gun with his hand and pointed his finger to his head and then pointed his gun-finger at me."

Emma's head snapped back, just as her head did when the boy threatened her that day.

"You're kidding? What did you do?" Jolene leaned forward, concern on her face.

"Well, my heart was racing like Seattle Slew and I said, 'Please, have a nice day,' and I turned toward the counter to ruffle through papers as if I had work to do and couldn't be bothered anymore.

"But the guy continued to stare and then, in another threatening voice, said, 'You're a mouthy little bitch, aren't you?' Then he turned to his friends and in a low voice said, "Come on, let's haul ass out of this rat-ass store." The boy swooped up his items, items that I knew he had no intention of leaving for any refund, and the boys quickly left. The lead boy yelled over his shoulder, 'Watch your back!'"

Jolene's eyes flashed deep interest in the suspense, much like she had read a story with the ingredients of a well-received Stephen King novel.

"Oh, my gosh...you were only fourteen, and you could do that? What happened then?" asked Jolene. "Did the gang leave? Just like that?"

"Not quite," Emma said, as the memory flooded into her mind and her body braced itself for the most difficult part of her story.

"At closing time, Grandpa came up to me. I could see the concern tightened his lips. He told me I couldn't leave the grocery.

"At first, I was angry. What more did he want now? What task could be so important that I needed to stay? I had put in a full day's work. I just wanted to go home.

"But it seemed like the gang was going to make good on their threats, and they waited outside of the store for me to leave. Grandpa told me he would escort me home every night after work, as the gang wouldn't give up that easily. He instructed me to walk, keep my eyes straight, not to look down at the road in submission or give the gang any attention, no matter what they yelled from their car."

"Wow..." was all Jolene could say.

"Grandpa showed up every night for a week, sitting in his truck outside of the store and waiting. And every night I walked confidently toward home without giving the gang any attention, no matter the words they yelled at me. I was confident because Grandpa was a scary guy to go up against, even for that gang. Grandpa showed until the night he told me he would not be there."

"No way would Grandpa leave you alone," said Jolene.

Emma paused in her story to brace for the next part. The next part hurt her the most. She took a breath and continued with the most troublesome part of her story.

"Grandpa told me to continue to do as I had the previous nights and that I would be fine. But to tell you the truth, on that day, he abandoned me. But I did as I was told and sure enough the gang continued to harass me, and I continued to keep my eyes forward and I just kept walking toward home." Tears welled up in Emma's eyes, remembering the hurt at the moment and having to find her courage within.

"Oh my God...what happened then?"

"Nothing, they just left—never to return." Emma said matter-of-factly.

"So, Grandpa Frank left you to face those guys all alone?" Jolene asked, incredulous. "That doesn't sound like something he'd do."

"Yep. He sure enough did."

Grandma looked at Emma, surprised. "That's not quite the entire story, Emma."

Emma looked at Grandma suspiciously. "What do you mean?"

Grandma grinned large. "Do you remember what else you did that last night when you thought your grandpa wasn't there?"

Emma looked at Grandma. "And...how do you know what went down that night?" she asked suspiciously. "Are there any secrets left in this family?"

"Just tell the entire story." said Grandma, enjoying the moment fully.

"Well, yeah. I left a little something out. I wouldn't go down without doing something dramatic-like." Emma laughed, realizing the secret she thought secret and crazy was up for the telling. "It wasn't my finest moment."

"So…don't leave me hanging here. Finish the story," Jolene said.

"Well, the idea came to me while I paced the store, you know, assessing the situation of having to face the gang alone. I kept playing the scenario out in my mind and while I thought the idea was crazy, I also thought it might just work. Then, I thought, *what the hell, just do it.*

"So, before I left the store, I took some tomato paste from the shelf. You know the kind with the pull tab? I popped it open and ceremoniously smeared it all over my head and face." Her idea embarrassed her now from the lameness of it, but at the time she thought if the gang led her as a goat to slaughter, then she might as well look the part. Laughter, a small self-conscious laugh at the memory of smearing the tomato paste all over her, bubbled up, and she felt relief.

"You did what?" asked Jolene.

"I painted myself with tomato paste, then I held my head high and walked out the door."

"I was so proud of you," said Grandma. She laughed. "Your grandpa didn't abandon you! He hid in the field next to the store with his shotgun. He saw the whole thing go down. He was never prouder of you. You were so brave." Grandma laughed, her eyes watering. "Your grandpa said that with the illumination of the half-moon, the tomato paste had a blackened-blood look and created such a sight to behold. Frank said Emma looked like she had her skin stripped away from her face. And, with the white of her wide eyes, she seemed like a demonic animal. Crazy's difficult to ignore. Grandpa thought that maybe the young men decided they better leave her alone as they were dealing with a demented person. You know, someone not quite right in the head."

"You must have looked like Carrie at the prom," said Jolene. "And for the classmates of Carrie, it didn't work out well for them, either." She laughed until her eyes teared. "So, what happened after you left the store?"

"Well, the gang sort of made this stunned and collective gasp, then they mumbled among themselves some. They yelled from their car that I was one crazy bitch and they drove off. I guess the thing that stops a bully is to have either true confidence or to show them you've completely lost your mind and have no fear."

"Your grandpa helped you to find and develop your inner male with the help of his outer man, and it helps that you're bred and buttered here in Taylorville." Grandma said. "From that day on, you've let no one cross you." Grandma looked at Jolene. "She's always stood up for herself and others."

"But that is not exactly true, is it, Grandma?" Emma's eyes flashed with anger. "I wasn't there for Mattie, nor Jolene for that matter."

Grandma stiffened, her body slightly rising on her crate of Johnnie Walker.

Jolene placed her hand over Emma's trembling one. "Emma, you've been there for me in more ways than you know."

The three women sat in silence for a moment. The smells of lavender and sage strong in the room.

"Well, it's true we've raised you in this harsh town, but you never made me prouder than that night. A reputation for being tough can always come in handy. Now, I know the two of you, being stubborn as you both are, will not let this Mattie thing run its course. And maybe you shouldn't. But I think you should apply the same type of solution Emma did with the gang. Meet violence with courage, kindness and guile—not vengeance."

Maybe Emma could see the purpose Grandma had in bringing up the story of the gang. But for Emma, the biggest take-away was Grandpa had been there for her when all this time she resented him for making her face the enemy alone. What else was in her mind that distorted her current reality? She hated to think of people she had misjudged because of her assumptions. So, if she had misjudged Grandpa, her own flesh and blood, who else did she see wrongly? Could it be Wade?

33

Grandma Rose rubbed her palms along her thighs and stood up from her crate of liquor.

"How about we smudge ourselves and the tavern? It's time to smoke out the darkness that seems to have gathered around our light," she said.

Emma's mood softened. When Grandma Rose smudged, she was more reasonable. Emma walked to the shelves for the smudge sticks. Jolene followed to stand by Emma and searched among the jars for a lighter.

"I know we pray and smudge to help protect our family and the surrounding space, but Grandma, there is so much wrong in our town. It will take more than smoke to cleanse its soul."

"Yes, meanness lives in many men," said Grandma Rose, sighing. She stood in silence, her head down and lips pursed in thought.

"I wish evil didn't have to happen in my life," Emma said wistfully.

When Grandma Rose spoke again, her voice resonated with calm and compassion. "So do I, but it's not for us to decide. Our decision lies with what action we take when we face the evil in another. Do you just want to be another spoke in the wheel of violence? You must do your journey work to find your answers, the both of you." Grandma paused a moment, deep in her mind. "It's time to call upon the angels to clear out the dark again, dear. It will help you, and Jolene, to get right in this situation and your challenges. It will help us all to heal." Grandma dropped into a chair and watched the girls with her shiny blue eyes while Emma and Jolene gathered the supplies.

Jolene walked to the back wall, where Grandma Rose kept her jars of herbs and medicines, and an idea eased into her mind, like light creeping into a dark room from the crack of a slowly opening door. Jolene, too, had joined Emma and Grandpa Frank's informal book club and she realized that Grandma Rose's blue light-filled eyes reminded her of the tired fisherman from *The Old Man and the Sea*, the man who never gave up his fight against the Marlin. The tired fisherman lost his fight against the sharks that ate his prized Marlin, which he had hung from the side of his skiff before he could reach his village. He'd lost his fight, but his eyes remained as blue as the sea he loved, like Grandma Rose's. Even though he lost the fight, the experience alone revealed aspects of the fisherman's soul which never would have found expression if he hadn't engaged in the fight. So, in actuality, though the fish got away, his spirit remained undefeated and strengthened for future challenges.

Maybe Jolene needed to fight for Mattie and give voice to abused women. And through the fight for Mattie, she'd be fighting for herself for once. Maybe an aspect of her personality needed that expression, too. Jolene hadn't given up, not at age six and not at age eighteen. Maybe she needed to have the fight before she could surrender to the forces of violence, as Grandma advised. The fight was an important step in her getting closer to surrender, and through that in her obtaining the wisdom Grandma Rose spoke about.

Then, as if Grandma Rose were reading Jolene's thoughts, she said, "Just like Mattie, you both will have to face your darkness, and maybe battle it, before you come to peace. And I believe you will do it soon."

Emma did not question Grandma. When Grandma spoke from her quiet place, she seemed to access a veiled truth.

34

Emma joined Jolene at the chest. She remained silent as she lifted down the old woman's ornate wooden chest from the top shelf. When she raised the lid, a shelf folded out. The scents of cedar, orange, lemon, lavender and rose— rose being the highest quality of all medicinal flowers and herbs—filled the air. The chest contained certain objects and talismans that Grandma had collected over the years: a beautiful eagle feather, an owl's wing, precious stones, rocks from the riverbed, sand from the banks of the Wabash, trinkets representing the sun and the moon, blessed-holy water, and special concoctions made from herbs and flowers. These things supported Grandma's shamanic practices, a healing practice of Mayan origins, but Grandma never referred to herself as a shaman. She just respected nature and her intuition. She could tease the healing property from anything that grew, died, or laid in her path because she was a natural healer.

In her life, objects magically appeared in her path, and she would always say, "Here's another gift from Mother Earth." She would bend to grasp the object and tuck it away in her pocket. In her mind, each object she saw in her path was because she needed to own the power the object represented. She had considerable gratitude for the gift that life offered, a reminder for her to keep developing her gifts.

Emma grabbed the talisman bag from the chest. The pouch was a small black velvet purse, with tasseled threads to tie close the mouth. She referred to the bag as the power pouch. It contained three favorite talismans: a silver pendant of a wolf, a small silver rose, and a tiny wooden monkey. The wooden monkey was a Mayan symbol of the scribe, the village writer who wrote of the Mayan mysteries, their stories and history, and who became regarded as a healer of the Mayan people.

In Emma's classes, she had studied Mayan mythology. The Mayan villagers revered their scribes, and today, societies considered these writers as modern-day priests or psychologists. These people inspired Emma for their understanding of the earth's existence in relationship to the universe. The scribes knew the forces of the universe as told by the heavenly bodies of planets and their relationship to the earth and how those forces influenced life on earth. They knew when to plant their crops for the best yield, when to marry, and when to conceive a child for the strongest of offspring. The Mayans were the wisest people in her book.

Grandma had found the tiny wooden monkey when she visited Mexico as a young woman with her husband. The Mexico trip became the only time Grandma left Taylorville, other than on brief trips to Darwin. It was on that trip where she learned her shamanic ways and came to respect the Mayan traditions. Grandma had added the monkey scribe to her talisman bag, along with the wolf and the rose pendants.

The rose pendant represented Grandma's heritage as a Ford, her strength and power as a woman. It was through the rose image and its power that Grandma found the courage and intelligence to run her own business and be independent in her thinking. Grandma said roses have the highest vibration of all flowers and herbs and are therefore used for healing. The Rose name ran throughout the women in their family, presented to the first-born girl. Emma's mother insisted on not giving her the first name Rose, but Emma's father urged her mother to give the middle name Rose. Her mother said she wanted Emma to determine her own destiny and not set the forces upon her through her name as a dictating influence. But Emma believed her mother simply wanted another way to defy Grandma.

The third talisman, the wolf's tooth, represented the pack's importance, the family and otherworld wisdom. Emma understood the power of the wolf and its reminder to listen to her own intuition. She selected this talisman and held it to my heart. Jolene selected the wooden monkey. They took a smudge stick, a bundle of dried sage grass, and lit the end with a long wooden match, selecting an abalone shell to hold under the burning grass. Emma and Jolene waited until the grass caught and smoke wafted up toward the ceiling.

The abalone shell felt rough in Emma's hand. The smudge stick burned slowly, tiny embers burning on the ends of the dried blades of grass. Then, she fanned the owl wing to disperse the smoke and cleanse the room. A pungent smell filled the space. As they smudged, they repeated the Lord's Prayer. Emma smoked out her worries. She smoked out the pain of her dad's death, the fear of loneliness in times of challenge, the blackness that feeds on a child's innocence, a suffering town's evil, and the dark thoughts that gathered in corners and shadows of the tavern rooms. She prayed for protection from anything that did not have the family's and her friend's best interests at heart. She smudged the doorways and the windows against evil entering the tavern. The three women walked from room to room in communion while Grandma chanted her prayer.

They smoked away the haunts held in a gathering place that had seen more than its fair share of suffering. Grandma, holding her smudge stick high, cleansed Emma by waving the smoke over her body from head to foot. A light grey cloud enveloped her and then dissipated languorously away. Then Grandma smudged Jolene by raising the stick high above Jolene's head and fanning the smoke over her body. Then, not forgetting Miss Henry, Grandma ran a few passes over her while she sat at the slot machine. It was the only time Emma witnessed Miss Henry still at her slot machine. Miss Henry closed her eyes in prayer, and the moment affirmed Emma's theory, the old woman had more than half-a-mind.

35

Jolene and Emma stood at the tavern's back door in silence. Both girls looked up at the evening sky, then looked at each other. Emma held her palms faced up, fingers wide in a gesture of confused defeat.

Jolene sighed heavily. "You know, I won't let it go. It'll take years of smudging to erase what I witnessed that day with Mattie. What I've lived through with George wasn't even as bad. It's different when the abuse is happening to someone else—someone you care about." She said this with renewed focus and purpose, fueled by rage, partly because of Mattie's situation and partly from her own abuse. "I do what I do to help keep Vickie safe and not feel helpless." Images of George flashed through her mind and then seeing Mattie huddled in her nakedness brought her vulnerability to a new low. "Wade has to pay for what he's done. I can do something with Wade."

She looked at Emma with a pleading look. "You won't leave me to do this alone, will you? You're with me on this, right?"

"I don't know, Jolene. Maybe Grandma's right. Maybe we should leave it be and figure this out. All three of us could go on. Maybe we should focus on helping Mattie get over it."

Jolene's thoughts of helpless Mattie triggered her own feelings of vulnerability. There were times in which she felt naked and huddling in a crowd of people. Yet, she had to go to school, perform in swim practice, and worse...go home to sleep. How many times did people turn the other way to her own abuse? Too many to count. And no one called George to task. Which only let the abuse continue.

"Mattie won't just get over it. No amount of wisdom from Grandma Rose will reverse what happened to her. And it will keep happening unless we make Wade pay."

Emma stood, deep in thought. Jolene could see her struggle. Jolene took a deep breath to measure her voice. Anger was not what she needed to convince her friend.

"Emma, I know that Grandma Rose has an influence on us, mostly because she's typically right, but we can do this without violent intent. We still need to do something, though. Don't leave me to do it alone. I can't. I need you."

Emma reached behind her shoulder, touching her tattoo. She imagined that Jolene's tattoo stung, just as her own was stinging—a reminder of their sisterhood promise. Emma pressed her lips together and nodded. Jolene smiled with pressed lips, not convinced by Emma's response.

Jolene turned to walk home to her own nightmare before Emma changed her mind. Emma's lack of enthusiasm felt like an abandonment. She didn't enjoy resisting Grandma Rose's wishes, either. But, at this point, she didn't care if Grandma was right. She had a powerful and simple reason to take revenge. She wanted to once and for all to do what felt right to her.

Jolene admitted she had made mistakes in her past. Maybe one of them was remaining quiet when the Department of Human Services questioned her about George's abuse. Maybe this time she'd make the right decision. Jolene stopped and stood a moment longer, looking up at the sky and absorbing the last silent moments as she witnessed the oncoming night's darkness chasing the remaining day's light on the west horizon. The light winked out over the edge of the world, then she put her head down and walked home.

36

Mattie plodded past the wrecks along the lane, her head down, humming to herself.

"Hey, girl!" Wade's voice shot down the lane and Mattie's head snapped up. Wade shuffled toward her from the top of the drive, carrying a dark bundle under his arm.

"Yes, Wade," said Mattie, in a wobbly, barely audible cadence.

"Come here, girl. Look what I've brought you."

Mattie slowed her walk into tentative steps.

"Come on, hurry up. I ain't got all day." He felt exasperated at how little appreciation she showed for his gift.

Mattie sped up her shuffle to a slow walk.

"Come on, come on," Wade said. He was becoming even more exacerbated, but he tried to soften his tone all the same. "Lookie at what I have for you. A gift."

The gift thrashed around, wanting down. Wade put Fido on the ground and Fido wagged his tail, trotting over to Mattie. Mattie looked at the dog and a big O formed on her mouth. She squatted down and began petting Fido, who tried jumping into her face with huge licks.

She giggled. "What's wrong with his eye? It's closed over," Mattie said, concern wrinkling her face, though her smile continued to shine through.

"Probably a stick. You know, they say that anything is better than a stick in your eye," Wade said with a thoughtful tone in his voice.

"And now he has one less eye to worry about poking with a stick, right, Wade?"

"That's right. His name's Fido, and he's yours," Wade said, a smile warming his face.

"Wow, he already has a name...and he's all mine?" Mattie asked. "You're not teasing me?"

"Of course, I'm not teasing you. I don't torment like that." Wade saw teasing as a negligible way to inflict misery, so why even bother?

"I can keep him, then? Like, forever?" Mattie looked up from Fido to Wade gaging his expression for any sign of deceit.

"Of course you can keep him. I don't know about *forever*, unless you die before he does, then I guess it's a forever promise to you."

"Thank you, Wade. This is the best gift anyone's ever given me."

"You can call me Dad, as it seems there's no one else stepping up for that job."

"Ok, Wade."

"So, he's yours and you have to take care of him...you know, feed him and all."

Mattie, satisfied, squealed as she picked Fido up in her arms, hugging him. "I will."

"Well, then, come on, let's introduce him to our new home."

Wade placed his arm around her shoulders as Fido squirmed in her arms and they walked together toward the house, the new silver shingles contrasting with the darkening moonlit evening.

37

Grandma, so often the poised woman, gracefully positioned her hand on her crossed knee. The gesture was reminiscent of flapper girls from the 1930s, a gesture of aloofness and class, as if nothing sinister could touch her, not even a bout of lung cancer from all the smoking she did. Grandma always remarked that she'd smoked for sixty years, and no Surgeon General would influence her to do any different. She sat on a carton of Johnnie Walker and patted the other box. Emma sat down with her legs sprawled out in front of her and pulled her black cotton shift tight over her legging clad knees.

"My, my girl. You'd think one of the Beatles was arriving for a visit. It's just a boy showing up for your first date. Keep reminding yourself of that...he's only a boy. You're distracting me from reminiscing about my past good times. Take a few deep breaths to calm yourself down a bit." The faint sound of the slot machine dropping coins drifted in from the main room.

"Grandma...The Beatles? Really? Maybe if you told me Drake was waiting at the door, then I'd really flip out." She laughed.

"I don't know this Drake fellow. Anyway, I can't believe you asked your date to meet you at The Dam Tavern. Why not meet you at home? I mean, it's right next door."

"Because the dating rule is that you never meet someone you don't know yet at your home. That way, they'll won't know where you live." Emma paused. "Besides, I told him to meet me in front of The Dam Tavern, not in it." She bit her lower lip. "It's about time for him to show. I'll wait out front." Emma stood, smoothing down her shirt and tucking a few strands of her hair behind her ears. She walked to the front, glancing over at Miss Henry nested in front of the slot machine, the bars clicking into their slots. Grandma rose off her box of booze to follow.

"Really, Grandma?" Emma asked, opening the door and sitting on the stoop.

Emma hadn't been waiting long when a green '66 Mustang pulled up to the front and Nate emerged from the car. Emma caught a movement from the tavern window as a hand drew a blind back. She swallowed her irritation, choosing instead to smile at Nate.

Nate strode up to the stoop, and Emma stood to greet him.

"Hello. You said you have something in mind to do?" asked Nate. Emma smiled, knowing his jumping into a question about their activity revealed his anxiety about their date. Knowing that he, too, felt anxious allowed her to ease into the moment. Her jaw relaxed, turning her forced smile into a genuine one.

Grandma opened the tavern door. "Hello, I'm Grandma Rose, Emma's grandmother."

She extended her hand out for Nate to shake. The faint rolling of the slots drifted out from the open door. Grandma held the door ajar as she invited Nate in.

Nate looked confusion, briefly glancing at Emma before shifting his gaze back to Grandma Rose. "Hello, I'm Nate."

"Why don't you step in for a moment," Grandma said, holding the door wider.

Nate took a tentative step forward, hesitating a moment before walking in. Emma followed Nate, rolling her eyes at Grandma to express her displeasure. She never felt ashamed by Grandma Rose. In fact, she was always proud of her family. But, beside sophisticated Nate, she saw a stark contrast.

It seemed perfectly natural the way Grandma Rose scanned Nate from head to toe, just as she would appraise a rare bottle of Johnnie Walker whiskey. Nate's charming looks took Grandma back some, told by the way she tilted her head and smiled. Soon, Emma dropped away from her earlier irritation and embarrassment to feeling a little happier knowing Grandma was pleased. Nate stood much taller than Emma remembered from the library. Standing six feet four, he dwarfed everything in The Dam Tavern. He filled the space with his presence.

"Welcome to our humble home, Nate." Grandma remarked, eyes bright with disbelief, as if she were looking at a Greek God.

"Whatever, Grandma. This isn't home, but The Dam Tavern".

"So, what do you two have planned?" Grandma Rose asked, ignoring Emma's comment. "It's a glorious day today."

"Emma has something planned. She told me what to wear," Nate said, turning to smile at Emma.

"Well, that takes guts, not knowing Emma or what's planned. But hey, I'm not one to spoil a surprise." Grandma's attention never left Nate. "You're welcomed to stay for supper tonight...if the date goes well." Grandma smiled, and Emma could tell that she liked Nate with her invitation to supper.

Emma felt the heat rise to her face and turned toward Grandma. "Don't you have work to do or something?" Emma, her head tilted, and she looked pointedly at Grandma, hoping she'd get the message.

"Yeah, I do, but don't rightly feel like doing it none." She smiled sweetly at Nate. Emma swore Grandma was flirting.

"Come on, Nate," Emma said. She wanted to leave before Grandma said anything more, turning her own face an even deeper beet red.

Outside, Nate helped her into the passenger side and inserted the key into the ignition before his door closed. He jammed the car into first gear and immediately lurched into a nearly impossible U-turn. The easy forcefulness in how Nate drove stirred something unfamiliar in Emma—lower than her stomach, almost like a raw ripple of sensation. She liked the sight of his powerful hands grasping the leather-bound steering wheel with their long, slender fingers. His blue shirt with the double pockets on the front emphasized his wide, muscled shoulders and brought out the blueness of his eyes. He made the boys she had gone to high school with seem so boyish and thuggish.

"So, where to?" He asked, glancing Emma's way.

"Follow the river for about half a mile."

Nate glanced a little longer at Emma, a smile growing on his face, and he tipped his head down to laugh, enjoying the mystery of the adventure he was on. "Are you going to tell me what you have planned?"

"Have you ever been noodling?" Emma asked, observing his response.

"Noodling. Is that something you'd do in a Chinese restaurant?" He asked, laughing. "I see an image of people sucking a long noodle into their mouths."

"Not quite. You do it in a river and it's quite dangerous."

"I'm not sure that narrows it down any. To me, anything done on the river is dangerous." He said this, glancing over at her and flashing a smile, causing Emma's heart to skip. In her mind, dating Nate was doing something more dangerous than any activity on the Wabash.

38

Nate pulled his Mustang near the river's edge under a grove of trees. Emma opened the door, jumping out to not be in close proximity to him. His masculinity made her body tingle as if she had taken a swig of Grandma's best whiskey. She rounded the car and grabbed his hand, leading him down to Grandpa's rowboat, which she had hidden earlier under the brush. Nate pushed the boat into the Wabash. She climbed in and shoved them off the bank.

The river current flowed enough to create little white caps atop the muddy brown water. Emma expertly handled the oars to steer the boat into the current. The river carried them downstream with no need to use the small trolling motor mounted on the transom. The rocking of the boat and the nudging of the river helped to quiet Emma's stomach butterflies.

As they floated downriver, Emma explained that noodling was how people who lived on the river caught flat-nose catfish. She had a spot where the granddaddy of all catfish spawned every year. He even had a name, Jaws. Jaws was a sixty-pound catfish. A legend and a rite-of-passage for any river angler to catch-and-release Jaws, though she didn't tell Nate anything about Jaws. She didn't want to spoil the adventure. Or frighten him more.

"You want to find a place that has large rocks or limbs, like an abandoned beaver dam." Emma steered the boat to the river's edge by a mound of limbs piled high. "Okay, this looks like a worthwhile spot."

"What do I need to do?" Nate asked, his tone serious. "I've never been fishing before."

"Really?" A question flashed through Emma's mind like lightning through the sky. How did someone live without catching a fish now and then for dinner? Then, she realized, he was born into a family who never worried about having to fish. He oozed wealth. He drove a nice vintage car that appeared expensive. "Well, Nate, we're not really going to fish. We're going to jump into the river and you're going to noodle the fish."

"You want me to strip down to my boxers and noodle a fish? And I don't have a clue to what that even means." He looked at her incredulously.

"It means you're going to stick your hand into his spawning hole, wait until he bites down on your hand, then you will wrestle him to the surface."

Nate glanced into the murky river, then at Emma, his face revealing a look of disbelief. "I am going to do what?"

She nodded, and he pulled his shirt off, exposing a taut, muscled upper chest. He rolled his shirt into a ball and removed his Nike sweat pants over his shoes.

"Take your shoes off, too," said Emma.

"Are we going into the river?" Nate asked, staring over the side into the Wabash's muddy depths. "Isn't it cold?"

"It's cold, maybe about sixty-five degrees, but we won't be in long."

Nate responded by shivering and not realizing he did so. His body was tight in expressing its reluctance, but to Emma he seemed game to try it. Emma tossed a pair of goggles at him, and she placed a pair around her neck to dangle.

"Catfish spawning holes are typically along the river bank," she said, directing them.

Nate nodded. His expression was a mixture of determination and hesitation.

"When you noodle a fish, stick your hand into his spawning hole, then push your hand into his mouth and grab him by his lower jaw," she said. "Then, use your other hand to hook him in his gills and lift him out of the river. Be careful not to get your hand caught in his gills, because he'll clamp down and it'll get stuck there."

"That sounds like something to avoid," Nate said.

She grinned. "You don't want to get your hand stuck because you'll need it later. You could easily lose a finger or two in the gills. And you also want to be careful of the tail. The tail is where his power lives. He can swipe his tail side-to-side to roll you over. You don't want that happening, because you can drown, especially if the fish has more power than you." Emma watched him, curious how he would respond to her next statement. "So, if he's a big one, use your legs to circle him and hold him steady."

"Wait a minute. How large do these fish get? You sure I can do this?" He stared at Emma, his eyes searching her face for any signs of doubt.

"Of course, I'm here and I'll help. I'm your noodling buddy," she said, laughing. "And we may encounter the catfish named Jaws."

"How big is Jaws, anyway?"

"Maybe, about this big," Emma said, holding her hands about twelve inches apart.

Emma had already removed her top, pulling it over her head and revealing her sports bra, and then she tugged her leggings off, exposing her swimming briefs. She stepped over the boat's edge and into the Wabash, which rose to her waist. Nate followed and immediately broke out in goosebumps, shivering. He looked as if he was in pain.

"Well, if he's only about twelve inches long, I think I can handle him." Nate said doubtfully.

"It'll be fine." Emma tried to be reassuring, as she knew he probably had never ever been in a river before. "Okay, now. Do you see that hole right there between the branches?" Emma pointed to a spot within the tree limbs, an opening close to the west bank.

"Yeah." Nate had stooped over and was peering between tree limbs.

"Put your goggles on and duck your head under. You should see the catfish in his spawning hole. You want to locate the fish's mouth. His bottom lip will be white against the dark water."

Nate submerged his head, and only his backside remained exposed above water. He rose, sputtering.

"I see him! He's huge! Way bigger than twelve inches."

Emma gave a slight laugh. "I guess he's grown since the last time I saw him."

Nate recovered his courage and resolve and threw his shoulders back in preparation. "Now what?"

"Thrust your hand into his mouth and clamp down on that lower lip and pull him out. It'll feel like sandpaper, but pay it no mind. Grasping him that way won't hurt you or him."

Nate took in a deep breath, preparing to submerge himself once again to do the noodling deed, but when Emma moved easily in the water, he released his held breath slowly and remained standing.

"When you get him out enough to place your free hand by his gill, stick it in the open flap and pull harder."

"What?" Doubt registered on his face again. "This appears more difficult than you first indicated," said Nate, while he watched Emma slowly walking away from him.

She laughed in her light way. "You're doing fine. I'll be on the other side, blocking his escape route."

"How do you know he has an escape route?"

"All you big boys do," Emma said, laughing.

She made her way to the back of the mound of limbs; the river moving around her legs like silken fabric. Her right leg planted down into the mushy bottom and into an opening she knew was the back end of Jaw's spawning hole. She felt a surge of excitement run up her body, matching the water bubbles from her movement in the water. She loved an adventure, and her attraction toward Nate was exhilarating.

"Remember, I'm here to help, as your noodling partner." She enjoyed saying the word partner as it sent a warmth through her body in contrast to the icy river. "Okay, you ready?"

Nate nodded, adjusting his goggles and submerging his body.

Within a few seconds, white water splashed high above the brown river, catching the sunlight, showing the struggle that occurred beneath. Nate's feet kicked and twisted hard above surface. Then his feet went under, and when he rose, he rose like a Poseidon warrior hauling in a fighting sea monster from his watery domain, Nate's right hand in its wide-open mouth and his left hand in its gills.

During the struggle, Nate and Jaws had moved to deeper water. Jaws rolled and Nate went under, and the thrashing ensued. Emma's excitement reverted to worry, wondering if Nate would drown under Jaw's body weight. She didn't know if he was a strong swimmer. Then she saw his head as his feet found their purchase on the riverbed. Nate stood and dragged the thrashing big fish to shallow waters, circling Jaws' body with his legs to help quiet the struggle.

Emma let out a loud hoop and ran through the river, reaching Nate and to help him subdue the large fish.

Nate laughed after the battle ended. "Oh, my God, he's a monster! I wish I had my cell phone to get a photo of him. My first fish!" He turned to Emma. "What do we do with him?"

"Turn him loose and wish him well and hope he has better luck next time," Emma said, her laughter reaching her eyes to mix with the admiration she felt.

Nate looked at her, somewhat disappointed, to let his prize catch go. But he did as he was told and released Jaws, giving him a little nudge. Jaws swam to deeper water, and they watched as he returned to his spawning bed through the escape door.

"What do you call this again?" Nate said, a serious and proud look on his face.

"Foreplay," Emma said, with a wink.

Nate turned and looked at Emma. He grabbed her and pulled her close to him, kissing her long and intimate.

Her first actual kiss from a man.

"I wanted to kiss you the moment I met you," he said. "It's more than I imagined. Now that's out of the way, I won't be nervous the rest of the day," he said. He reached down and kissed her again, this time his lips lingering a little longer.

She marveled he would be the one anxious about kissing her because he seemed so much more worldly than her hillbilly nature. She wanted his kiss to go on. It felt so warm and her whole body relaxed into his. Here was a man who accepted her no matter which side of the Wabash she lived and his acceptance was intoxicating. She wanted this man at her side as she ventured out into the unknown world. Knowing that this courageous man stood beside her, she knew she could conquer any challenge life threw at her and achieve her highest dreams.

39

Nate and Emma walked back to the boat and jumped in, rocking the boat and making the retrieving of their clothing difficult. Emma slipped her shift over her head, tugging it down over her arms to use for cover while she removed her soggy wet sports bra and then her swim briefs. She replaced her wet clothing with her dry undergarments and leggings. She accomplished this act with ease and swiftness.

Nate watched, amazement in his eyes. Without the need to address it, she turned her back toward him and gave him the opportunity to change into his dry clothes.

"Well, this date has reached the top of My-Best-First-Dates-Ever-List," Nate said this to Emma's back.

"Well, I bet that's saying something, for I'm sure there's a lot of competition." Emma turned to see his response.

"Maybe," said Nate with an impish grin. He smiled and looked at Emma with his intense blue eyes that shone with admiration.

They headed back to the car, using the trolling motor against the current. Emma was having a great time until the anxiety hit. She worried about what might happen when the date ended. She did not want it to end. Did Nate? Would he want to see her again?

Luckily, Nate delayed the oncoming disappointment when he looked at her and asked, "Walk with me?"

She nodded, her face brightening. She steered the trolling motor in the opposite direction to the east bank and away from the car. They strolled toward Fairbanks Park. He took her hand and assisted her out of the rowboat, which they dragged out of the river. As he walked beside her, she was keenly aware of his physical presence, the way his eyes captured the sunset dropping closer to the horizon and the lightness contained within his large body when it moved. He walked like an enormous cat, comfortable in its innate ability to move its body and at ease in its surroundings, even if unfamiliar with the terrain.

They walked in silence and she noticed how comfortable they were in not having conversation, just being quiet. He seemed to like it, too, as he grabbed her hand and folded her arm into the crook of his arm. The intimacy heightened her vulnerability. The urge to ask a nagging question conflicted with her fear that asking it could ruin the moment. Jolene's voice inside her head saying that remaining in silence and not knowing was worse than risking and asking for an answer. So, she went for it.

"So, were you afraid when you came to pick me up?" she asked. Her brain monitored the structure of the sentence and she wondered if she spoke correctly. Earlier, she noticed, during the noodling, that she had lapsed into the hillbilly twang, something she constantly tried to correct. She wanted him to see her as sophisticated and intelligent, but eventually she became who she was—an only somewhat educated hillbilly.

"Sort of. I didn't think about where you lived until I crossed over the bridge." That nervous chuckle again came from him.

"You mean you weren't ashamed of dating a River Rat until you crossed over to the west side of the Wabash?"

He snorted and laughed his brief laugh, more uncomfortable with confronting the shallowness of those who allowed a river to separate in more ways than one. "The simple response to your question is no. But I have to admit, I was a little uncomfortable driving into Taylorville. Then I saw you on the stoop of The Dam Tavern, and my unfounded worries about Taylorville disappeared."

She laughed, her eyes turning away from his, and her face became serious. "I'm not so sure those things are unfounded," she said. "I mean, since you've met me today, we've already committed one crime." She laughed when she saw his look of confusion and shock. "Noodling," she said. "It's against the law in Indiana."

He laughed. "I'm relieved. I thought my life of crime would be more serious."

"Oh, but it is serious. The Indiana Senate is meeting to discuss whether to dismiss the law."

He scratched his head. "I don't understand what the problem is? It's like if I want to stick my hand into a hole and catch a fish, then why can't I?"

Emma admired this man who thought similar to her. The lightness of which he spoke regarding her hillbilly ways made her feel safe and accepted. The only people who ever made her feel safe were Grandma, Grandpa and Jolene—and those relationships she had developed across her lifetime. Nate, she knew one afternoon.

"I think it has to do with the destruction of the catfish's spawning beds."

"Oh," he said. "Well, I am pretty sure he destroyed me more than I destroyed him."

He laughed. She liked his laughter. It had a way of putting her at ease.

At the end of their walk, when he escorted her to the boat, he drew her close, enfolded her in him, and ran his hand behind her head. She could feel his heart beating and her breath caught. She looked up into his eyes, and her mouth opened slightly. *Oh no, he's going to kiss me again.* Before she could pull away, he reached down and kissed her lightly on her lips, a long and slow kiss. He kissed her as if he didn't want his lips to part from hers. All her anxiety left, and she felt the softness and fullness of his lips. A butterfly sensation, like so many others spoke of, fluttered her heart and moved south to tingle areas that felt the arousal of a man for the first time. It was a night of so many firsts.

40

Sy pushed The Dam Tavern door open and stepped into the smoke-filled room. The way he opened the door with such force belied his outward persona of a chill, standing-in-the-back-of-the-room type of guy. When he strode to the bar, eight or ten men looked his way. When he gave a nod, they pivoted their heads, pretending to be interested in the goings on at their table. Two mussed women with makeup-smudged racoon eyes danced, moving to nineties pop music braying from a jukebox in the corner. All that noise competed with the jangly sound and whir of the spinning reels coming from the slot machine as Miss Henry, dressed in her black chiffon dress and wearing pearls, sat on her stool pulling the crank.

"Oni vse klouny," Sy said to Rose, muttering under his breath and smiling at the thought of secretly passing judgement on the other patrons, for he knew Rose wouldn't speak Russian.

Rose tilted her head and replied, "No, they're not clowns. Only poor hard-working people wanting a brief respite."

Sy studied her, surprise written over his face. "So, you speak Russian?"

"Nyet." Rose picked up a dish towel and shined a pint glass. "My only Russian word. I'm just good at reading the energy underlying any words spoken in any language."

Her eyes penetrated into him, and he knew that little escaped this woman.

"A yorsh?" She asked, sitting the polished pint glass down on the bar in front of him.

Sy pinched his lips together, displeased that he had misjudged her. He felt off-balanced. He prided himself on knowing people inside and out within moments of meeting them. There were times his life depended on it. "Sounds good." Sy loved to savor a yorsh a little at a time, as the drink was his favorite.

Rose grabbed a bottle of Absolut and poured two three-finger shots into the pint glass and then reached down for a cold Guinness buried in the ice chest to top off the drink. She sat it in front of Sy and lifted her 'fizzy' water to drink in a toast. "Best luck in all our plans," she said.

Sy lifted his drink in the toast, and in the Russian tradition, downed the first drink in one go. The next one he would savor. Rose poured him another.

"So, the rumors that you have an ability to see beyond the surface of things is true, eh? What do you see when you look at me?" he asked her, genuinely interested in her opinion.

She laughed, then her smile faded, sobering Sy. "I don't profess to have such an ability."

"You see nothing in me. Am I right?"

She shrugged. Her eyes shifted, taking in the dagger prison tat alongside his face and the serpent rising on the other side of his neck. He reached for his glass with fingers tatted with crude-like numbers. Her eyes, taking in his tattoos, would tell her he was a man far from nothing, but no way could she comprehend what business he had in Taylorville.

Rose didn't respond to his question, which Sy took as a response. She remained looking at him while she picked up another glass to shine.

"That's good." Sy took a sip of his second yorsh.

"I'm curious why a man such as you lives or spends time in quaint Taylorville?" Rose looked at him with interest. "Unless you're completely taken in by the charms of Dottie?" Rose looked at him with focused interest. "Love can be unexplainable in that way."

Sy threw his head back and laughed, not because he thought she was funny, but because he believed she looked deep beneath the façade and into the truth.

Rose continued to shine her glass with a towel, her eyes slightly closed and her gaze shifted to Sy's right shoulder—a stoned, sleepy gaze. She poured Sy a third yorsh.

Sy shifted on his bar stool. He started to sweat. He gave a slight sideways nod of his head in response. It was all he could do. The heated room of stinky air made by the recycled breath from the mouths of chain-smoking drunks made him woozy. He downed the rest of his drink. Sy stood and threw down some cash, tapped the bar with his fist as if he didn't have a care in the world, and walked out of the tavern, his stride a little uneven. Rose made a strong yorsh, evidently.

Once outside, Sy breathed in the fresh air, reviving himself. For the first time in his life, he had thought he was going to faint in front of a bar full of dumbass drunken men and in a town where appearance was everything. The old bar woman intrigued him, but he needed to remind himself to make his next few weeks uneventful. To have things go differently would be dangerous. Yet, he wondered if the woman had worked some magic on him to embarrass him or put him in his place. He'd never met someone who had this effect to strip him of his power with no offensive or aggressive action, and definitely never a woman. All she did was to see right through him. No one in his life had ever done that. He needed to keep an eye on her.

41

The preparation for Emma's meditation began in the early morning, down by the Wabash on Flattop Rock. Maybe the river would give her the answers she sought. "I call upon compassion," she said. "I call upon unconditional love and innate harmony, too. Protect me well as I journey." Then, her incantation complete, she placed the jaguar pendant that Grandma gave her from the smudging ceremony onto Flattop Rock and became still as she lay on her back.

In order for her to enter the unseen world in her meditation, she had to let her imagination take full rein. In her mind, she selected a port of entry into the unseen world. The portal was a large hole in the side of the holler behind her house—one she had discovered as a young girl. The hole was just large enough for her to curl up and fit nicely in. She had used this hole in the ground as a place where she could get away and be alone for a while, like a little cave. The smell of the earth always quieted her, and she enjoyed the aloneness she felt huddled in her hole. Now, she used this hole in her meditative journey and squeezed into the opening. Soon, she was deep into her meditative state and entered into familiar but distorted dimensions of time and space.

As had been her experience in previous meditations when she used this hole, it enlarged within her mind. Today was no exception. Tiny white plant roots sprouted from the ceiling and brushed the top of her head as she stood upright. She walked upright for a few hundred feet, going deeply into the hole that twisted and turned as it undulated on a downward slope further into the earth. As she moved further into the tunnel, it tightened, and forced her to crawl on all fours, the sides of the tunnel squeezing along the length of her body. Then the tightness forced her down onto her stomach, and soon she slithered along like a serpent.

This part of the journey stifled her breathing, as she hated tight spaces. Her mind clutched, and she was afraid she would panic. Her breath came in shorter and shorter bursts, and soon she would suffocate and die. Where would she exist if she died in this other world? Would she die also in the physical world, or would her death just occur in this other dimension? Maybe she should return by backing out. At this point, when she could no longer endure any more, she squeezed out of the hole. After she gathered herself and looked around, the world she viewed looked much different from Southern Indiana.

This Other World had mountains, valleys, and a vanilla sky with two suns. She stood on a mountainside looking out over a valley and at a cerulean blue lake down below. The plants grew lush with shiny green leaves the size and appearance of large fans. Ferns as tall as a man grew wildly.

She felt a pair of eyes on her and jumped slightly when an old grey wolf came into view. His presence comforted her, though. The Wolf sat still on his haunches and had the most startling hazel eyes—or were they blue? He felt like a friend.

She approached the Wolf, and he looked at her. He spoke to her telepathically. The Wolf turned on the path and headed down the mountain. He paused and looked back. "*Aren't you going to follow?*" The words sounded like a male voice, not coming from the Wolf's mouth but inside of her head.

She nodded at once. Then he trotted off, moving swiftly along a path lined with tall pine trees that could easily top any ten-story building. He moved faster than any earthly wolf or animal. The smells wafted earthy and woodsy and the air crisp, a world clearly not contaminated by humans.

She kept pace with the Wolf. The ground moved quickly beneath her feet. Distance in this Other World seemed different from that in her physical reality. She and the Wolf could cover four times the distance in half the time just by walking. And she was not even rushed. She easily matched the stride of the Wolf as he took her through another series of twists and turns along a heavily wooded trail. As they traveled, they encountered the changing of the seasons—spring, summer, fall, and winter.

By the time they reached a campfire in a small clearing, they had already walked through snow for a while, their breath smoking. The Wolf sat at one side of the fire and indicated with a glance that she was to sit at the other side. The daylight receded, and within minutes, the blackest darkness enveloped the camp. But then the campfire blazed, and the darkness receded back into the pines. The only light came from the orange and yellow fire and the two bright white moons, each the size of a hunter moon, with one higher in the sky than the other and directly above it.

As she looked into the eyes of her otherworld guide, the Wolf transmitted the most profound compassion. There was a familiarity in his gaze that she could not immediately identify. The Wolf had eyes the color of Grandma's. Emma reached into her pocket for the Wolf's tooth and medallion and palmed them both, at the same time inhaling the smoke of burning wood. The Wolf stared at the fire without blinking, and she finally understood and followed suit. As she gazed at the fire, her mind stilled, and she entered the depths of the fire, seeing every nuance of color: blue, yellow, burnt umber, red, ochre, white, and orange. Her senses heightened, yet a feeling of profound stillness permeated through her mind and body.

The Wolf spoke again inside her head. *"What questions do you have for me?"*

"I want to know what this place is. Second, ever since I was a child, I had a feeling there was something within me, something that made me different, maybe something that made me feel wrong. My mother left me. My father died. I'm alone. I want to know why that is. My third question is, I want to know how to defeat the darkness and struggles within me."

She looked at the Wolf, half-suspecting she would not get answers to her questions. She felt on the verge of tears, admitting her own vulnerability to being so different and consequently alone in the world. Rarely would she allow herself to feel exposed and defenseless. It was this world she entered. Maybe she was mad, because she knew none of her friends who meditated like this. And, she felt vulnerable to be in the presence of an all-knowing-wisdom of the Wolf and that the Wolf would value her enough to share his knowledge.

The Wolf's head dropped as he sat on his haunches. "The answer to your first question is that this place is as real as your world—it just has unique properties, many of which you have experienced. Time, for instance, is more fluid here. It may speed up or it may slow. Distances are not consistent. What happens here has consequences in your world, though, regardless. Actions taken here may play out similarly in your world. Also, what happens in your world affects this world. We are interrelated, after all. Welcome to the animal world."

If wolves could smile, he now appeared to do so as his lips stretched further back on his jawline, but he bared no teeth. "You will see the forces of your world here in the forms of animals. Animals will feel familiar to you, representations of your world." This feral animal spoke so matter-of-fact and so calmly. How could the Wolf be so at ease with these revelations, talking about different worlds as natural as describing the subtle uniqueness of different strains of roses?

"Now, as to your second and third questions. Become yourself, love yourself. Then you will not notice you are different. Allow God and the Devil to play within you. Don't run from fear, understand? This inner darkness, whatever you may call it, is not to be defeated, it is to be accepted through your surrendering to it." The Wolf paused and stood to his full height; a height rather large for a wolf. In that moment, he towered above her while she remained sitting. "Try to relate to the other who you may see as the Devil at the level of their fear rather than staying at the level of the conflict. If you do this, then you will relate to the other with kindness. You will never resolve the conflict if you stay at the level of seeing them different and at the level of the conflict. You understand?"

"You are telling me that God or Pure Love is always within me, as well as the Devil or Corrupt Fear. One can't exist without the other. I must allow both by having compassion for the Devil that I see in another, as this is the Devil who resides within me."

The Wolf smiled and nodded as if pleased.

For a moment, a feeling of disbelief entered her as she noticed how intelligent she appeared in this Other World. She understood what the Wolf explained, but she didn't think she could sustain this knowledge when she returned home.

"Be careful. Can you find the force within you that can enable the two opposing lives to live together? You must remember, The Beast can devour The Lamb. Darkness can consume your mind through your resistance to your fear. Overcome your fear. To remember this, you must learn to become responsible for how you interact with others. Responsible for what you project out onto your world. Responsible for your judgments on others, such as envy and greed. You do this and you will find your way. You will overcome your darkness."

Her eyes glassed over as she became overwhelmed again. This world faded, and she could smell the earth of her hole in the ground and then feel the hardness of Flattop Rock along the length of her body. She existed in both worlds simultaneously and this experience almost took her to the brink of madness. Her vision focused on the fire in the animal world, drawing her complete attention. Her left hand slightly trembled when she lifted it to her brow.

Her hand returned to her breast and her right hand clasped over it to keep it still. The fire in the imagined world calmed her, and her trembling hand quieted. The animal world returned completely, and she sat with the Wolf. This Other World's wisdom proved vital for her world. Fear overcame her with the thought that she could be destroyed if she navigated through challenges in Taylorville without care. With this fear, she felt the hardness of Flattop Rock. She drew her attention to her heart once again.

The Wolf stretched out on his front paws, his hindquarters high in the air, and he gave an audible sigh as he dropped on his haunches. "Your journey here is complete. There will be another guide for you soon. You do not need me any longer. On the next leg of your journey, you will encounter challenges, some involving violence. These violent experiences are to assist you in understanding Good and Evil, in understanding how you can relate to both simultaneously within your mind."

The Wolf broke off eye contact and stared once more into the fire. Emma waited. Her heart beat faster as she panicked about having another guide. She didn't want a new guide. She felt comfortable with the Wolf. Her vision faltered under panic and again her earthly tunnel loomed in front of her. She quickly slowed her breath, focused on the fire, and she sat once again with the Wolf.

"You are to gain the wisdom of knowing that violence and love are of the same oneness, the two sides of a coin," the Wolf said. "You must strive to know the Truth of these two forces. You understand violence, then you will understand love. You are the Revealer of the Truth, as am I. That is why you are here."

As his eyes met hers, the Wolf half-smiled. The Wolf referred to the veil-bearer, the condition of her birth, the gift that gave her the ability to see below the surface, the same as Grandma. The connections between this world and her earthly world made sense.

This time, understanding her destiny and its deeper purpose, didn't draw the angry reaction that it had in the past. Every human being had a deeper purpose in life, there for his or her discovery. Emma had a wise grandmother who helped her to discover hers. She acknowledged she could enjoy this other "animal" world. It exuded a peaceful and beautiful landscape when you grew accustomed to its rules.

The Wolf continued, "Your task is to synthesize this information to the level of knowing the Lamb, or the Light representing virtue, and knowing the Beast, or the Dark of deceit and manipulation. All are at a sacred level. Violence is also of a Divine nature. Are you at the stage where you value and can be the Lamb, or at the stage where you need to choose to be that of the Beast? The third stage, a more difficult one to arrive at, has no choice. Do you understand?"

Emma studied the Wolf's face and, surprisingly, she nodded. "Yes, but I won't keep this knowledge for long after I return."

In fact, the understanding danced at the edge of her consciousness, threatening to tumble off and into a black void of non-remembrance and confusion.

"Something about the Beast and the Lamb," she said, her mind losing focus once again. If only she could simplify it and remember to sacrifice to both the Light and the Dark, to stay with her vulnerability until she was One.

The Wolf nodded. He heard her thoughts. "You will remember the wisdom when you need to. Your challenge is to witness people cast out their darkness as a matter of survival. They will cast out their evil to people whom they judge, cast out the dark thoughts they harbor through acts of greed, vanity, and selfishness. They will see themselves as righteous, since they have power, money, and fame. But eventually humanity will need to confront their darkness as outcasts and understand it is the other side of the same coin—that what they see as darkness outside of them is the same darkness within them—darkness they have masked not only from others but themselves. Understand this one thing and you will transcend your fear by embracing the thing others show fear of. In this way your darkness will transcend. Or, integrate within you. This is important. Do you understand?"

Emma nodded, slowly. She fought the urge to look distractedly at the forest and the size of the leaves on the tree closest to her; many grew as large as a small child. The words of the Wolf did sound familiar. All of this reminded her of her reading of Jung and his theory of the projected shadow and dreamwork, but the understanding of his concepts eluded her then. Now, she was understanding.

The Wolf spoke to her throughout the Other World night, reiterating the message. The Wolf's speaking comforted Emma.

She focused her mind on the beauty of the night sky, the two moons, the beautiful fire and her love for her wolf guide. Her blood rushed through her veins, yet her heart continued to beat as steadily as before.

Soon, though, the influx of information became too much, and her body collapsed like a rag doll, and she lay curled on her side. A diffused and permeating weakness entered as the vitality of her body slowly ebbed away, like the sands of an hourglass draining from the upper chamber to the bottom. The fire had burned down to scattered flames among the embers.

The Wolf spoke, telling her that the weakness she felt was because she was undergoing a physical change, one that would help her maintain this new wisdom. His eyes shone with intensity, and she could not tear her gaze away. The Wolf's eyes stirred something familiar within her. Emma knew these eyes. A tingling sensation now coursed throughout her body, her strength returned and her mind remained as focused as a laser.

The Wolf aged during her time with him. He lay down and placed his head between its front paws. His eyelids drooped. The light dimmed within his eyes, as if the life from a vibrant living thing drained slowly away like water swirling out of a sink. His breath labored a shallow wheeze.

"Grandma, don't leave me. Don't die," Emma called out.

But the Wolf's half-lidded eyes did not widen with her plea. The old grey wolf sighed. His eyes closed completely, and his breath became imperceptible. Then came the final shallow rise of his chest. Emma felt totally alone and lost in this new and different world without the Wolf.

Her body shook from the cold, and her breath escaped as sobs. A feeling of devastation settled in at the passing of her mentor and companion. How much of what happened here also happened in her real life? The Wolf said the two worlds interacted and affected one another.

A hawk cawed, and she lifted her eyes to see if she could see the bird in the dark sky. The cawing continued, but all she could see was blackness, and the darkness was the same whether or not she opened her eyes.

The cawing then sounded like her alarm, as she slowly returned to the reality, first, of her Flattop Rock, then the sound of the Wabash, and beyond to Taylorville. She opened her eyes and realized she was lying on Flattop in exactly the same position she had been one hour earlier. That hour had seemed like years in the Other World. She reached over to turn off the alarm and then lay on her back again. Strangely, she felt quiet, with no extreme emotions except a slight disorientation.

When she returned home, Grandma sat at the kitchen table. Her eyes worryingly searched Emma's face.

"So?" she asked. "How was your journey?"

"You know I don't do drugs and have never, right Grandma?" Emma asked, with a look of wonder on her face.

Grandma nodded.

"Well, that was some serious trippin' going on." Emma smiled, then added, "You know, don't you? You've been there." Nothing was a secret from Grandma.

"It's a beautiful place, isn't it?" Grandma asked, beaming as if she had returned from a weekend revival herself.

"So, you were there?" she asked. "The same place?" she added.

Grandma nodded. "Yes. The world of the two suns and the two moons, the animal world—"

"The Wolf?" Emma interjected.

Grandma slowly rose from the table and stretched her arms, and began gathering the breakfast plates. She had yet to answer Emma, but a sadness overcame her expression and her body moved with a tiredness where before peace and a bounce showed.

Emma had her answer. The Beast will access her through her fear or her seductive desire. To find some compassion or acceptance of that fear was her first task. Now she needed to see if strength existed within her to put it into practice. To change the course of what she saw in her journey world, she needed to act in this world.

42

"Tell me about yourself," Emma asked Nate after they entered the pizza place and settled into a booth. She realized that if she began talking because of her nervousness, chances would be that she would slip into her back-woodsy, hillbilly twang. That thought horrified her. Nate needed to carry the conversation. That was her strategic plan to hide her ancestors.

Nate smiled. "So, are you my psychologist?"

"I am. I'm here to analyze you." Emma felt enjoyment and more at ease playing this game that gave her curiosity a structure to explore harmlessly. "See if you're worth the time of an unsophisticated and poor girl not even out of high school." This was as close to baring her deepest vulnerability of her roots as she could go.

Emma grabbed a napkin and a straw and pretended to take notes. Nate straightened his posture in the booth, readying himself to be amused.

"Not much to tell," he said, sitting back in the booth. "I'm in my second year of electrical engineering. I love being near water, in water, or on water. Even the Wabash. And I like to read." His reference to the Wabash River and noodling brought a smile to his face. Emma felt a connection to him, knowing that she helped to create that experience for him, one he wouldn't forget easily.

Emma attended to her speech, careful of her words, and allowing herself to enunciate clearly. "What do you like to read?" she asked.

"Oh, philosophical or esoteric stuff. I just finished *Meditations* by Marcus Aurelius." He mis-pronounced the Roman philosopher Aurelius as "Aurorelous."

Emma smiled. "Aurelius."

Nate laughed. "Excuse me, Dr. Conner. I was giving the French pronunciation of the Roman Emperor."

Emma smiled, taking note that Nate could laugh at himself and make a joke. She sat her Coke glass down and leaned in. "My dad gave me that book after he finished it. It's on my nightstand."

"Is that a self-revelation from counselor to client, Doctor?" Nate's eyes shone with enjoyment at their role-playing. He twirled his Coke glass between his hands.

Emma laughed. She felt some esteem when he referred to her as 'counselor'. "Dad would go around and say, 'You have power over your mind–not your outside events.'" She bit her lower lip hard and looked away, blinking fast, remembering that he wasn't around anymore. "I believe he said that to taunt us since we live in Taylorville, where the unexpected could happen. Grandma would just shake her head and smile.

Grandma thought Dad could be right. Or maybe half-right and half-crazed. That's an excellent combination to have in our town."

She laughed, reaching up to tuck a strand of her hair behind her right ear. She watched Nate intently, taking in his minute responses. Nate's opinions of Taylorville were unknown to her, and while she didn't want to know because she feared he would see her in a different, more diminished way, she had to know. "Maybe Dad wanted to stretch my beliefs. Loosen up my mind a bit." Emma adjusted herself in the booth, sitting back in her seat.

Nate's eyes lit up. "I understand what you mean. The book had me thinking outside of my box. Who is God, exactly, especially when you consider the vastness of the universe?"

Emma hoped he thought the same as she: that God was a cosmic expansion and unfolding, and not a man with a white beard passing judgment on humanity.

Emma finally breathed, releasing her breath over her lips, not wanting Nate to know she had held her breath after revealing so much about her family. She hadn't even gotten to the bad stuff yet. Nate seemed oblivious either way, incapable of anything but simply staring into her eyes.

Emma broke the awkward silence and pointed the conversation back to him. "So, your parents raised you?"

He shook his head. "My mother divorced my dad when I was two. I don't know my natural father." Nate looked down at his pizza slice and picked it up to take a bite, guiding the flimsy slice to his mouth. Moments went by and, after a few swallows, he continued. "My grandparents did most of raising me. They helped Mom. She didn't have a job, so they pretty much paid the bills until my mother remarried when I was eight years old."

"So, you get along all right with your stepfather?" Emma asked.

"Yeah. We get along fine," Nate said, taking another bite of his pizza. From the shortness of his answer, Emma figured he might not be telling the complete truth. His refusal to look at her indicated as much, at least.

Perhaps for that reason, he redirected their conversation. "I would like to know something, counselor, if that's all right?" he asked Emma, prompting a smile. "What drives you to read Carl Jung at seven in the morning?"

"Well, I've an interest in psychology," she said slowly. "In particular, I want to understand why people hurt other people. I figure it has to be a subconscious thing. Jung understands the subconscious. So, I'm studying Jung. I think the answer to most of life lies in his views of the disowned shadow of our mind, the part of us we're afraid to recognize which exists within us, and sometimes if we are paying attention to our judgments, we can see our shadow in others." She wondered if she had gone too abstract. Maybe Nate would think she was pretending to be intelligent. She needed him to see her and who she was truly and not some psych-geek. But maybe he could see through the façade and to her insecurity? "So, anyway," she said, quickly. "I read him a lot."

Emma studied Nate's face to see if he had lost interest. She had rattled on about a subject that most people would find boring. No one in her small world showed interest in anything esoteric, except for maybe Grandpa and Grandma. Nate studied her and nodded, so she took a risk and continued.

"It gives me a different perspective of the darkness in the people who surround me. You know, that which we deny within ourselves has a way of building up and becoming part of our reality through the people we meet in our experiences. We see those dark qualities in others and then judge them, believing we are not that."

She paused for a moment, realizing an important connection. She said it out loud, more to imprint it on her memory rather than to enlighten Nate. "Grandma calls it mirroring the darkness within ourselves. The Indians called it Wetiko, The Beast." So, Grandma understood Jung better than Emma thought. She allowed this realization to sink in a little more.

Nate's eyebrows rose a little. "Wetiko and Jung's psychology of the disowned are the same?"

Emma shrugged, not yet putting it together herself. "I guess modern psychology has its roots in ancient mythology. Anyways, reading Carl Jung helps me go through my day and face the challenges, because I figure that, somehow, this one very smart man had a theory to explain it all. It'll satisfy my need to know the mystery behind life. Once I figure out his theory, that is."

"Damn, girl. Who even has these thoughts?" He sat across from her, shaking his head back and forth, his long fingers lightly tapping the rim of his glass covered in condensation, before sliding down and grasping his Coke to bring to his lips for a sip, his eyes never leaving hers.

"Well, I guess I do," Emma said.

Her mind continued to reel, but this time not from her realization of a connection between Carl Jung and Grandma's wisdom. She wanted to experience Nate and forget for a moment the depth of the minds of people. She watched the lushness of Nate's lips when he sipped his Coke and a warmth spread between her thighs. Her eyes wandered to Nate's face and his startling blue eyes, wondering if he grasped what she spoke about, but more curious if he was aware of the feelings he stirred up in her body. She hadn't realized a discourse of Jungian theory could be so arousing to her.

Nate nodded—perhaps understanding why she needed to escape her life amongst the poor and violent by diving into Jung. Or maybe he understood what he was doing to her body.

"So tell me," he said. "What do you see, Dr. Connor?" He asked with a serious expression on his face and his hands gesturing toward his body.

"Is this a trick question?" she asked.

His face broke into a bright smile. "No. I'm really interested," he stated matter-of-factly. It intrigued her to see if he contained enough perception to apply Jung's principle to what she said. Few people, she believed, could.

She crossed her arms. "I see a man who's confident and at ease with himself in his own skin." Nate tucked in his lower lip and gave a slight downward nod in a pleased response. She thought for a moment and continued. "You're intelligent. You're champing at the bit to take on your life as an independent person, free from the influence of others, unable to wait to see what new adventure the future holds."

He nodded again and smiled.

Emma pressed on. "And you're used to getting your way and things come easy for you." She said this last sentence with a somewhat fast clip to her speech, unsure how he would accept the observation, because she didn't see it as a compliment but more than a critique of his opulent and spoiled lifestyle.

He smiled again.

"And you're willing to break the law to impress a girl." Emma laughed.

"So, is this your darkness?" he asked, his smile even broader.

She grinned in response and marveled at his astuteness. "Be gentle," she said.

He continued. "If you are projecting your darkness, and you seemed uncomfortable with how you see me, then you're not sure of who you are. You don't recognize nor do you accept your own level of confidence and intelligence." He paused and thought for a moment, then added, "And you're afraid of what life has in store for you. And you're somewhat angry that I may have privileges that give me an edge to finding success."

"See, it was a trick question," Emma said, wondering if she had revealed too much of herself to him unwittingly. It didn't occur to her he would grasp Jung's shadow concept so astutely and quickly. It hadn't occurred to her he could read, through her projections, parts of herself that even she wasn't totally aware of and wouldn't reveal to others so readily.

"No, when I saw you sitting in front of The Dam Tavern, I knew then I'd met my Cinderella," he said, laughing through a rash of embarrassment reddening his face.

Emma grabbed her straw and pretended to write on the napkin. "Believes in fairytale endings. Rule-out Eros complex." She bit on the end of her straw and pretended to think.

Nate, laughing, said, "So, Dr. Connor, can you give me your professional initial assessment?"

Emma considered him for a moment, bit down on her straw, and pretended to write again. "Patient comes from a divorced family, but that didn't bring financial stress, as mother came from money, and he was a trust-fund baby. Father wasn't around much and family became important to him because of this initial abandonment. He lives in a castle, is the only child, a Prince, heir to the throne—and is looking for his match in a Cinderella, a replacement for the mother whom he loves dearly."

Nate looked at her seriously. "You're damn close to your assessment, Emma. Now, analyze this. I think I'm falling in love."

Emma couldn't believe the words coming out of Nate's mouth. His admission threw her by complete surprise. Maybe she wasn't as well-versed in assessing people as she thought she was. She looked at him, serious now. "But, I'm not a princess, Nate. Far from it."

He looked at her and kindness shown in his expression. "That's where you were wrong in your analysis; I'm not looking for a princess." Nate reached over and held her hands in his. They sat in silence for a moment until Nate broke the silence. "Let's hang out at my house," he said, getting up from the table.

A strange stirring fluttered in Emma's belly. Going to Nate's house would indicate that she would probably meet his parents. She felt nervous that his parents wouldn't like her.

She proved right in her intuition. The meeting changed everything. Putting it in terms of the ancient Native American, the Wetiko beast was unleashed as Nate's old grandfather.

43

Nate's green Mustang sped along Ohio Street. Outside, beautiful homes passed across the window. The serenity and safety these homes offered in their nicely manicured lawns and paved driveways spurred a sense of hope and possibilities in Emma's heart. Interestingly, this wealth flourished just a few short miles from Taylorville. Maybe, as they drove alongside these stately homes and she sat next to Nate, a college guy interested in furthering his opportunities, she could only believe that her life was taking a turn for the best. Maybe she could one day go to college and live a life far from the poverty and all the hurt it brought to the people of her hometown.

The grand homes of Darwin had wide expanses of yards. Most houses had two or three stories, with terraces circling the top floors. Some even had a widow's walk. While the Darwin homes were not even close to the spectacles of the

Long Island houses described in *The Great Gatsby*, Emma wondered what Daisy must have experienced living in one of those homes.

For her, though, it wasn't the opulence of the Darwin homes that enticed her as much as wondering if people living in those homes lived without a worry, and without worry were the people nice to one another. Wealth like that could liberate a person. No, the elegance of the homes and the material wealth did not intrigue her as much as the imagined lives of those breathing within.

As they rolled up to his stately home on Ohio Street, Nate reached over and lightly kissed her again, as if he knew she felt nervous. Emma needed that kiss to blunt her anxiety. His home, after all, was infinitely more beautiful than she imagined. The two-story house would look perfectly set at the end of a long drive lined with weeping willows on a grand Southern plantation.

Craftsman evidently built the home with care, Emma thought, when Nate opened the black teakwood double doors. Oak floors flowed from the foyer to living room to dining room without division. A lit, glistening glass chandelier hung from the foyer ceiling and gave the appearance of sparkling diamonds suspended in the air. It was the first chandelier she'd ever seen in real life, aside from pictures in a *Home and Garden* magazine or in a movie, or music video. A fire crackled within a fireplace, easily warming whomever lay upon the elegant furnishings placed in an intimate arrangement around.

Nate's grandfather, lounged in a comfortable chair with the evening paper in his lap, smiled when his only grandson entered the room. From his seating position, he looked to be as tall as Nate, wearing wire-rimmed glasses that hid his startling blue eyes that drew attention from the shiny, balding head.

Nate stood slightly in front of Emma and made the introductions. At hearing her last name of Connor, the grandfather, president of one of Darwin's banks, sat upright in his chair, placing the paper in his lap. Nate's grandmother and mother entered the room, hearing Nate arrive home. Both women wore full skirts and blouses with flat shoes, dressed for a casual night out even though from all appearances they had spent the evening at home.

Nate's grandfather asked, "Are you related to Frank and Alice Connor?"

Emma nodded. She was innately suspicious of speech, because she could "hear" with remarkable accuracy what lay behind it. Her meditations had made her sensitive to the intent behind people's words. The way he said her paternal grandparents' name and his slight, cat-like smile told her she intrigued the old man as a predator-to-prey attitude. The tone of his question also told her he geared up for something, and she alerted herself for the cat-and-mouse game of wits he planned, for it probably would not bode well for her, as it never did for the mouse.

The women had drawn their heads back at Emma's nod and the grandmother gasped in her own response to the grandfather's question and her answer. The women's smiles hardened into stone. A sickening pit in Emma's stomach grew, for this sharp response to her family's name wasn't heartening. Meeting Nate's family wasn't a good decision, after all.

Then Nate's grandfather let loose a slight laugh, amused at the scene building around him. The women's response behind amused him, and his smile grew even more, as he enjoyed this introduction to his grandson's date.

The intention behind the grandfather's question was clear. Maybe there would have been a time she would have felt appreciative of his challenge if she wasn't so nervous, like the times Grandpa's friend Bill had jostled her. It was apparent that Nate's grandfather enjoyed the discomfort of his wife and daughter, and using Emma to enact his newly devised scheme distressed her.

"Your grandparents are real characters. They live in Taylorville, isn't that so? On the west side of the Wabash?"

"Well, my paternal grandmother is dead, but my maternal Grandma Rose and my paternal Grandpa Frank are still alive."

The two women's bodies tightened and became rigid. The expression on their faces mirrored each other and their lips puckered in unison. They clearly had not known she hailed from Taylorville.

Even though Nate's grandfather used her family to taunt the women in his household, she liked his straightforward approach. That part of him was honest. The honesty she could appreciate within him. A person knows what they are confronting in another. The problem didn't exist with her family as much as he understood his problem lived with him. The judgments of his women, the constant gossip, and his own built-up resentment toward them.

If Emma had enough gumption to go toe-to-toe with the old gentleman, she thought he would admire her ability to hold her own, but two confrontations in one day were about to do her in. The old man's smile widened. "And your grandmother owns that tavern over there, doesn't she?"

Emma nodded, unable to find her voice. She was proud that her grandmother ran her own business. She marveled that Nate's grandfather could state that fact with such degradation, a man who worked hard for his own living and living with women living off of him.

"I heard rumors she's a witch," the old man said.

"Rumors only, unless you see a spiritual woman as witchy. She can quiet her mind with meditation, and with that, find solutions to her challenges," Emma said. "That's all."

"But your other grandmother, the one who was married to Frank, now she was a pistol. I have to admit your grandfather's an intelligent man, yet from what I've experienced, he doesn't have the best luck at playing poker or picking quiet, demure women."

The old man intended to insult her. Nate's grandfather studied her as if he could gauge her IQ and assess her genealogy and her prowess at gambling. If he knew Grandpa's poor expertise at gambling, then he must be a member of the Eagle's club where her grandparents, while both alive, spent their weekends dancing, gambling, and drinking. No wonder he knew so much about her family.

She risked and chose her words wisely. "Well, my grandfather Frank is no fool. He has a hard time being any good at any *foolhardy game*. I'm sure you understand, loving to play poker at the club and all." Emma smiled.

The old man recoiled at her covert reference to his choice of pastime.

"My late grandmother Alice worked hard and played harder and she didn't follow anyone's rules but her own. She loved having a good time. It was all she could do to deal with the harshness of poverty," Emma said, and waiting a moment before deciding to add on, not caring what Nate thought of her exchange with his grandfather. In that moment, if he didn't value her in all her qualities, then he wasn't the man for her. "And Grandma Rose sees her bar business as a way to give people healing energy in our community, an escape from their hard lives through her meditative practices and energy work. Some may see that as 'witchy'; I see her work giving those a respite when they have no resources to find it for themselves. And, I guess for those who can't meditate or accept her energy work, she offers them an easier route through drink. Grandma does not act from greed." Emma tensed, waiting for his response to her concealed criticism of his character with her last word.

The old banker's smile widened, and he nodded his head. "I take it you're much like all three of them."

Emma gave a nod, understanding that his comment wasn't a compliment, but smiling in reply anyway, for she considered it a compliment. She understood the direction this conversation was headed. She'd heard it all her life—about the fact her grandmother owned and ran a tavern, about the fact her paternal grandfather mismanaged a grocery which left him in poverty, about the fact her clothes weren't good enough, and that she was the daughter of a drugged-out whore of a mother. She'd been called 'trash' or a 'redneck' all her life. It meant nothing anymore. Just like the children's lesson, she believed that whatever outsiders said out of meanness would bounce off of her, since she was rubber and stick to them since they were glue. But, anymore, each time judgment occurred against the people she loved, she felt more protective toward them.

If this wasn't Nate's grandfather, she wouldn't have any trouble going after this pompous man in more descriptive characterization of his choices in life. The idea he called her trashy in front of a man she would like to impress left her confused. Her anger intensified at how the old man played with her. Her smile widened, and she could feel the sweat soak into her new blouse. She channeled her rage into an inner war of thoughts. Even though she could appreciate the old man's straightforwardness before, how dare he assume her folk were stupid and her family not good enough for his grandson? While she could hold some semblance of her own with Dottie or Wade because she was prepared and they understood the rules of her town while this situation was overwhelming. She released the naïve hope that Darwin people might have the decorum to avoid shaming their grandson's date. Wealth didn't increase a man's character.

Emma saw Nate's face redden. But from what? Out of shame for his family's behavior? Or out of embarrassment for being with her? Emma knew, regardless, either reason did not bode well for the two of them.

The older of the two women—his grandmother, she assumed since Nate hadn't introduced them—broke her silence with a cough. "Nate, can we speak with you in private? Will you excuse us, Emma?"

The grandmother turned on her heel without waiting for Emma to reply, exited with stern and stiff strides into a side sitting room, Nate's mother following.

Nate reached over and squeezed Emma's hand in reassurance. But he didn't say a word, as if unable to find his voice, and followed behind the women, closing the door to the sitting room.

The old man watched her in silence. Shrill voices erupted from the closed room and a low voice responded, only to have the angry voices interrupt once again. Nate's grandfather sighed, appearing too weary of the game that he put in motion. He reached for his folded paper in his lap, shaking it free, and began reading, dismissing Emma without a word.

"You know," Emma said, allowing tears to flow freely without swiping them away. "Fitzgerald once wrote, '*Poor boys shouldn't think of marrying rich girls.*'"

The old man looked up at her. She could see he took a renewed interest in her.

"Maybe, in your world, it's also true that rich boys shouldn't marry poor girls." As Emma said this, her chin rose. "And, I would like to add...it could be a poor girl's mistake and eventual ruin to marry a rich boy."

She firmly believed that now. A rich boy to a poor girl would only offer her a crutch to finding her own independence.

"Well, you're not silent now, are you?" The grandfather asked, his air of superiority rising off of him like steam on cow shit.

"Don't mistake my earlier silence for weakness, sir. You may judge the fact that I was born on the wrong side of the river, but I did nothing to you to bring on the insults."

Emma wiped away her tears and remained looking at Nate's grandfather.

"Do you really hold out hope that someone like Nate would eventually love you?" He asked.

An awkward silence followed his question. Emma allowed the question to hang without response in the stillness. The sitting room, where Nate, his mother, and grandmother sparred, had also grown silent. Emma knew that the occupants of that room could probably hear what was being said in the library.

"I guess you should have raised Nate to be a better man," she said, raising her volume. "One thing's for certain, though. Nate had no choice in the family he was born into. But he did choose to date me."

Anger flushed across Mr. Lucas's face. "Choose you? One date? And you think he's crazy about you?"

Emma pulled back. Mr. Lucas wasn't finished.

"And what does this illusion of yours get you?" He nodded toward the sitting room. "That's the sound of Nate coming to the right decision for himself and his family."

Mr. Lucas shook his newspaper open to the sports section and pretended to read, indicating to Emma that the conversation was over.

So, what started out to be the most perfect second date ever became one of the worst days of Emma's life, second only to her father's death. She squashed her belief that people with more education, opportunities and richer life experiences could differ from her downtrodden kin and instead act with more civility among one another. There was something to fear regarding evil within men who have the comforts of life, yet intentionally strike out and hurt others less fortunate. They cloaked evil in the authority that position and money brought and therefore more effective in manipulating others to their dark deeds. With Wade, she expected the meanness. He didn't cloak his aggression in politeness. Wade understood that if you crossed someone, you risked the payback, while monied people bought themselves a way out and may not serve any consequences.

The mustang pulled up to the stoop of The Dam Tavern. Emma and Nate had driven from his home in complete silence. Now Nate leapt from the car and walked around to meet her at the passenger door. Emma searched his face for any warmth he had felt toward her before, but she saw none. "No need to walk me to my door, Nate."

"Emma, I need time to figure things out." Nate fidgeted with his hands and then jammed them into his front pockets. It gave him the excuse not to touch her.

"I think you have. You just wanted to have a fling with the girl from the other side of the river. You're going to marry some rich girl your family approves of, one who can advance you in life. Right now, you just want to find an easy way out of this situation with me." She turned to go, then swung back around. "And I'm going to make it easy for you. Bye, Nate."

Nate dropped his head in a half-nod goodbye and walked back to his car. The Mustang's taillights disappeared around the corner. She caught sight of them again as he turned out onto the main road to Darwin, finally losing the red lights as he traveled along the bridge and crossed to the east bank of the Wabash.

44

Instead of walking home, Emma turned toward the path to Flattop Rock, where she sat watching the Wabash River catch the light from the moon. A large splash drew her attention and Emma's head turned in time to catch a large catfish leaping out of the Wabash and swimming downstream toward her, its scales like armor plating, a dart of silver in the shallows, making the act of navigating the current look simple.

The sound took Emma back to when she was five years old. To her mother, Maggie, diving into the water, her white shirt soaking in the brown river and her white sneakers looking wavy under the water.

Emma dove into the memory herself.

"Stay there, little girl," her mother said. "Don't move. Grandma Rose'll come for you and she'll take good care of you. Mommy has got to go away now. There's nothing left for me to live for in this town."

Terror froze on Emma's face and her expression squeezed into a puckered expression, so much so that her eyes disappeared, forcing the tears to run down her cheeks.

Maggie raised her arms over her head and slipped silently under the river surface.

"Mommy! Mommy! Mommy!"

Emma's legs bounce up and down on the large rock, but she didn't move. Mom told her not to. A minute cranked by, and Maggie still didn't surface. Emma's eyes dart up and down the Wabash, looking for a flash of white. She felt alone, afraid to speak or yell.

Then, hands grabbed her around the waist and tickled her. Emma caught her breath, terror registered on her face. Though it didn't need to be.

"Here I am! You really did miss me, huh?" Maggie said, laughing and hugging Emma to her wet and soaking chest. "So, you do love your mommy, don't you? Don't fret. I'll never leave you."

The memory struck an abandonment chord and rang out as a tied note to the rejection she currently felt. Nate's ability to go from a strong connection at dinner to being barely recognizable and cold at the end of their date was difficult to understand. Emma vowed that from that day forward, she would never allow herself to be that vulnerable to anyone, especially another man, ever.

Her hand reached into her pocket and pulled out her cellphone. Tears flowed freely now, and at times, turned into sobs. Her journey work was all but forgotten. Life just kept getting more challenging, and she doubted the value of it.

She texted, "*Jolene, he has to pay. I'm ready. Let's do this thing.*" Emma wasn't sure herself if she spoke in reference to Wade or someone else. But did it matter?

45

Two weeks later

The tavern room didn't swim before his drugged-out eyes, but he did, through it, as if it were liquid. Wade desperately tried focusing, but to no avail. A familiar face crossed his vision and the girl who gave him the drink with unkept promises bent over him, dark hair tumbling. Wade didn't understand what was happening to him. It was as if he watched a movie. He was conscious. He had not passed out. It dawned on his drugged-out mind this girl had done this to him, rendered him helpless, a man who had faced many mean-ass O.G.'s in his time.

The girl stood straddling him before reaching into his back pocket and removing his wallet, rifling out three twenty-dollar bills and throwing them on the bar. "No need to stiff Grandma Rose of her much-earned money," she said.

Then she turned and grabbed him by his ankles and struggled to turn him with his feet toward the door. She dragged him by his boots across the floor and behind the bar. The girl grabbed the liquor bottle she had used to drug Wade and turned to place it on the counter where the liquor bottles were stored.

The front door opened and slammed shut, and the girl's body startled, but she didn't look around. "Hi Emma, hurry over here and help me."

"No. Not Emma." The voice was deep and he could tell from her surprised expression that she wasn't expecting Sy.

The girl spun around and looked up and into the face of Sy. Her shoulders slumped.

"Where's Wade? I was told he's here and to drag his ass home."

Wade gathered an internal strength and was able to finally muster out a moan.

"Nooo," the girl said, long and slow, covering up Wade's whimper. "Wade's come and gone."

Wade could see Sy's reflection in the backbar mirror. Had he heard him? He watched as Sy took a few steps into the bar. "That right?" Sy looked doubtful and glanced around the tavern's main room. His eyes lock on the one empty glass on the bar. The girl gathered the glass and turned to place it in the sink. Wade could tell that it took all she had to turn her back on Sy, because her confidence had drained before his eyes.

Wade watched as the girl swallowed hard, turned and pushed back at Sy with hard eyes to quell his suspicions. "Of course. Why would I cover for him? We made last call. He finished his drink and left, cussing up a storm, like he normally does."

Sy stood for a long minute, coiled and ready for whatever action his mind decided on. He measured her up, then relaxed, dropping his arms at his side and turning toward the door.

No, don't leave me, man, Wade thought.

"Damn, the guy. He's going to be trouble for me yet. Mark me." Sy jerked the door open and strode out, slamming the door behind him.

After Sy left, the girl waited a few more minutes to ensure she was in the clear. Then she pulled Wade down the couple of concrete steps to the side of the street, his head banging each step hard, his arms flailing about in twisted, unnatural ways. Terror seized his heart and birthed dark thoughts in his compromised mind. He was in trouble, and he had no idea why. He'd done nothing to this girl. Right?

A truck braked to a sudden halt, sending gravel and cinders to pelt his unfeeling body. Another youthful face crossed his vision—a blonde-haired girl this time. Wade blinked, his eyes wide now. He recognized her. She was the granddaughter of Rose and a friend of the other girl. She, too, walked his daughter from the bus stop the day he taught Mattie a lesson. His muddled brain was trying to make sense of all of this. Was he here all because of *that day*?

The dark-haired girl was aiming something at him that shown with a red laser dot. Dear God, was that a laser sight for a pistol? He was about to die. A shot between the eyes if she was efficient and didn't miss. Was this real, or merely the result of some delirious drug trip? He tried to speak and not even a mumble could he push through his frozen lips.

This girl—Emma, he remembered now—spoke to him, bringing her face close within inches of his. "Don't worry, Wade. No need to be afraid. Yet."

The fright must have registered in his eyes, because his face was immobile. It was as if his face and body did not exist—a sensation that brought on a whole new level of panic within him.

She turned off her cell phone camera and the red light disappeared. "This is our insurance policy...you know, in case you want vengeance." She tapped the phone with her forefinger before putting it in her back pocket. "Wade, you won't do anything knowing that we can release this video of how two girls bested you. Dottie won't do anything either when she knows this video will be released for all who have a Facebook account to view. Her family will face shame. Not good for the reputation of your family, now, is it?" Jolene turned toward Emma and laughed. "Who says revenge isn't sweet?"

Emma dropped the tailgate of the truck, her expression dead serious. "Grandma. Violence is violence in her book, no matter if the intent is justified.

The girl acted annoyed, but was smiling, "*Okay, Martin Luther King, Jr.* Grandma Rose never experienced this feeling of the need for justice. Retribution begins and justice is ours. And don't forget, justice is blind."

"I know, I know. I've got to think about Mattie. We're sisters, deeper than blood."

"That's right. Our tats sealed that deal and our fate. We shed blood with each other."

The girl patted her shoulder, and Emma patted hers in response.

"Well, we're in this now." Emma said.

"Yeah, so let's haul ass." Jolene said, squatting next to Wade.

Emma turned and looked down at Wade. "Look at it like this, Wade. Another unfortunate by-product of your built-up karma. Your ass is about to be mine." Emma then turned to glance at Jolene. "Karma's an easier pill to swallow than revenge."

Jolene rose, looked down and gestured with her head toward Wade. "Won't be for him. Karma...revenge, it's the same, isn't it?"

Emma shot the girl a look. "Not really, Jolene."

Jolene, the name of the girl who had slipped him the mickey, and the one whom he would mark her image in his brain forever, pulled her t-shirt by two points away from her breasts, emphasizing the printed word, "The short...you've been fugazied." Then she laughed.

He most definitely wouldn't let her off the hook for this little nightmare.

And with those words and the laughter fading into the darkness and overtaking his senses, his heart pounding like a skittish racetrack filly, he lost consciousness.

46

Emma and Jolene made their getaway, going about three miles an hour on the slippery, rutted back roads of Taylorville and into the smaller village of Toad Hop. They decided on the round-about route to avoid running into Grandma Rose on her way back to the tavern. The truck bounced over ruts, bottomed out over a dip in asphalt and bumped over a curb or two. Jolene repeatedly swiveled, looking through the rear window, ensuring Wade wasn't sliding around in the back. Emma bottomed out over an uneven rut. "How's he doing?"

Jolene glanced back. "He slipped slightly to the right and lifted off of the truck bed a few inches. But I guess since he's paralyzed, he's not feeling the hurt. He's lying on his back, not moving, now. Just keep going to the main road."

The words Grandma said at the smudging rung in Emma's head—the whole knowing your intention thing.

Were they doing the right thing, taking Wade out of town and into Darwin and risking exposure? Jolene's premise was that she did this for all women. Well, were some women placing themselves in bargaining positions and not realizing what it was they bargained for? Emma couldn't think of that perplexing question and redirected her thoughts to her immediate world. Emma's intention was retribution for Mattie, plain and simple. Was that a bad thing to call for?

"Did you grab the op bag?" Jolene asked.

Emma nodded. The old Ford drove out of Toad Hop and onto the highway, heading east to Darwin.

"Oh, my God! We did it!" Jolene said, exhaling, as if there were no more risk to take and they were heading home, the situation complete. "Now, I understand what drove Jack Bauer to take the risks he took," Jolene said, making the noise of the television series score of the twenty-four-hour clock ticking down.

"Jolene, stop...you're making me nervous."

"It's fine, Emma. We're doing exactly what anyone from Taylorville would do for their sister."

"But, we're not in Taylorville anymore, are we Jolene? We're in Darwin."

"It'll be fine," Jolene said, the light of adventure shining on her face.

"I'm not sure about that. They follow the law here." Emma bit her lower lip but continued driving.

The old Ford drove over the Wabash bridge and into Fairbanks Park, right outside downtown Darwin along the river. Emma drove the truck into a secluded place under a tree. Both girls exited the truck and ran to the tailgate. Emma jumped into the bed and hoisted a folded wheelchair, handing it to Jolene.

"You think Bill will miss it? He won't be getting it back, you know."

"I know. It's his old one. I found it in his shed."

A hit of morality struck Emma. Stealing from Grandpa's crippled diabetic friend didn't sit well with her, either. They had carried out a whole series of dubious decisions to get to this moment. What was it Grandma said? 'Sometimes, it takes making a whole lot of wrong decisions to get to the right place?' Emma hoped she was right.

Jolene unfolded the chair.

Emma checked on Wade for the first time since loading him into the truck. His eyes were wide open and blinking, shifting side-to-side and crossed at times, as if he tried to focus on them.

"Looks like he's slowly regaining consciousness," Emma said. "I wonder if he knows what is going on. It seems like he does."

"I'm not sure I didn't give him too much of that drug. What is in that Devil's Breath, anyway?" Jolene asked.

"Hell, I don't know. I only saw Grandma use it once, and that was to help Harry when he almost sliced off his fingers with that electric saw and refused to go to the hospital. He told Grandma to knock him out real good. He was out for over twelve hours, paralyzed. Knew everything going on, though. When he could talk, he said he couldn't move anything. The terror of the drug was worse than the pain of cutting his fingers, he said."

Jolene nodded and grinned in satisfaction. "Good, that's what we want. For him to feel what terror feels like and the shame afterwards. If that's all we achieve for Mattie, then so be it."

"Well, pretend he sees and hears everything," Emma said, grabbing the op bag.

"Get ready for some real shit to happen. We are in this now," Jolene said, nodding to affirm it to herself, not realizing she stated the obvious. She rummaged through the Op bag, pulling out the items they would need. She set aside a cotton housedress, a wig, and makeup. "Do you want to take his clothes off, or should I?"

"Leave on his underclothes?"

"Well...yeah." She drew out this last word with a surprise tone to it. "That is, if he's wearing any."

"Then you take off his clothes. I don't want to see an old man's pecker."

Emma tugged Wade's boots off, tossing them aside.

Jolene unbuckled Wade's belt and yanked his pants down; as expected, he wore no underwear. Emma averted her eyes, sickened at the sight of his flaccid penis, very much a symbol of his current situation. Jolene gave it no mind and removed Wade's shirt.

Wade lay nude on the bed of the truck, and Jolene's heart lurched, but quickly hardened, when she saw tears gathering in his eyes. To separate herself from her sympathetic nature, she remembered Mattie's nude body as Wade sprayed her from the hose. Her heart hardened even more.

She leaned over him. "How does it feel Wade, stripped of your dignity in front of two girls?" She paused, flinching, as if she expected obscenities to fly from his mouth. "Now, you have something in common with your daughter, if I could define her as that, because you are not father material. Oh, no...that you're not. Your humiliation should be only about one-fifth as terrifying as hers, as you stripped her naked in front of ten people."

"Here." Emma dropped the clothing on top of Wade's body. "Let's cover him up. I don't know who is more traumatized, him being naked or me having to see him naked."

Jolene positioned Wade's body against the side of the truck bed and grabbed the housedress, averting her eyes and keeping them locked onto his face. She snapped the dress on after much pulling and tugging. "This is hard work to dress someone who can't move," she said, speaking to him in such a way as if a mother speaking to a child getting ready for church. Jolene put on his boots. Then they dragged him off of the truck bed and heaved him into the waiting wheelchair.

47

The girls wouldn't stop at the housedress. No, they needed to make his transformation as complete as possible. Jolene grabbed the wig and makeup. "You have the honors of doing his makeup. You're better at it."

With unpracticed precision, Emma painted Wade's fingernails with a red nail polish she had picked up at the dollar store and retrieved the jewelry from her bag. The fake pearls fastened around his neck and the pearl earrings clipped on his ears, giving him a crass look with his facial stubble. She painted bright red on his lips, outlining them to be bigger and puffier, then applied bright blue eye shadow, making the eyes gaudy. His look fancied the character Dr. Frank N. Furter, the cross-dressing alien from the *Rocky Horror Picture Show*.

"Can't have you looking more beautiful than the women in Darwin, now, can we? There's no shame in feeling like the belle of the masquerade ball," Emma said, then laughed a quiet, uncomfortable laugh. It all felt like a funny joke told at a funeral—a situation that resisted humor, yet at the same time called for it.

"No, you need to know what it feels like for others to judge you when you're your most vulnerable...just as you made Mattie feel standing naked in front of those men," she said, turning to Jolene. "Right now, the way I'm feeling when I think of what happened to Mattie, I'd castrate him myself," Emma said.

"Damn straight," said Jolene, as she sat a short curly blonde wig on his head. The girls looked at each other and burst out laughing at Dottie Malone's favorite affirmation. Then Jolene sobered from giggling, "Finally, the Emma I know, righting the wrongs in the world." She straightened the blond wig, tugging it down. "This is the best the Salvation Army could provide. Sorry, Wade. I was going for a Daenerys Targaryen look, you know, Mother of Dragons. But you have to settle for Maude. Besides, it may garner you more pity. It makes you look older."

"Yes. In case you haven't caught on to this lesson, since you're a mastermind at giving them from what I've heard told. This lesson is about you having empathy for the many women who cross your path and who feel shame from the hands of abusive, frightened, little men like you." Jolene said.

Tears gathered in Wade's eyes and something else shone through. Maybe understanding, maybe fear? Or both? The moment was enough for Jolene to pause, and she leaned in, her face close to his.

"If it helps, Wade, we know what you're going through and I have compassion for your suffering," she said. Even though it sounded like an enlightened declaration, Jolene knew it was far from compassionate for Wade. "We won't let you sit in this getup for too long, just enough for you to see others witness your shame. At least you don't have to suffer through twelve years of abuse."

Wade, seeming to have felt a sense of Emma's and Jolene's resolve, sank lower into his chair.

With heavy-handed application, Emma drew a thick line of eye liner around his eyes, and using the lipstick, she applied bright rouge on his cheeks. "There. He doesn't look half bad."

Both girls, as if on cue, grabbed their hoodies from the cab, pulling them over their heads, tucking their hair and tightening the hood close to their faces. They then pulled on black sweatpants over their clothing to make themselves as unidentifiable as possible. Jolene was sure law enforcement would classify what they were doing as breaking the law. Maybe the crime would be an abducting offense. She and Emma bet Wade would not give them away because, given the circles in which he ran, a girl getting the best of him would end his career. Either way, she and Emma were committed. They had the recording. There was no backpedaling now.

48

Jolene pushed Wade's wheelchair through the town square at a leisurely pace. Darwin still maintained its nostalgic, nineteen-fifties feel, even though over six decades had gone by since that era. She and Emma rolled Wade by the dollar store where a person could get a great soda fountain drink with scoops of vanilla ice cream topped with rich dark chocolate, crushed nuts and a cherry. They rolled past the pharmacy and then the beautiful movie theater named, appropriately, The Grand.

When Jolene was younger, she had imagined herself as a princess, and The Grand as her castle, where there was no King George. For each movie showing, ushers escorted patrons to their seats to enjoy the movie, and every movie began when the lush, heavy red velvet curtains retreated to reveal the screen.

Once, the Grand brought back a showing of *The Titanic* and she, Emma and Grandma Rose donned their most beautiful summer dresses and went to an evening showing. The Grand's great staircase in the lobby spiraled up to the second floor and reminded Jolene of the ending in the movie where the immortal Jack Dawson waited for Rose at the Titanic's elaborate staircase, after she had lived her life by following her dreams.

Well, Jolene had a similar promise to herself. But she was no Rose. Grandma Rose had the same resilience as Titanic Rose even—Jolene wasn't sure she herself could withstand even the tenth of adversity those women faced. That was why she and Emma needed to take a stand against an adverse situation, hoping it would make a difference to stop the violence in town. Anyway, this was their moment, the moment after the Titanic sank or a husband dies leaving you to support yourself. They were on their own now.

The girls wheeled Wade a few blocks east on Main Street to the First City Bank, one of the most historical—and most notorious—buildings in town. In a former life, the First City Bank was a hotel, once called The Darwin House. The Darwin House played host to all kinds of shining lights, perhaps none brighter than Al Capone, who stayed at the hotel while overseeing his prostitution and river gambling operations on the Wabash. Since those days, the new owners had converted the hotel into a major downtown office building. The First City Bank stood four stories high and was built from the finest limestone in the United States, obtained from a stone quarry in the area. The bank, with its notorious gangster history, offered a splendid setting for Wade's public shame. A place of crime to pay for a crime.

Jolene parked their charge in front of the bank, trying her best to avoid the bird droppings that splattered around the sidewalk. The wheelchair brake applied easily enough, and Emma placed the cardboard sign on his lap. Emma leaned down and whispered, "No more shame-by-proxy; Wade, you're going to own responsibility."

The shock of this moment registered as alarm in his blue eyes set within his frozen face. "He looks just like prey does when I'm about to release an arrow or pull the trigger on my shotgun."

Jolene draped a sash over his head and across his chest that read, "Miss Ogynist," and then placed a plastic gold crown on his head. Wade continued to register the shock in his eyes at each indignity the two girls dished out to him.

"Someone will pick you up later, I suppose," Jolene said, smiling. "Until then, enjoy your day. And remember, this is for Mattie."

"Oh, before I forget, one more thing," Emma said, digging deep into her pocket and grabbing the last little surprise—a handful of sunflower seeds. She spread the seeds in Wade's lap. Food for the birds.

"Wow, you sure thought of everything, didn't you?" Jolene asked.

The birds cooed from their perch at the top of the four-story building, anticipating the meal below.

"And they're right on time," Emma said, smiling. "Love it when a plan comes together."

Satisfied, they walked across the street to the Blue Water Coffeehouse, the only place opened at this early morning hour. After disposing of their sweats in the bathroom trash, they sat down at a table with a view.

49

People hurried into the bank, giving Wade a wide berth. Some people walked by slowly, cautiously, dropping dollar bills in the side pocket of his wheelchair, not taking the time to read the sign. "Will you look at that?" Emma sipped the cappuccino she splurged for the occasion. "Those Malones can turn any activity into a moneymaking business. They sure have the life of Riley."

"Is panhandling against the law?" Jolene asked. "Maybe he'll get arrested?"

A young woman pulled out a chair next to their table and sat down with her iced coffee and several books. She must have been a student at the university, judging from the medical text she opened up. Her face had a worried frown as she watched the scene unfolding across the street, each moment increasing her restlessness. She looked over at Emma and Jolene. "What's that about?"

Emma didn't want to engage in the conversation. Her nerves were on edge and she couldn't wait until this was done and over. She remained quiet and was thankful when Jolene answered the woman.

"I don't know. It looks like someone is helping a poor handicapped person," Jolene said, as she sipped from her mug, keeping to her and Emma's agreement of anonymity in the matter.

"Where you girls from?" she asked.

"Taylorville," said Jolene.

"Taylorville?" She asked with a mixture of amazement and trepidation. The woman's knee rose and fell rhythmically under her small tabletop.

"Yeah. Why?" Jolene asked, both she and Emma's attention drawn away from Wade for a moment at the anxiety in the woman's voice.

"Because I'm from Chicago and my momma told me to never cross the Wabash Bridge into Taylorville and never speak to anyone from there." She opened her eyes big and round as she looked them up and down, assessing the threat. "Momma said my chances of surviving the town were slim to none. I could be lynched if I were a man and terrible things done to me as a woman. Worse than Chicago."

Jolene shrugged. "I can understand why your momma said that. I don't think any stranger should visit Taylorville. We don't take lightly to strangers. No one really trusts new people."

Emma wanted to add that there were other reasons other than violence to not live in Taylorville or visit, for that matter, but thought she'd not extend the conversation.

Jolene's unsympathetic responses to the expression of violence seemed out of character for her. The student's concern made Emma feel that the whole abduction of Wade was wrong. They had somehow entered a parallel universe where she and Jolene were the cold, vindictive, violent, and action-oriented people—no different from the abusive men. Maybe Grandma was right. Maybe their malintent would grow into a darkness within themselves.

"But, wow. You heard about Taylorville way up in Chicago, huh?" Jolene asked.

The woman nodded. Jolene's face lit up, as if experiencing a brief moment of pride that her tiny town's reputation extended that far, albeit for dark reasons.

"There's some jacked-up-strange going on there with that woman in the wheelchair," said the student with a half nod of her head toward Wade.

"Yeah," Emma said, feeling her guilt grow as the woman continued to talk. The actions she and Jolene had carried out in revenge didn't seem in alignment with the teachings of Jesus, either.

"That woman seems to be in some kind of trouble. She hasn't moved, and now a few people have gathered around her." The coffee patron's voice took on a slight tone of alarm.

Before long, a couple of women bank tellers came out to look at him. One woman, her hair pulled back into a tight silver bun, approached Wade, leaned over, and spoke to him. He did not respond as far as she could tell. The teller pulled out a wadded Kleenex and wiped his cheeks. It seemed she intended to wipe away his makeup or pigeon dropping, and then Emma sat up straighter in her chair and strained forward to get a clearer look. The realization hit her. *Oh, he's crying, and that woman is wiping away his tears.* Sympathy was not the reaction she wanted people to have toward this child abuser and she didn't want to be feeling it herself.

The bank teller stood up and called out to one of her co-workers in the bank. A young teller came to the door, and the older woman spoke to her. Soon, the younger woman went back inside. Within a few minutes, she reappeared at the door, said something to the teller standing at Wade's side, and then both women walked back into the bank.

Once the tellers left, a pigeon, enticed by the sunflower seeds and not minding the gathering of people on the sidewalk, swooped down and landed in Wade's lap to peck at the snack. Other pigeons, not wanting to miss out on easy food, perched on Wade to snatch a seed, squawking at each other to establish their domain. The birds dove in, pecked a seed, and flew away, skittish. People continued to slow down their steps and stare. Some pulled out their cell phones to take photos. Others hurried on down the street as if Wade carried a disease.

"Oh, my gosh. Now that isn't right, taking pictures of a woman in a wheelchair as if she was a circus sideshow," said the college student. "Before long, it'll be all over the internet."

Emma and Jolene nodded in response, as if on cue in an effort to disguise their shock. Emma's body quivered with anxiety and her stomach lurched. The entire scene had unraveled out of control. Their insurance policy would be void and repercussions from the Malones were guaranteed to occur.

She realized how ineffective their insurance policy truly was from the get-go.

"Well, I was going to go across the street to help the poor woman, but it looks like someone will take care of her." The student pushed back her chair and walked to the coffee shop window to get a closer look.

"There's a sign in her lap." She pulled out her phone's camera and brought the image closer. "I can't believe what it says." The tone in her voice registers alarm. "Is this some kind of joke, you think?" Then she brought her phone down slowly, pity filling her eyes for the woman across the street, and not waiting for an answer, grabbed her belongings and left the coffeeshop.

More pedestrians gathered, gawking at the invalid dressed in women's clothes, wearing snakeskin cowboy boots, fake pearls, and a bad blond wig with a live pigeon as a topper. Soon, the small crowd swelled to a small mob of business owners and shoppers, standing beside the streetlights in front of the bank. Lawyers. Merchants. Ragged street people. All wondering what the fuss was about. In the midst of this scene sat Wade, silent and immobile, no longer visible to Emma through the many people clustered around him.

50

Wade could only move his eyes as he passively watched the crowd gathering around him. This had to be his worst nightmare, to be trapped in his body and unable to move. This must be how that paralyzed science fellow felt, Stephen Hawking or something or the other...how could that man have stood it for all those years? Maybe he'd talk to Rose about it. She'd know who Hawking was and would understand his torture. Did he piss himself? He could smell urine. God, the shame of it all. Damn, his thoughts were all over the place, first thinking about a scientist and a future topic he could discuss with Rose.

Wade's body wasn't the only thing he couldn't control—his mind wasn't working right, either, as it jumped from one subject to another. He forced his mind to focus, and he tried to scream, but nothing came out. The surrounding crowd just stared, whispering their dumb comments to others. Oh God, when will Dottie arrive? He never thought he would pray for her help and never thought he'd need her to rescue him. Not in a million years. Damn, his thoughts were ping-ponging all over the place.

People were snapping photos of him. A vain thought ran roughshod over all the others during this time of crisis. A stifled laughter bubbled up in his belly. He couldn't believe he was stopping traffic and dressed as a woman. The inanity of the situation almost made it bearable. That was some kind of mickey that girl Jolene gave him. Certainly, different than the ones he himself had slipped to other folks in the past.

But, when the cell phones came out and people started recording his situation, he felt fear course through his body in a more intense way. That's when he felt true dread. Not about the girls. Hell no. He could handle them later if he wanted his comeuppance, but people would see the video, mock him, destroy his professional reputation and one Senator would have a deadly score to settle. He was in more deep trouble than Taylorville or Darwin mocking him.

Any retribution delivered by him and the Malones wouldn't straighten out this situation and the damage done by these girls. Rose's granddaughter. Could he really harm her? She was Rose's blood. Yet, he had a reputation to keep up, and all he could do was watch passively while the phones began immortalizing his humiliation. These idiots would post it on their social media, and he'd be a laughingstock, never to work under contract again. Who would take him seriously? Hell, forget about not getting any more work, he would be a dead man before the week was out if certain people caught wind of this. He may need to have more than a sit-down with those two young idiot friends of his daughter. Learn them a lesson.

But that girl, the one named Jolene, had an insurance policy if this didn't get out. Sure, it was bad enough to have a couple of women take advantage of you. But teen girls? He'd never be able to live it down if her video got out. Reputation ruined. Career ruined. Unfortunately for her, the passersby' videos of him dressed in drag would be enough to devalue her insurance policy.

But that was the least of his worries. His mind turned once again to the larger threat: the Russians. If they somehow saw these videos and identified him, he was in major trouble. The Russians would want to break an egg, and now they'd know exactly how to locate the hen house. Hell will rain down on me, was all he could think about as he watched people snapping their photos.

A female bank teller came into view, stooped over so that her face was directly in front of his. A look of pity turned her lips downward, and she appeared uncomfortable. "Ma'am, your sister is on her way."

How could he have forgotten already? It must be the drugs or the trauma of it all that he blocked it out, and then he'd remembered. He was dressed as a *woman*. Tears filled his eyes. He felt beaten and weak. Those girls, Emma and Jolene, they were the ones that had done this to him. His life ruined. The videos exposed him. He was a sitting duck and vulnerable. Tears ran down his cheeks. The bank teller reached over to wipe them away with a soggy Kleenex. At least Dottie was on her way, he thought. He sure hoped that she would recognize the implications and come straight here. Knowing her, though, she would not want to interrupt watching one of her soaps. But, on the other hand, she loved drama. And this was definitely more drama than any reality television show could dream up.

While Wade was having his disjointed recollections in the pastimes of Dottie, the eighty-eight Oldsmobile drove right up and stopped in front of him. Dottie leaped out and ran toward him, pushing through the crowd. She stopped in front of his wheelchair, looking at him, then the sign and her face registered shock. She grabbed the sign and ripped it into pieces. "How dare they? You look like a...a...joke. What's going on here, Wade?"

All Wade could do was stare at her, motionless and expressionless except for the tears that flowed down his rouged cheeks.

51

The cappuccino weighed heavily, like someone had just shoveled mud into Emma's stomach. Dottie had arrived to take Wade home.

"Well, let's leave, now," Emma said to Jolene, giving her a stern look, hoping to convey how little she wanted a rebuke.

"Yes. Let's go," Jolene said. "We executed the plan...easy-peasy. Wade suffered the pain he's caused other girls. Maybe the message will reach others, too."

"Makes me queasy," Emma said, shaking her head in doubt. "You think one person can even the scales of justice here?"

Once outside the coffeehouse, they began their walk back to Fairbanks Park.

"Maybe not, but, for Mattie, I believe Wade's paid for the pain he's done," Jolene said. "Yep, no shame-by-proxy here; he's owning his, and Taylorville will take notice."

"Taylorville? I think the entire city of Darwin will notice in a few days, and what if it goes viral?" Emma asked. "What will that mean for us?"

They walked in silence. Emma lost herself in her thoughts. Pity for Wade overwhelmed her, softening her heart. Empathy wasn't standing over a well and looking down at your friend, nose-level in water and saying you understand. Empathy only came from being in the well yourself and maybe, just maybe, being so helpless to not be able to get yourself out. Compassion, a whole different level, would be to hold the suffering of her friend in the well, as if in the well yourself, and take action. She wondered if they'd done the right thing with such revenge in their heart?

Jeez. She cannot hate the same way others hate. She tried to, and she'd failed. Things would be easier if she could hate. Then, this plan of retribution or this public statement they were making would feel more like a victory. An image of Wade in the well clamored for recognition in her mind demanding consideration, and a then a flash of Wade holding Mattie against her will, nude, overtook the image. He's done wrong, and he's getting what he deserves. She wouldn't forget about what started them on this journey of revenge. Better yet to think positively. Better yet to think that their actions brought things into *balance*. With the whole town, too. She remembered the day the town boys made fun of Mattie. Everyone—the men and the boys—needed to learn a lesson. It was simply the right thing to do, and they did it.

They had made mistakes, though. She didn't want Darwin to know she and Jolene were behind the scheme and she wasn't sure if they had made any unexpected oversights. Hollowness seized her stomach. Neither she nor Jolene expected the crowd to record Wade on their phones. Maybe Wade needed to carry his shame only in Taylorville, where folks understood the act of vengeance as a settling of sorts. But, if revenge felt like this, so dark and so wrong, then it really didn't set things right, did it?

Grandma encouraged them to make a statement without violence. While they hadn't done physical violence, they caused suffering to another human being. Wasn't that violence? Emma couldn't deny that it wasn't violent. When they brought pain to Wade, then they acted out of their own darkness and aggression. Nothing could justify acts with no awareness. There was no free will in that. If they were lucky, maybe the situation would be okay. She and Jolene would have the outcome they planned, one where Wade would carry the pain he inflicted, carry his shame. Maybe she made something out of nothing and everything would be alright. The hairs on the back of Emma's neck stood up, and a sensation tingled down her spine.

Well, nothing could be done about the events they had set into motion. What was done was done, and she needed to forget about it. The whole matter seemed settled in Jolene's mind. Maybe she should take Jolene's lead. Emma would follow Jolene's lead and act as if nothing had happened. Emma knew she sounded like that engineer guy from the *Titanic*, Thomas Andrews, who reassured Rose by saying, "Sleep soundly young Rose, because I have built you a good ship and you have all the lifeboats you will need, although you won't need them." Nothing good came from the reassurance of that very smart man.

52

The bar appeared empty except for Miss Henry sitting quietly on her stool, feeding quarters into her slot machine, receiving three-ping dings of defeat, only to drop another coin in for another go at it. Her eyes fell closed when she pulled the lever, as if she willed the bars to stop in her favor. Emma washed mugs in the sink, her head down and appearing to be having her own Zen moment to reflect.

"Hi, Miss Henry!" Jolene said in a louder-than-usual voice, doing her best impression of an Elaine Benes herky-jerky dance move. "Watch this, Miss Henry! I've got the moves." Miss Henry paused before dropping her next quarter. Jolene made her best 'see-I-told-you' look at Emma, and Emma shook her head and smiled, wiping her wet hands on her jeans. She turned to give Jolene her full attention.

"Can you believe we did it? According to the news, the security footage shows two teen boys wearing hoodies pushing Wade down the street. Darwin's in the dark and Taylorville is keeping their lips sealed." Jolene did a spin in her dance. "Let's celebrate!"

Emma nodded toward Miss Henry. Jolene gave her best slanted smile, to a Don't-worry-about-her-I-don't-think-she's-comprehending-look.

Emma grabbed two champagne glasses, pulled out orange juice from the small bar fridge. "Mimosas on the way."

"See, I told you. You had nothing to worry about. We're fine."

"Yeah, I guess you're right. I'm sorry that I was so up-tight."

Jolene pulled out her cell and showed Emma her Twitter account.

"One million and two-hundred thousand likes and thirty thousand re-tweets—all in one day. Can you freaking believe it?" She felt excitement over her notoriety.

"You're kidding, right?" A look of concern flitted across Emma's face.

"Do you think Wade remembers anything?"

Emma nodded. "I think he remembers everything." She poured the mimosas, and laughing, sat the drinks down on the bar.

Jolene grabbed a glass and danced over to Miss Henry and sat the mimosa in front of her slot machine. "Miss Henry, we're celebrating an achievement this morning. Drink up my friend and join us in the celebration."

Emma sat another drink down on the bar. "Let's have a toast, my friends."

Jolene held her glass up in a toast and rapped a song on which Emma joined in on.

"Hold on my sisters, Hold on tight,
We'll soon blow this town,
but till then, we'll be alright."

The girls laughed.

"For Mattie!" Jolene said and clinked Emma's glass and turned to clink Miss Henry's, who appeared content sipping her champagne in front of her slot machine.

"Boy, doesn't revenge feel good?" Jolene asked.

Emma laughed in agreement.

53

A hand slammed down on the bar behind her, which startled Emma. She jumped and spun around, the champagne glass raised, to find Grandma looking at her with a stern expression. Grandma's hand rested hard on the front page of the Darwin morning paper. "Child, what have you gone and done?" Grandma's eyes shifted to Emma's hand, pulling the champagne glass to her chest. Miss Henry stopped dropping coins in the slot machine and swiveled on her stool to watch the scene unfold with concern on her face. She was attentive now.

"What do you mean? We brought things full circle with Wade without using violence. It's over, Grandma. I had planned on telling you this morning." An uncomfortable feeling slithered from deep within her throat, and she coughed.

The paper grabbed her attention, even already knowing what she would see on the front page. The morning edition was worse than expected. Grandma moved her hand away. There, in the center of the front page of the *Darwin Tribune*, was a large photograph of Wade in a housedress, sitting in his wheelchair in front of the bank with a pigeon perched on his head. The photo was a close-up, and you could see the sash, which read "Miss Ogynist" and the sign Emma had placed on his lap. It read, "I abuse women and children. I'm a hoser. Please hose me off."

"Brought things full circle? What the hell does that mean, anyway? I thought you wouldn't take revenge. Now, the police will be involved...there could be legal charges."

"Grandma, I was trying to avoid violence, like you said," Emma stuttered. "You know, don't do the eye-for-an-eye thing. We didn't. He wore a dress. We didn't threaten him with a gun or anything."

"Isn't revenge violent? Wasn't it a vengeful heart that drugged and took Wade to the city, then sat him in front of a bank? That's not violent? City folk won't understand our ways. If the law investigates further, they will expose your identity. They could arrest you for kidnapping. You won't be going to the university then, will you?"

Emma stared at Grandma, and for the first time, her emotions spun out of control. She hadn't thought this would jeopardize her college dreams.

"You're messing with a force, the folks of Darwin, who live outside of how we handle things in this town," Grandma Rose continued, sternly. "You girls did exactly what not to do—create drama and cause harm to another." Grandma jabbed at the picture of Wade with her index finger as if she drilled a hole through the tabletop. "You're tampering with a man's fate and you've set into motion a chain of events that you can't control." Grandma's body shuddered as if Death had breezed over her.

"Grandma Rose," Jolene said, butting in. "Blame me. I'm the one that drugged Wade and forced Emma to help me. It was all me." Jolene's face registered defeat and worry. She turned away to study the floor tiles.

Grandma rubbed her forehead with the fingertips of both hands. She did this gesture when she was being flooded with information, or when she had a very intense migraine. "Your actions weren't that far or no different from the abuse he does."

Emma didn't have the courage to tell Grandma her confusion about how they could have settled things without violence. "I don't know."

Grandma regarded Emma; her eyes unwavering. "Oh, dear child. What were you thinking?" She rubbed her forehead with more force while she circled the kitchen in her consternation. With everything they had faced as a family, Emma never observed Grandma, anxious to the point of not being able to sit still. Her eyes dropped to the paper, and she collapsed in the chair. "I'd thought maybe you would make a different decision after our discussion." Grandma now put both hands over her eyes and began rubbing.

Emma felt her anxiety crawl under her skin and enter her bloodstream. A million fire ants trekked along her veins in search of the large picnic she served up for them inside her heart. She looked over at Jolene, her face pasty and white.

Grandma's ignorance of what was required to set things straight without violence demanded a high level of consciousness. Life was tough with all the expectations placed on her—working, taking care of her friends, trying to figure out how to get to college and living in a poor, mean town *and* doing it all while pleasing her grandma. The anger rose within her. "I thought outside of the box...no, wait, I wasn't even seeing a box."

Grandma looked at Emma, appearing to not comprehend anything Emma said. "Don't be a smart ass now. This is serious."

Emma sat her glass down hard and some mimosa flicked onto the photo of Wade, blotching his picture. Grandma closed her eyes, and the change in her demeanor alarmed Emma, and her anger drained, but the anxiety within her shook her body. Now she felt concern. "Are you seeing something, Grandma? You'd tell me if you were...right?"

Grandma sighed without answering and without opening her eyes. Her fingers migrated to her temples and began rubbing small concentric circles. "You not only will have the whole town talking about it, but I am sure Darwin is wondering how a drugged man ended up alone, downtown, and dressed in drag." She shook her head, and a weariness came over her, and Grandma again placed her head in her hands, with her elbows resting on the table. "Well, you have one thing right. I suspect the Malones will be tight-lipped to the police about any of this, even though I'm sure they are quite aware who's behind it. They wouldn't risk any police involvement and have the law digging into their life."

Grandma sighed and shifted away from Emma for a moment, then she looked at Emma. Her eyes narrowed and lips pressed together in a stern, straight line.

Emma sat down on the bar stool; her legs unable to support her weight. She felt drained. Her plans for a celebratory drink were forgotten. The newspaper, with the now-infamous photo, blurred in her vision, emphasizing the mimosa splatters that ran the print into small ink blobs. *Oh my God, what have I done?*

Grandma sighed a tired, old woman sigh, and shrugged. "My concern is that the actions you've taken have escalated the situation. Now, someone will pay. It's karma's way." Her eyes shifted over to Miss Henry, who watched the scene before her unfold, the slot machine forgotten.

Grandma's fingers tapped out a hoof-beat rhythm on the newspaper, and that slithering feeling that stuck in Emma's throat doubled in diameter. It threatened to cut off her air supply. She searched in vain to find the words to express her oppressed, awful regret. But all she could do was simply apologize.

"I'm sorry," she said, her head hung. Those words were all she could muster. She'd hoped they'd settled the situation with Wade. It seems instead that they had started something else entirely.

Grandma nodded and lifted her weary body out of the chair. "You are young, darling, and don't always see below the surface of things. Hell, most adults don't see the very thing that's put in front of them. At least your plan was imaginative; that is an improvement, at least. But because your heart was full of revenge and fear, you only ended up perpetuating the wheel of injustice and violence." Grandma sighed. "I will meditate with this in my morning practice." She leaned over the bar; her palms pressed onto the bar top, letting it support her weight.

Grandma stopped speaking for a moment while seeming to contemplate the possibilities of the acts of her and Jolene. When she spoke, her voice had the cadence, a cadence which indicated she spoke with a wisdom.

Without lifting her head, Grandma Rose said, "Things happen for a reason, child. Fates destined you to engage forces outside our way of life." Grandma swept her arms wide around her body. "All of this holds a larger purpose that extends beyond Taylorville and our hillbilly ways," she said. "I want you to remember. Things unfolded the way they did to serve a larger purpose. It was not your fault. It was destined to happen." Grandma lifted her head, her eyes meeting Emma's. "Promise me at least one thing: no matter what happens, you will remember this."

Grandma grabbed Emma's forearm. Her fingers pressed into the flesh as if to sink the information more deeply into her mind.

"I understand," Emma said, nodding. "But you're not seeing trouble brewing for Jolene and me, are you?" The fear crept in again at the urgency of her words.

"I'm so sorry about this, Grandma Rose," Jolene said, with fear creeping into her expression, her eyes wide and sad.

Grandma looked at her as if seeing her for the first time, still with that faraway look in her eyes. "If something will happen, it'll happen soon. Life will test you, sweetie. I think it's time for you to have a clearer understanding of the situation. You must sharpen your own senses for what's coming." Then Grandma turned to Emma. "Remember the world of The Wolf."

Emma felt taken aback. Jolene took a deep inhale of breath and her eyes filled with tears at the distress Grandma Rose showed.

Grandma walked around the bar and reached under to pull out the rifle. She looked at Emma. "You know how to use this. Your Daddy taught you how to hunt and shoot. I just want you to know it's here...in case trouble comes around. Okay? It would help if you both practice the shift to Ch'Ulel heart and brain."

Emma nodded through her nerves.

"The Malones may come after you, and I want you to defend yourself," Grandma Rose said, continuing. "The paper says Wade has no memory of the night before. That's probably not true. But the Malones will be tight-lipped, that's for certain. Maybe it's time to have a meeting with Dottie. She can be reasonable."

Emma thought, really? Accessory to a murder, Dottie? Emma nodded. "I'm not scared."

Jolene nodded, as well. "I'm not either."

Grandma looked at them both and nodded, though her eyes reflected she didn't believe either of them. "Then you're not as smart as I thought. I don't want you to be concerned. But you need to be prepared." Her glance focused on Miss Henry for a moment, a sadness washing over her face, reaching her eyes before giving everyone a nod. She returned the gun below the bar. Without waiting for any additional conversation from either Emma or Jolene, she turned and walked to the back room. Every step taxed her body, and she appeared to shrink in size before she disappeared through the doorway. Then Grandma did something Emma had never seen before: she closed her backroom door.

54

Wade woke in the spare bedroom at Dottie's house, staring up at the water leak patterns on the ceiling. He tried sitting up and felt the pounding of his head and the sluggish response from his body. His mind was fuzzy, but he recalled bits and pieces of the events. Slowly, he returned to the present and moved his body in little increments, starting with his feet and hands and then eventually his limbs. That's when his ears picked up the newscaster's voice on the television on his dresser.

"Wade Malone, a Taylorville man, was drugged and dressed in drag while people stood by and filmed his shame and humiliation. Authorities are investigating and following up on leads. More on this story at six."

Wade grabbed his head in pain and shook it in disbelief, causing his head to pound more. The important parts of last evening's events came to him—especially the part in which the passersby video recorded his peril. His picture and name would be all over the internet by now. He needed to get the hell out.

Wade stumbled into Mattie's room, grabbed her pink Barbie backpack. Mattie wouldn't be needing it anymore, so he might as well use it. He stuffed a change of clothing in the bag. Stepping into Dottie's room, he pulled her Glock from under her mattress, checked the chamber, and tucked it into his pants waistband. Dottie never changed her routine. Lucky for him.

Back in his room, he put on a flannel shirt, leaving the tail end to hang over the Glock. He wondered if he had time to square a few things out, but he shouldn't risk it. He grabbed a hoodie and the remaining stash of his cash that he'd taped to the bottom of a drawer and stepped out of the house. He took a deep breath, knowing this was the last time he would ever be home. After another deep breath to steady his head, he began the walk out of Taylorville. He couldn't risk an Uber. His mind's ability to process things was slow to recover, but he was thinking of the pertinent things to stay alive.

55

Jolene pulled out her cell phone and logged onto her Twitter account. The two girls walked along the Wabash and shared their feelings on the aftermath of what they now called the Wade Heist. "It's trending. Can you freaking believe it?" Jolene felt excited about the increasing popularity of their revenge, almost as if she hadn't heard a thing Grandma had said, even though it had made her cry. She had pushed Grandma out of her mind.

"I don't know, Jolene. I'm not sure that we helped Mattie, in any way, to improve her situation. Now, it seems this has spun out of our control. There are too many people involved."

The two friends were on their way to pick up Mattie from her home for their daily walk to the bus stop. They became silent, lost in their own thoughts.

As they approached the house, they saw Dottie standing against the porch railing. Her arms were folded over her breast to keep her flannel shirt from blowing open in the wind. Sy leaned against the house, his legs stretched out in front of him. One hand dove deep into his pocket, resting there, the other holding a toothpick to his mouth.

"Girls, I don't want you walking Mattie anymore. In fact, she won't be going to school. We'll need her to find a job. Having friends like you has caused her nothing but problems. Wade's gone missing. Looks like he left today. Don't know if he skipped town or something else. But, he's gone."

Jolene understood the covert message. With Wade disappearing, the money would stop coming in. More than likely, there would be no more monthly checks sent for Mattie's expenses.

"Is Mattie okay?" asked Jolene.

"Of course she's okay. She just knows the dire situation you put her in."

"Well, can't we see her?"

"Hell no. Didn't you hear me? I can't make it any clearer. You're...not...to...see...Mattie. If you do, there will be repercussions. If something happened to my brother, there'll be more repercussions. Am I making myself clear?"

Sy stood away from the door frame and walked over to stand next to Dottie.

"Yes ma'am," said Jolene.

"Okay, then. You girls just be on your way. There won't be a future need for you to walk up our lane again. Understood?"

Jolene and Emma nodded and turned to amble down the lane.

"Do you think Mattie believes we are the reasons for her misery?"

"Maybe. Mattie processes things differently than most people, so I wouldn't assume she can see the truth. Mattie needs Dottie, no matter how cruel Dottie is to her."

Jolene nodded at her own statement, deep in thought. Emma had mentioned the well analogy regarding empathy and compassion to her before. She'd been in that well with the water to her eyeballs. Hell, she was in that well now. Maybe that was why she felt no empathy or compassion for Wade. He'd put her there.

Emma stopped walking and turned toward Jolene.

"Jolene, we have to own our responsibility in this whole mess. I've been thinking that what we've done isn't much different from what Wade's done. Not as overtly abusive, but still not good. Maybe Grandma was right."

Jolene teared a bit, almost as if her best friend punched her in the gut. She just wanted to feel that she had stopped the bad things done by the bad men in her world. She wanted to feel some of that power.

"While Wade wasn't George, some part of me didn't care. That moment when I dragged Wade feet first out the tavern and into the street was a vengeance to all the wrong that's been done to me. And it felt good. I wouldn't take back what I did. For me, it was worth it."

"I can never assume to understand your difficulty, but I just feel empty now instead of angry. Now, I'm the victimizer. Just like Grandma says, the cycle continues and the wheel spins in the same direction." Emma said this with sadness in her tone.

"Maybe, but now Wade has paid for all he's done to Mattie and is carrying his shame." Anger punctuated the last part of Jolene's words, so much so that Emma's face registered alarm.

Jolene wanted to eliminate Emma's concern, so she softened her voice. "But I needed to experience the reclaiming of the power I lose to George every time he touches me. Don't judge me, Emma, for wanting that moment."

"I won't judge. I think I understand. But, please don't see that moment as resolving the things done to you but just a part of a path to redemption."

"Yeah. I know what you mean."

56

Wade walked toward the Wabash River Bridge. The sun was on its early ascent to midday and while the air was cool for March, sweat beaded his brow. His destination was Darwin and the nearest bus station since he'd forgotten that Uber doesn't service this shit-hole. Thank God for Greyhound. He had plenty of time to make the 3:00 bus out of town. His gait resorted to shuffling, and the physical effort it took to place one leg in front of the other seemed monumental. At times, he had to remind himself where he was going because his short-term memory recalled only a few seconds of past events. He headed toward the bridge. It didn't matter. If he wanted to live, he needed to get out of town.

As he approached a house, he looked and noticed Jolene sitting on her porch stoop. She glanced at him. He could see the shock in her eyes.

A rush of power entered him when he noticed her reaction. The need to learn her a lesson overruled his urge to leave town quickly. It was fated, his running across her like this. He wasn't sure if this need to square up resulted from the unleashing of whatever drug she had given him, but a newfound energy filled his veins. Even though leaving town made all kinds of sense, he could not suffer the humiliation of full surrender. The Malones never surrendered. An eye for an eye, a tooth for a tooth, ain't that what the Bible said? He reached for his Glock.

He walked over to Jolene on the stoop, his hand firmly on the Glock behind his back. She watched him with wide eyes, but did nothing, cemented in place. He stood in front of her and she lifted her head to look at him. He bent down, pulled the Glock from behind his back and waved the Glock toward the east.

"We're gonna take a little walk," he said. "Down to the river. Say one word or make one sound and you're dead. It's that simple. So don't even think about it."

Jolene said nothing. Wade looked deep into Jolene's green eyes, and the way her eyes registered first shock, then fear, and finally a begging of sorts, imploring him not to do whatever he planned. He understood that look. He had it before his father's beatings. It was the look a tough, angry guy had after you'd brought him to his knees, before he felt the shame, and then finally a helpless relief. She was at the relief stage. He knew she understood, somehow, that it would soon be over.

Jolene rose, and Wade shoved his Glock into the small of her back and stood close behind her. Then they walked.

Given the morning time of day, they passed no one along the brief trip to the Wabash. He smiled. She was compliant now, not the raging bitch from the night before. He was going to take pleasure in learning her a lesson. If she didn't learn now, life would only get harder for her. He finally had found his groove as mentor to all who didn't know any better and he never wanted to leave. He felt better already.

57

Late morning shadows worked patterns across the black and white tiled floor of The Dam Tavern. Miss Henry was the only customer in the late morning, as was typical, sitting in front of her slot machine. Her eyes would fall closed, and then a slight snore would wake her up to plug in another quarter. Even when Emma entered the bar, her presence didn't distract Miss Henry from pulling down the crank and listening to the wheels click into their stops. The television in the bar's corner played *The Price is Right*. The set was on so that Miss Henry wouldn't feel alone when the tavern's work required Grandma to leave the main bar area.

Grandma stood in the doorway to the supply room wearing her favorite tie-dyed skirt. She checked through all the boxes of wine, whiskey, vodka, and specialty liquors. Grandma appeared different in that moment, like a friend you encounter day after day, yet couldn't ever really know. A great outpouring of love radiated from Emma's heart for all the sacrifices Grandma, a woman who worked hard her whole life, had made for her. Emma walked over and her arms encircled Grandma from behind, giving her a tight hug.

"Whatever it is, it'll be fine, dear." Grandma paused in the checking of her inventory and studied Emma's face, reaching out to take her hand in hers. "You know, I love you," she said.

"I know...love will find its way through paths where wolves fear to prey."

Grandma looked at her with a blank expression. "Huh?"

"It's a quote from Lord Byron."

"Ah...whoever he is, he sounds like a man with wisdom." She half-smiled. Her mind seemed distracted this morning. "Now, here's the inventory list. You know what to do. I'm going next door to fix sandwiches for Miss Henry and me. Do you want anything?" Emma shook her head no. Grandma smiled, and her eyes lit up to their utmost brilliance, and just like that she was fully present. "It'll be fine, Emma. You'll see. Everything is as it should be."

Emma felt a profound stillness within her, and this feeling quieted her own momentary doubts. She didn't bring up her suspicions regarding the Wolf in her journey work. To do so would only make the foreboding she felt seem that much more real. Things would not be fine. There were so many unanswered challenges. Change was coming. She could sense it like the coming of spring after a long winter cold.

Grandma, though, who had aged a century in the last few days, turned and suddenly appeared childlike again. She walked as if her feet barely touched the floor and, like a fairy-child, she floated out of the tavern.

Emma started cutting the oranges and lemons with a small, sharp paring knife. The sounds of the lever on the slot machine forcing the reels to spin and then the clicking as the wheels stopped to reveal the play competed with the sound of the television, its volume turned low. The repetitious cutting movement and the consistent sounds lulled Emma into a peaceful state.

After a few minutes, Emma noticed the main room had fallen silent except for the droning of the television. Miss Henry must have taken a rare break to rest her arm. Emma's mind wandered to Mattie's humiliation. The disbelief and horror she read in Mattie's eyes was something that would never leave her. Soon, her mind drifted to a different place. The connections of Carl Jung's shadow of the mind and spiritual darkness spoke of the same—a warfare of the spiritual kind. After she finished with the oranges and lemons, she put the paring knife in her pant pocket and went outside to sit on the stoop for a few minutes of fresh air.

Alongside the tavern and the river's edge was a brush-wood of knotted branches where a few grey squirrels crouched, utterly still. One, alarmed, ran out into the road, and indecisive of which way to go, nervously switched one direction to the next before running back and into the thicket. Emma felt exactly how the anxious squirrel felt.

From the stoop, Emma could see Wade in the distance, hunched over, walking toward the town entrance. His presence disturbed her. Maybe it was the remnants of the red lipstick smeared over his face like a grotesque clown, or that he had Mattie's pink Barbie bag slung in a creepy fashion over his shoulder. He turned to glance her way, and she saw the white Tootsie Roll stick hanging from his mouth, which he swished from one side of his mouth to the other. She wasn't ready to confront him, and she wasn't sure she would ever be ready to speak to him.

He turned and walked toward her, swishing the Tootsie Roll back and forth, back and forth. The swishing Tootsie Roll triggered a memory she'd repressed, but it all flooded back in an instant. She played the memory as if she watched a movie, a horror film.

58

She was only four years old at the time and sitting on the tavern stoop playing with her new Barbie purse and Barbie doll. She struggled to get the blazer on Barbie, who was getting ready to go to work in New York City. Little Emma gave up her struggle and rifled through her Barbie pocketbook to find a Kleenex to dress her Barbie when a car sped by.

Squealing, the car slowed enough to do a U-turn a few feet in front of her and park across the street. A man, handsome with his dark, wavy hair, sweatshirt and jeans, stepped out and leaned against the door, crossing his legs at the ankles. He placed a cigarette in his mouth and lit it. Emma felt the excitement in the air that rolled off of him, and it made her anxious. She had seen this man with her mom several times. Her attention diverted from the man leaning against the car to another man who approached them, sucking on a Tootsie Roll pop. It was Wade, and she knew him slightly as a man who visited the tavern. Wade stopped and looked at the man by the car. His expression turned sour immediately.

The man by the car stood, grabbed his cigarette, flipped it out, and paced alongside the car. "Maggie! C'mon!" he shouted, staring off at The Dam Tavern door, without even acknowledging Emma. "The bus leaves in 30. Let's go!"

Emma began crying. She understood what the man said, and it wasn't good for her.

The screen door opened. Cowboy boots gave rise to tan skinny legs and a short jean skirt topped by a Cream T-shirt appeared over Emma. Whiffs of vanilla sugar wafted toward her. These legs and that scent belonged to her mother, Maggie.

Maggie stepped out on the stoop, frantically bending down toward Emma, bangles jingling on her wrist. Her mother's backpack strap dropped off of her shoulder and the bag tumbled down the two steps of the stoop.

"Jeeze...I've got to pull it together," Maggie said, reaching down to grab the strap.

"Mommy, don't leave. I'll be good. I won't make him mad. Pleasssse don't go!" Emma wiped her tears with her Barbie's tousled hair, which gripped in her grasp.

"Honey, Grandma will be here shortly. You love Grandma. She'll take care of you until mommy returns. I promise I'll call." Maggie took her thumb and wiped away the tears from Emma's face.

"C'mon Maggie!" yelled the man.

Maggie stood and anxiously gathered up her bag and, slinging it over her shoulder, ran to the car. She jumped into the passenger side, where the man had opened the door, all in a seemingly one choreographed movement. He slammed the door behind her and strode to the driver's side of the car, hopping behind the wheel.

Emma, still clutching her Barbie, held her face in her hands. She didn't want to watch the car drive away. The car started, and the engine roared, and the car surged forward. Wade jumped out of the way as the car narrowly missed him and sped down the road. He lifted a fist and shook his head. "Whore!"

Wade turned and walked over to Emma. He watched her for a moment with her head in her hands, bawling. He sat down and pulled his bandana from around his neck and nudged her to look at him. "Hey little girlie, your Barbie needs a dress. You want me to make one for her?"

Emma nodded, sniffling, tears rolling freely, but slightly distracted by her beloved doll.

Wade took the naked barbie and wrapped his bandana around the doll's body, tucking the ends in.

"See? She has a beautiful dress, and she's going to go places now."

Emma cried harder, remembering her mom and the man. "Like Mommy?"

"Noooooo...never like your mommy. Barbie, you see, she's got herself a career in the city. She can take care of herself, just like Grandma Rose. She doesn't need Ken."

Emma smiled; somehow this man made her feel better. Barbie had a job, and she herself had Grandma Rose, who would never leave her, because Grandma could take care of herself.

"Would you like some candy?" Wade asked, pulling out a Tootsie Pop and handing it to Emma, who grasped it in her fingers.

"*There you are, you son-of-a-bitch.*" *The harshness of the man's words ran down Emma's spine like the pointy ends of a fork and she hastily looked up.*

A man in his forties approached, wearing a flannel shirt under dirty overalls and oily work boots. His face was beet red and sweat ran down from his brow.

"*Oh, jeez. Dad is pissed,*" *Wade said, mumbling under his breath.*

Emma felt Wade shrinking beside her. She watched as the mad man stomped over and jabbed his finger at Wade and grabbing his shirt collar, lifted him onto his feet. Wade stood; his shoulder slumped as if his chest collapsed in at the sternum, in an effort to protect his vital organs for what was to come.

"*You're a douche-bag. What the hell you smokin? You back-holed the McCullen's yard, the wrong f'ing place, you jack-ass. Cost me more than two day's work and what you're worth...givin' me twice the work to do now.*"

The mad man lunged at Wade and drew back his fist, pummeling Wade several times. Wade half-raised his arms in a weak effort to break the force of the blows. The strikes folded Wade in two, and he rested his head on his knees. Not for long. The man drove his knee into Wade's face, and Wade flipped backward, collapsing on the ground. The man stomped off and jumped into his truck. Emma looked at Wade curled into a fetal position on the ground, his mouth busted and bleeding. Wade wiped the blood with his sleeve, smearing it around his lips and lower jaw. He looked like a sad clown.

Emma started crying at the spectacle as it unfolded around her. The violence and the staggering way Wade rose to sit up.

They remained silent for a moment, with only the babble of the full-fed Wabash as it made its journey south and her occasional sniffle filling her ears.

"Oh, honey. It's okay. No need to be sad for me. I'm okay."
Wade wiped at the blood that still streamed down his face. His eyes watered, whether from the pounding or his emotional state, and he wiped at their corners. "It was just a beating, that's all."
He pointed at her lollipop. "Take a lick, now. Everything's going to be alright."

He pulled out a Tootsie Pop from his pocket and slowly unwrapped it, taking his time, as if he studied a specimen he'd discovered from an archeological site. He twirled the candy between his thumb and forefinger before popping it into his mouth, then he turned and looked toward the Wabash as if deep in thought.

The sound of the Wabash River brought Emma back to the present. The rustle, swirl, and bubble of the river flowing over tree limbs and boulders called to her. The river was her constant, and it had witnessed her mother leaving and the kindness of Wade even after his father's beating. Oh, the stories the Wabash could tell. She felt a kinship with the Wabash at that moment and that feeling lifted her into seeing life from a higher realm of connectiveness.

The memory of Wade comforting her brought in a side of him she had not remembered or seen since. This side of Wade she'd witnessed as a child at first befuddled her and then soon disturbed her. How could he have been so kind to her as a child and years later done what he'd done to Mattie? Those actions were as if they arose out of two different men.

If he had gone to the San Francisco as he had said, then what type of life could he had lived that brought out that mean behavior? Because even his abusive life as a child hadn't corrupted him. He had been nice to her when she was at her most vulnerable, seeing her mother walk out of her life forever and abandon her. But, for Wade, maybe the physical abuse of his father sat the foundation of something more sinister to come in that was a dark, creepy, insatiable drive to power. These two parts of Wade flashed in her mind like both men were in one of those revolving doors you'd see when walking into a fancy hotel. The question in her mind was which Wade would emerge out of that rotating door?

59

The smeared lip-sticked face of a weary-looking Wade quickened his step as he approached The Dam Tavern. Emma stood, turned and entered the tavern, walking behind the bar and hoping to escape any encounter with Wade. She wished he would go on his way. She didn't want to confront him, especially since she had so many conflicting feelings regarding Operation Humiliation and she could only assume the Wade she would confront would be the power-driven one.

The sound of Miss Henry getting off of her stool drew Emma's attention.

"You okay, Miss Henry? I can walk you home if you're ready."

Miss Henry waved her away with a flick of her hand and headed to the bathroom door.

Wade entered and stood at the bar in front of Emma. He didn't say a word. He took the lollipop out of his mouth and tossed it on the bar. He pulled his smokes from his shirt pocket and tapped a cigarette out, then put it in his mouth. He withdrew a match from his matchbook and struck it on the bottom of his boot. When he held the flame to the tip of his cigarette, he inhaled, then blew the smoke out slowly through his mouth. His eyes animated suddenly like coals fanned beneath the bellows, bizarre slow actions from a spectacle of a man half-crazed. Emma knew something sinister was about to go down.

She reached into her jean pocket and felt the paring knife, wolf's tooth, and the medallion. Renewed strength flowed, and she stood in front of Wade. Her hands pressed on the bar to steady their shaking. Vulnerability settled into every cell of her body at being alone with Wade in the tavern's solitude.

"Wade, I'm glad you're doing okay," she said.

"Beer. I'm due one, don't you think?"

Emma turned to retrieve the beer and placed the bottle before Wade.

He sucked on the cigarette until the tip burned a deep fire red. Then, with his left hand, he took the cigarette out, and in a fluid motion, he grabbed her wrist with his right. Emma jerked her hand, but couldn't escape his grasp. Rage contorted his features into the look of a demon.

With his fingers wrapped tightly around her wrist, he placed the burning tip of the cigarette firmly onto the top of her hand. At first, the depravity of the act startled her, and the pain didn't register, but quickly, she felt the heat, and yelped, trying to snatch her hand away while the cigarette burned into her skin. The smell of tobacco mingled with burning skin shocked her enough that she drew back, but he held fast. She whimpered, understanding things were about to get much worse.

The struggle to control her reaction was foremost while she processed her options. Her reflex screamed: flee. Her eyes searched desperately in the distance to the front door. Perhaps she could outrun him if she was to break free. No, he would catch her before she could open the door. So, her options dwindled to one: stand her ground.

Wade watched her. On his face, he seemed...happy? Pleased? He had a single-minded purpose. She dismissed any idea of trying to make her escape by running. She had to be smart.

Still holding onto her wrist, Wade jumped over the bar in one swift, graceful movement and twisted her around so that he pressed her arm between their bodies. A flash of metal blade swished in an arc as the knife came down and pressed into her neck.

Her mouth opened to speak, but she could not produce any words. The fear overwhelmed her. She worried if she said anything, that her words would trigger Wade to pull the knife toward him and slice through her throat.

"Scream and you're dead. Understand?"

Emma nodded.

"Okay now, start walking to the back door. If you try to run, or anything at all, I'll yank this knife back and forth in one swift motion until I hit bone. Understand?"

His mouth was close to her ear, his lips almost brushing the lobe. The sweet, acrid smell of candy and cigarette smoke with his musky smell of sweat almost made her vomit. She swallowed hard, knowing with terrible certainty that leaving the tavern would bring her death.

"Yes," she said. "I understand." Her mouth was dry and the words sounded deep and raspy to her own ears. She licked her lips.

"You was warned. And you didn't listen. Why didn't you fuckin' listen?" Wade's voice had a calm yet menacing quality, and it resonated so low and guttural that she could feel its vibration along her neck. The sound of his voice traveled up into the base of her skull, sending gooseflesh across her skin. She wanted to take her hand to the back of her neck and scrape off the slime he left when he spoke. But she couldn't, of course. He was in full command, speaking slowly, as if he had all the time in the world.

"Now it's time to pay. No one's gonna make me look like a dolt." Wade pulled her tighter to him and pushed her toward the back of the supply room door. "Move slowly. Any fast movement and I cut your throat, remember?"

She nodded slightly, and he wrenched her arm up higher behind her back, the knife pressing more firmly into her throat to emphasize his message. Emma braced against Wade's arm; her head tilted up, trying to keep the knife point from digging deeper into her skin. A shadow moved out of the bathroom and slowly to the slot machine. Pain stunned Emma, but she hoped Wade wouldn't notice the movement and put Miss Henry into any danger as well. He hadn't noticed.

"Walk to the river. If we're lucky, we may stumble over your friend."

"What do you mean? Where's Jolene? What have you done?" Panic rose from Emma's belly to her throat.

"Never mind about that bitch. She's paid for her deed; now it's your turn."

Emma's mind rushed with the possibilities, but she had to stay focused on the now.

They made their way to the bank of the Wabash. "Yep. If you was a man, I'd bash your teeth out, then feed them to you, one-by-one, like a baby."

Emma stumbled slightly and regained her footing.

"That's it, just keep your tight ass walking, just like your whore of a mother."

Her heart raced and sweat beaded on the soft hairs at the back of her neck. Dried leaves rustled underfoot, and a twisted vine wound down a smaller tree trunk like a snake strangling its way into the earth. Ironic what the mind focuses on when it's hyper-alert. She dropped her attention to her heart-center. Her panic subsided and she no longer focused on her fear of dying, but noticed she oscillated from wanting to live, from fear of dying, to being in the moment. She wasn't attached but could influence the direction of the next moments outcome.

As they walked, new options processed through her mind. Could Miss Henry, in her demented fog, understand that she was in danger and run and get Grandma? The thought of the paring knife in her pocket, quite useless compared to his hunting knife that pushed against her throat. But the small knife was a weapon, and she had it in her possession, if only she had a chance to retrieve it and find an opportunity to use it.

The Wabash, deepening from its winter's respite, rushed along to her right. Emma staggered with Wade directly behind her, through the thicket of small leafless trees, near the rabbit hutches, until they reached the trail alongside of the river that led to where the land steepened. At the top was Flattop Rock. As she brushed aside a sticker weed, she saw her to the left in the thicket brush. Jolene, face down, flat on her stomach. Her flowered patterned shirt was darkened, almost black with blood and ripped open. She wasn't wearing her jeans. Jolene's face was turned and angled toward the ground. Emma could see enough of Jolene's head, a bloody tangle of hair and flesh. Her hair, stringy and clumped from the blood, laid strewn across her face. Her eyes were closed and Emma could only hope that she was passed out and was not dead.

Emma took a deep breath so as not to react at the site of Jolene. She didn't want to give Wade that pleasure or power by intensifying her fear more, so she said not a word. From the site of the disturbed ground behind Jolene, it was possible she crawled her way to that spot, making her way to the tavern. That Wade didn't even indicate that Jolene was there meant he didn't know she was. Emma could not be of any help to her friend at this point. She had to free herself from Wade first in order to be of any good for the two of them. She spoke only in her mind, "Jolene, please be alive. Please be alive."

At the top of the slight rise, Wade whispered in her ear, "Over there," and shoved her toward Flattop Rock. Even at the height of her crisis, Emma thought about the irony that this situation between her and Wade would take place at her meditative spot. They walked almost as one toward the rock's edge. His hold tightened around her, so she had to rise on her toes to prevent the knife from cutting. Then he shoved her forward and away. She spun to look at him, right at the edge of her beloved Flattop Rock, with the river rushing behind her. He smirked oh-so slightly.

"You know, I'm going to kill you before we're done here. Just like your friend. Now, let's see your lips smile, bitch. That's the second most important thing you can do with them, and the first one ain't talking." Wade sneered and then grinned as if one of his buddies told a good joke.

A slow burn climbed from the base of her neck up to her hairline. Humiliation washed over her and distracted her thoughts as her fear rose. She felt the last reserve of her power seeping away. No possible way out of the situation, except for the small knife in her pocket.

Then she heard Grandma speaking to her. Grandma's words flowed into her mind, loud and clear. Maybe it was imagination that conjured up those words, but she didn't question their relevance. It may have been her own thoughts spoken in her voice. It didn't matter; the words rang of rationality.

"Ch'Ulel Heart! Don't let fear take over. Open your heart. Hold your power. Find the silence within, understand his vulnerability as well."

Emma's body relaxed. If today she was to die, she would die knowing that she had lived the best moment she could live at the moment of death, in the Ch'Ulel Heart.

Wade approached her. She turned her head to avoid his rancid breath, and his lips, meant to cover hers, brushed her cheek and trailed wetly down her throat.

"Take your pants off," he ordered, angry that his lips missed their mark.

He stepped back, his eyes running up and down her body. She nodded and unzipped her jeans, pushing them down over her hips. Kicking her shoes off, she pulled the jeans free from her legs. As she picked up her pants and folded them, she palmed the knife, pushing the handle up under the long sleeve of her blouse, the blade cupped in her palm. In her other hand, she grasped the tiny wolf's tooth, the only talisman she could grab from her jean pocket.

Wade motioned with his knife in a downward movement, showing he wanted her to lie down. She did as she was told, lying down on Flattop Rock. He grabbed his Glock from the back of his waistband and placed it in the top of his boot. He hastened on top, straddling her, his knees along her sides while he fumbled with the zipper of his jeans.

"You don't want to be doing this," she said, voice calm, but louder than a whisper so that her words could be heard over the rushing river. "I don't deserve this."

"Oh, yes, you do," he said, menacing. "You think you can hide behind your grandma and grandpa?" He snorted. "You did a bad thing...kidnapping me, tormenting me, shaming me, and starting the media circus that put me into all kinds of danger. This lesson will serve you. You need to be marked so that every time you look in the mirror, you will remember how you done wrong, girl. You never cross a Malone."

The knife he held in his left hand came down along her temple. She could feel the pierce of its tip into her skin, the deepening of the cut, but, curiously, she felt no pain. The knife slid along her cheek, ending just below the jaw-line. She could feel the warmth and wetness of the blood running down her cheek and onto the back of her neck. She could feel the skin on her cheek part and the tautness of her face before, loosened.

His hands on her legs made the muscles spasm, as if repulsed by his touch. They were hard hands, calloused. He touched her knees, then squeezed her thighs, creeping up higher to a place she didn't want them to go. She looked into Wade's face, looming down from above her. She had never seen a face like that—so drawn, so cold, so hard. His dark eyes glinted with bits of light filled with hate, devoid of any humanity. Her eyes looked toward the Wabash, asking for help from the river. Help me! Please help me find strength.

She prayed with her whole being and will. *Warrior of Light, True of Strength, Serenity and Presence.* Her arm limply stretched out toward the edge of the rock and her fisted hand opened to release the paring knife and the wolf's tooth talisman into the Wabash. The knife was the sacrifice and the wolf's tooth a gift to the powers-that-be. The items rode the current. Now, she watched as her salvation floated away, and maybe soon her body would take the same ride down the river. But at least she would be at peace.

Wade took the tip of his knife and trailed it in the opening of her blouse, stopping at the center of her chest. She wondered in that moment how that knife would feel going into her heart. She thought of the blood pulsing out as her heart beat. Wade wanted to draw out her terror, wanted her to feel afraid, in order to revel in his own power for a while longer. His carnal desire for vengeance, to see her writhe with fear of him, was here, written on his face, but she felt no desire to resist. She wasn't giving in to her own fear.

He wanted her to squirm. This need of his to achieve this satisfaction at her expense gave her a moment, a moment to dive deeper into her heart. In that additional moment, she could find an opening to get them both out of this situation alive. Her meditation training kicked in and she fell deeper into her Ch'Ulel Heart. She knew how to sit with fear from an open heart. Center, do not resist. She surrendered, and in doing so, she had not given up.

She knew the action she took would break cycles of violence in her struggling town. How this knowledge came to her, she did not understand. She just envisioned a stone when dropped into the Wabash, sending out waves of ripples in the raging river, conforming the water to its momentum of concentric circles, affecting her and Wade in its flow.

Her fear dissolved, completely gone. The scared part of her separated and sat off to her side, transparent, small and fragile, a husk of her former self, like the useless skin of a molten snake.

With sudden calculation, she gathered her strength and felt the force of her undisguised power. Her power concentrated itself in her heart. She was not to have power over Wade, oh no. He and she existed in this experience together, both sides of the same coin. She focused her attention on

Wade and looked deeply into his eyes. His eyes were dark and rimmed with redness. His hate burned deep; his meanness ingrained. She dropped deeper within him and saw his fear. She searched for the truth underneath his fear and dropped deeper. They were of the same mind. She descended even further down—until she reached the vulnerability of his smallest child-like aspect. A child who saw his world as never safe. A child who shrank in terror from those meant to protect him, beaten by his father, over and over.

Emma brushed up against the evil that overcame this child-like part, dark and alive. No desire or thought to outwit or overpower Wade entered her mind. His dark deeds served a purpose in their world. Her eyes met his, straight on and unwavering, firm but not cold.

"Do with me as you will," she whispered.

She bit her lip, waiting for the rape, though in complete acceptance of what life offered. Their eyes remained locked. She continued to see his child, fearful and child-like, trembling in the deep recesses of his soul. Compassion replaced all her fear.

It was then, within her mind, that she reached out and held the hand of the terrorized child within Wade.

Wade tried to push himself into her, but her body involuntarily clinched, making it impossible for him. His body shuddered. He had gone limp. All the violence that he directed toward her turned back onto him, weakening his libido.

Wade resigned and collapsed on top of her, panting, ineffective in his possession. The knife in his hand dropped to the rock. She lay still. She could feel Wade's erratic heartbeat on her chest. Some knowledge of great importance about violence and why men like violence flooded her mind. It gave them power, masking their own helplessness, and for a short time these men felt good, and could feel, for a time, like a real man.

"What have you done to me?" he asked, his voice full of surprise and surrender.

She glanced up over Wade's shoulder while he continued to lie motionless on top of her. Save for his heavy panting, she would have wondered if he was still alive. His whole body felt limp.

Then, a small, shadowed figure loomed above them, throwing dark cool shadows across their bodies. The gun barrel of the rifle pointed directly at Wade's head. Then Jolene's voice, firm and steady, "Get off her."

60

Wade rolled off and onto his back, fumbling with his pants, struggling to pull them up, his eyes wide in surprise at Jolene standing over him, holding the rifle from The Dam Tavern.

"I'm fine, Jolene." Emma said quietly, in an effort to ease Jolene's threat.

Jolene stood with her clothing disheveled, her shirt unbuttoned except for one and hanging to cover over the tops of her bare legs. She sported a bruise under her left eye, and her right eye swelled shut. Blood flowed from the crown of her head into her hair.

"Now, for you," said Jolene, jabbing her gun toward Wade without getting too close so he could reach out and grab the barrel. "I'm not fine. You son-of-a-bitch." The gun shook with Jolene's battle of rage.

Wade wasn't moving a muscle.

"Jolene, it's okay. Don't do anything you're gonna regret."

Emma grabbed her shirt to cover her nakedness. Blood ran freely down her cheek and dripped onto her shirt. Her eyes never left Jolene's shaking figure as she continued to battle with herself.

"Jolene, he's not worth it. I'm okay. You're okay. Look at me!"

Jolene cried uncontrollably, the gun wavering up and down as if she warred within herself for the part that wanted to end the man who trembled in front of her. Jolene's eyes shifted to Emma. Her eyes pleaded for help. She turned back to Wade, and the gun steadied as she held it with both hands pointed at his chest.

Wade remained quiet.

Emma knew by the look in Jolene's eyes that she would fight, fight relentlessly. She had enough and was ready to put a bullet into Wade's face.

"Jolene! We are Warriors of Light, True of Strength, Serenity and Presence!"

But it was as if Jolene was in another reality, not hearing Emma at all.

Footfalls sounded loud and clear over the scrabble, but Emma remained focused on Jolene. She only caught the sight of Grandma and Miss Henry as they walked haltingly to the side of Jolene, not too close to push Jolene in reacting. Grandma reached out and touched Jolene on her arm. "Dear, you don't want to be doing this."

The gentleness in the gesture moved Jolene to drop the rifle slightly. Her eyes closed tightly, and she sobbed.

Then things unfolded in slow motion. Emma caught a motion in Wade's direction. Wade had dragged his knee up slowly, reached into his boot and pulled out his Glock, taking aim at Jolene. Emma screamed. Then, in an action like that of a mountain cat, Miss Henry and Grandma leapt in front of Jolene, throwing their bodies between Jolene and Wade, as he fired the gun. Miss Henry's sleeve tattered as the bullet ripped through her garment and her arm. Miss Henry dropped and Grandma followed behind, both falling with the momentum of their leap and the impact of the bullet.

"Miss Henry!" Emma yelled, knowing Miss Henry was shot but not knowing the extent of her wound.

Jolene screamed and aimed her rifle once again at Wade. Wade grabbed his backpack and hightailed it into the woods, toward the main road. Jolene dropped the rifle, unable to pull the trigger.

"No! No!" yelled Emma, as she rushed over to where Miss Henry partially laid over Grandma in a heap. Miss Henry rolled over onto her back and tugged at Grandma's arm. She wasn't moving. Miss Henry sat up and touched Grandma's cheek. She looked up at Emma, despair on her face, all the energy leaving from her body.

"Help! Get help!" Miss Henry shook her head and then slumped over weeping.

Emma ran and dropped at Grandma's side. A red spot expanded over Grandma's chest. Emma, in her despair, threw her head back in a silent open-mouthed howl, the blood from her cheek running down her neck. She hurled her body forward and collapsed over Grandma's quiet form.

Emma raised up, lifting Grandma into her arms. Her head jerked back again into a silent, open-mouthed scream. Finally, she let out a mournful howl as Grandma's blood drenched her own top.

"Please don't die, Grandma. Please don't die."

A slow smile radiated over Grandma's face. "It's okay, my dear. My final sacrifice." she whispered, and a last breath escaped from her lips.

"Oh..no! I failed you, Grandma. The Wolf warned me, and I failed youuuu...." Emma wailed.

Jolene sobbed quietly.

"It's my fault. Oh my God, it's my fault." Jolene repeated these lines over and over between sobs.

Dottie's truck screeched to a halt, and gravel pitted the area. Dottie jumped out from behind the steering wheel and Sy followed, bounding from the passenger side. With a determined stride, Dottie rushed over to where the women crouched. Sy followed. Dottie assessed the situation within a minute, looked over at Sy and said, "Go find him and get him out of town." Sy nodded.

61

Sy, driving Dottie's truck, pulled up to a Wade walking across the Wabash bridge, pink Barbie backpack slung over his shoulder and his clothes in disarray. "Where to, Bud?" asked Sy.

Wade opened the passenger door to the truck and climbed in. "To the bus stop."

Sy smiled. "You look like hell, man. You sure made a mess out of things, didn't ya? And what's with the smeared paint around your lips?"

Wade grunted in return and took his sleeved arm and rubbed across his mouth.

Sy drove the truck to the next turn and punched the gas, speeding onto a rutted road that ran alongside the river. The old Ford jostled and shimmied, rose and fell over the ruts. Wade turned to face Sy, a guarded expression on his clownish face. "Hey man, what's this about?"

Sy pulled the gun he had at his side, aiming it at Wade's chest. He stopped the truck near the river's edge. "Get out!"

"Sure man. No need for the gun," Wade said, opening the door and stumbling out. "I don't get why—"

Sy fired the gun, hitting Wade in the chest.

Wade dropped, and Sy calmly walked out of the truck and stood over Wade's inert body. He took aim and shot again, for good measure. Sy walked to the truck's bed and pulled out a concrete block along with rope. He uncoiled the rope and tied one end to the block and another around Wade's waist. As he worked, he mumbled to himself. "Dumb-ass. You didn't think I'd be hanging out in a dead-end town with your pain-in-the-ass sister because I wanted to, now did you?"

Sy squatted next to the bound Wade, shaking his head at the senselessness of his act of murder.

"The Senator sent me down to keep an eye on you, as insurance, just in case things got out of hand. All you had to do was lay low, but you totally screwed that up, didn't you, buddy?"

Sy stood, his head bowed and looking down at Wade. "Got the call from the Senator seconds after the news hit. 'Take him,' was all the boss guy said. Just tying up loose ends...no offense, Wade, but you became a loose end."

Sy dragged Wade's body, feet first, to the Wabash.

62

Emma sat with Grandpa in the back of the store as Grandpa flipped through her book, *The Old Man and the Sea*. It had been two months since Grandma's death, and Emma moped around, not wanting to take part or engage in anything. She embodied the perfect image of the walking dead. Even though the media had hyped up Wade's appearance in drag, no one could identify the perpetrators who pushed Wade in the wheelchair. When Wade went missing, the hype died down. The law had no interest in investigating crime in Taylorville. Another drama cycle that soon ended, and people went on with their living.

"Did you finish reading it?" Grandpa asked, nodding to the book he held.

"Ah...yeah." She attempted to return her focus to Grandpa, and she looked at him with dead eyes. She wanted to be fully present with the one person left alive who was really there for her now, and whom she knew loved her deeply, but the pain of losing Grandma kept her in a withdrawn state. Maybe she was afraid to love someone again because they always ended up leaving in one form or another.

"Okay. So, what did you take from it?" Grandpa studied her face and laid the book on the table. He tapped the cover with his long, lean, wrinkled finger.

She remembered the story that she had finished a few days before Grandma had died. She was prepared for Grandpa's routine discussions about a book he gave her to read. "Oh, just an old fisherman, doing what he always does, fishing for whatever he can catch to make a living." She felt an annoyed at the question, like her opinion on a book was important in the grander schemes of life and death. Death put things into perspective.

Grandpa's face dropped, and his eyes studied the book's cover, disappointment clear in his demeanor. His disappointment reached her and she felt the pang in her heart. It saddened her she had such a negative effect on him. She thought for a moment and decided to put in the effort for Grandpa.

"For real, though," she said. "The old fisherman, battles a huge marlin for three days before he is able to defeat it, but then in his effort to tow the fish back to shore, the sharks eat it. I guess the old man worked hard for nothing and death destroys any effort toward a happy life."

"So, it's about the futility in our lives?" he asked, looking at her, hoping that maybe she had more to offer than the obvious state of her mind.

Emma grinned. It was always easier for her to start with the simplest of ideas before expanding her thoughts in deeper ways. A part of her enjoyed seeing Grandpa's emotions rise and fall, much like the old fisherman's skiff on the vast ocean—payback for all the lessons taught, for his and Grandma's need to make her responsible. She also felt some of the life return to her when she thought in deep, philosophical ways about the motivations and intentions behind living things.

"No," she said. "Hemingway, I think, speaks of how the world is full of predators and no living thing escapes struggle until they die. When you encounter your greatest opponent, the challenge is to find worthiness and love for that opponent, to understand their weakness. The old fisherman found his worthy opponent—the marlin—during the last days of his life, and he admired the persistence of the marlin to fight for his life. When the sharks circled, the fisherman, tired from his fighting of the marlin, had to sacrifice his prized fish to the sharks. Death is our final opponent and we'll have to submit, won't we? Not much different from living here, don't you think?"

"Well, that sounds fatalistic, now doesn't it?" Grandpa said. "Surely, you got more."

Emma looked at Grandpa and smiled an easy smile. "That I do. Death is inevitable, but some of the best men— or *women*—will refuse to give in and actually fear its power. So, they remain slaves to their own fear. The story tells that it's possible to transcend even the fear of Death and you can do that, as you learn with any opponent, with love and respect for that of what you see in the opponent. No need to fight when Death comes. Find the part within you that can greet it." Emma looked over at Grandpa, tears in her eyes. "Die with purpose at your heart, even if it is for the sacrifice to another."

Grandpa nodded, pride shining in his eyes. He reached over to wipe a tear that dropped from her face and followed the scar that ran alongside her cheek. "Now, that's beyond me. I just thought it was a story about never giving up." He laughed quietly at his simplistic but profound thought, thrown back into her face.

"Whatever you say, Grandpa." She stood. "I'm on my way to meditate at the river."

"Good. That's good," Grandpa studied Emma. "You doing okay, Baby Girl?"

"Interestingly enough, Grandpa, I'm doing...*okay.*" She oscillated her hand, expressing her doubt in her own statement.

Grandpa nodded and watched through the large store window as Emma walked toward the river.

Emma stepped up onto Flattop Rock, hand over her heart as she breathed in the swiftly flowing Wabash. "I call upon my Light Warrior of strength, serenity and presence." Even though terrible things happened on her rock, she still found it peaceful on the rock's overhang above the river. It was one place she felt the presence of her grandmother.

Her gaze followed the river upstream to the opposite bank. A pink object protruded between a boulder and log. She strained her eyes and could pick up the pink Barbie backpack, Mattie's pack that Wade had taken with him that last day. She pulled out her cell and snapped a few pictures. A brown dog, with one eye missing, pulled at the bag. He tugged until he wrenched the bag from the boulder. Then, the dog dragged the bag away and into the woods, his tail wagging at his find.

Emma looked at her cell and attached a message to the photo of the bag. She wanted Dottie to know as Mattie continued to live with Dottie and that Sy character. She wanted to make sure Mattie was safe.

Looks like the bag Wade took with him on his way out of town. Just wanted you to know. Make of it what you will. My guess is that Wade's at the bottom of the Wabash.

A return message,

Don't you dare pretend you have Mattie's interest in mind? Not when you set your revenge in motion. Now, your grandma's dead. Wade, he's gone, some place where no one will find him. Just leave us alone. We don't want no trouble.

Emma turned to go home. Maybe Dottie was right, everyone needed to leave them alone.

63

Sy and Dottie exited the truck and walked toward the house. The new roof looked out of place against the peeling paint of the sideboards. Sy mentioned something that Dottie found funny, and she laughed. Sy smiled and stepped in front of her, leading the way to the porch. Dottie reached over and grabbed an axe the roofers left behind and called out to Sy before he was to step onto the porch.

"Hey, Sy!"

Sy turned, unable to draw back quick enough as steel flashed, and the axe buried into his head. He didn't even have the time to question what the woman he planned to leave soon intended to do with the ax.

Dottie watched as Sy crumbled to the ground. "It's our way," she said. Dottie bent over Sy to ensure he no longer breathed. Fido ran toward Dottie and sniffed at Sy's boots. He looked up at Dottie with his one eye.

"Well, Fido. One assassinated by gun and one by sharp blade." Dottie's expression turned into a frown. "Same difference, both men dead, huh, boy?" She ruffled Fido's head and stood to retrieve a shovel.

64

The grocery was in order. Grandpa couldn't stand disorder. He needed the cans of goods in line like a well-trained regiment, the meat in their proper categories, chicken and turkey with the poultry group, beef with red meats and the catfish and groupers with seafoods—or 'river food' as he referred to his fish supply. Order was a matter of efficiency for him.

After a while, Grandpa went to the front of the store and sat in his high-backed rocker on the porch. Soon, Emma and Jolene joined him, their sadness permeating the air. Jolene's face had a slight scar over her left eye from Wade's abuse and she still walked with a stiffness in her athletic body. The doctor sutured Emma's facial wound, and the long gash welted on her face like a bad makeup prosthesis on a horror movie set.

Grandpa took out his pipe and reached for his tobacco. Slowly he put it in, tamping it lightly, sighing with the heaviness surrounding him. He lit it with a match, turning the match slowly in the bowl, puffing lightly until it glowed red. He drew deeply, studying his pipe.

"I'm sitting here with the mystery women who carried out a perfect revenge, dressing a misogynist in drag," Grandpa said, looking at Emma and Jolene, both who looked miserable, leaning on the railing. Doubt registered on his face whether he should bring up what everyone refused to speak about, which took events down a dark path. "We have our secrets, don't we?"

"Yep. We sure do." Jolene said, her eyes filled with tears as she stared off down the street at a couple of children walking toward the grocery. Apparently, Jolene didn't want to speak more about the situation.

Grandpa, giving up on that subject, glanced over at Emma. "Whatever happened to the fellow you went noodling with?"

Emma's gazed looked as if it was a thousand miles away as she stared across at the Wabash. Her fingers traced the red long cut from her temple to her jawbone and a promise of a forever scar. "Ah...you know, Grandpa, I think I'm too wounded to be in a relationship. What with being abandoned by a mother like Maggie, and it seems trouble and violence follows me no matter what I do."

Grandpa shook his head, hard. "No, now, that's not true. You're more like me and your grandma. That fellow's crazy not to see the value in a girl like you."

The three sat in silence for a moment, staring out at the town.

"Haven't seen hide nor hair of that Sy fellow," Grandpa said, moving onto another subject.

Emma and Jolene looked at each other and shrugged, not caring anymore.

"Just like Wade, probably had too much excitement from our small town. Guess he headed back to Chicago," said Emma. "Too bad for Dottie, I guess."

"Hmmm...yeah. Maybe our women here in Taylorville are a little too much for the men." Grandpa laughed a gentle laugh and took a long puff from his pipe.

"It's our way," said Emma. She looked down the road at Dottie's approaching truck. "Speak of the devil."

The truck drove by, slowly. Mattie sat in the passenger seat and gave a tentative half wave with her fingers and a slight smile. Her dog Fido hung his head out of the window, his tongue flapping in the wind. Mattie looked happy. Fido was a loyal friend to her.

"Well, I suppose the two of you plan to go to college of some sort...ain't that right?" He waited a moment and received no immediate response. "Jolene, you still have that scholarship and you'll be leaving soon, right?

Jolene nodded and her face lit up with her plans finally coming to fruition.

So, what's your plan, Emma?" Grandpa asked.

"I don't know yet, Grandpa. Haven't worked my plan out completely. I'll need money to go to college. The tavern won't sell for anything, if at all. Who wants to buy a tavern in a town like this? The house, I could sell, but also for not much money. Who here has the dollars to spend to buy a house?

This town's got me, that's all I can say." She thought for a moment and felt pensive, then added, "Grandma says...used to say...to have patience, that my time for good karma is close to coming about since I've experienced about as much bad as anyone my age."

"Well, I'm sure Grandma was right about that. She typically was," said Grandpa, sitting back in his chair and rocking. For a few moments, the only sound was the creaking of his rocker.

"She used to say that a person's selfless sacrifice will help our town better itself and herald in the good," Jolene said, tears filling her eyes. "I just wished I'd made different decisions when it mattered the most. Then Grandma wouldn't have sacrificed for me. She'd be alive." She turned her head away from the view of Grandpa and Emma and bit her upper lip, tears spilling over as she looked off into the distance.

Emma didn't want to hear talk about Grandma's sacrifice. The way she saw it, she and Jolene made a great deal of mistakes placing Miss Henry and Grandma into danger, as well as themselves. The way she saw it, they were not Civilon-bull-like in their handling of things. The hurt of Grandma's death was overwhelming and she couldn't let herself think about it. She would grieve in her own way, like everyone else in Taylorville.

Grandpa nodded and remained silent, his attention to his pipe. His silence indicated that he'd given up on trying to get the two most important people in his life to find some moments of happiness in their lives to return to being ordinary teens. So far, so non-ordinary.

Jolene leaned back on the railing and crossed her arms over her belly and hugged it tightly, her one dim red eye moving around from Grandpa Conner to Emma. Her arms dropped to their sides, and she relaxed even more into the railing. Emma didn't know or better yet didn't have it in her to comfort her friend.

"I'm going home, guys. I'll catch up later," said Emma.

Emma rose from the railing and hopped off of the porch. As she walked down to the road to the river, she wasn't quite out of earshot to hear Jolene ask Grandpa, "Emma has the deepest thoughts. She's weird that way, you know, Grandpa Conner?"

"Yep. That's what I love about her," Grandpa replied.

"Me, too."

That put a gentle smile on Emma's face. She wasn't alone, after all.

The moist sand near the river had swirling depressions where deer had bedded down for the night. Emma's father had taught her the signs of the habits of the animals in the woods, in case she needed to track for food. Near the base of a hickory, a pile of hickory nut shells laid where a squirrel had finished a meal and probably had stuffed a few in its cheeks. She walked further along the Wabash, stopping to watch the river flow. She placed her hand over her heart and closed her eyes. "I'm a Light Warrior of strength, serenity, presence, *and compassion*," and a deep peace came over her.

A car's engine revved up from across the river on the east bank boat ramp. Emma looked and watched as Nate's Mustang pulled to the river's edge. Her fingers reached up to touch or maybe to hide the red, ugly wound running down her cheek, marring her physical beauty.

The driver's door opened and Nate jumped out and walked to the front of his car, lifting himself up and sitting on the hood. He looked across the river and his posture straightened in recognition of Emma. A tentative smile crossed his face. He lifted his hand in a wave. Emma, hesitantly, waved back.

QUESTIONS AND TOPICS
FOR DISCUSSION

1. In the first few pages of the book, we are introduced to the character Rose. What are her character traits that demonstrate the level of wisdom in the woman?

2. Wade was physically abused as a child by his father. Emma was abandoned by her mother at the age of five. Jolene sexually molested by her foster father. How did each of these characters deal with the violence in their past and in their culture? Were there any redeeming qualities they found by living in this type of violent and poor sub-culture?

3. How does Wade and Dolly reveal aspects of loyalty and humanity in some of their interactions with their family and community?

4. Nature and setting contribute greatly to the atmosphere of *Shame-by-Proxy*. How does Lowe convey both the harshness and the beauty of their world? How does the Wabash River play as a character in the novel?

5. The book speaks of Jung's approach to projections. How do Jolene and Emma project onto Wade? What are Wade's projections onto Emma, Jolene and Rose? Who is able to

withdraw their projections and find a way for psychological wholeness?

6. How does the process of Ch'Ulel Heart become a way to an enlightened soul?

7. Why is violence considered the extreme expression of a compassionate heart and mind? How is violence the opening to a compassionate heart?

8. Using the philosophy of the Ch'Ulel Heart, apply it to a scenario such as joining a march to save the planet. How does marching to save a planet actually contributes to the person/collective consciousness in keeping active the dynamic to destroy the planet?

9. Check out the meditation of heart centering on the authors page at Amazon.com.

ABOUT THE AUTHOR

 **M. C. LOWE** is the author of the fiction book *Shame By Proxy*, the first of the Proxy trilogy. Her second book in the trilogy is, *Dream By Proxy*. Born in Southern Indiana, she now lives near Boston. The violence she witnessed in her world and her philosophical, consciousness and psychological study of the subject inspired her to write this story, *Shame By Proxy*.

www.ingramcontent.com/pod-product-compliance
Lightning Source LLC
Chambersburg PA
CBHW061924170626
46813CB00006B/2291